Slow Man

Slow Man

J. M. Coetzee

LARGE PRINT

This large print edition published in 2005 by
RB Large Print
A division of Recorded Books
A Haights Cross Communications Company
270 Skipjack Road
Prince Frederick, MD 20678

Published by arrangement with Viking, an imprint of Penguin Group (USA)

Publisher's Cataloging In Publication Data
(Prepared by Donohue Group, Inc.)

Coetzee, J. M., 1940-
    Slow man / J. M. Coetzee.

    p. (large print) ; cm.

    ISBN-13: 978-1-4193-7597-2
    ISBN: 1-4193-7597-0

1. Amputees—Fiction. 2. Nurse and patient—Fiction. 3. Women novelists,
Australian—Fiction. 4. Large type books. I. Title.

PR9369.3.C58 S556 2005b
823

Printed in the United States of America

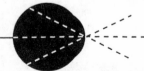

**This Large Print Book carries the
Seal of Approval of N.A.V.H.**

CHAPTER 1

The blow catches him from the right, sharp and surprising and painful, like a bolt of electricity, lifting him up off the bicycle. *Relax!* he tells himself as he flies through the air (*flies through the air with the greatest of ease!*), and indeed he can feel his limbs go obediently slack. *Like a cat* he tells himself: *roll, then spring to your feet, ready for what comes next.* The unusual word *limber* or *limbre* is on the horizon too.

That is not quite as it turns out, however. Whether because his legs disobey or because he is for a moment stunned (he hears rather than feels the impact of his skull on the bitumen, distant, wooden, like a mallet-blow), he does not spring to his feet at all, but on the contrary slides metre after metre, on and on, until he is quite lulled by the sliding.

He lies stretched out, at peace. It is a glorious morning. The sun's touch is kind. There are worse things than letting oneself go slack, waiting for one's strength to return. In fact there might be worse things than having a quick nap. He closes his eyes; the world tilts beneath him, rotates; he goes absent.

Once, briefly, he comes back. The body that had flown so lightly through the air has grown ponderous, so ponderous that for the life of him he cannot lift a finger. And there is someone looming over him, cutting off his air, a youngster with wiry hair and spots along his hairline. "My bicycle," he says to the boy, enunciating the difficult word syllable by syllable. He wants to ask what has become of his bicycle, whether it is being taken care of, since, as is well known, a bicycle can disappear in a flash; but before those words will come he is gone again.

CHAPTER 2

H e is being rocked from side to side, transported. From afar voices reach him, a hubbub rising and falling to a rhythm of its own. What is going on? If he were to open his eyes he would know. But he cannot do that just yet. Something is coming to him. A letter at a time, *clack clack clack*, a message is being typed on a rose-pink screen that trembles like water each time he blinks and is therefore quite likely his own inner eyelid. E-R-T-Y, say the letters, then F-R-I-V-O-L, then a trembling, then E, then Q-W-E-R-T-Y, on and on.

Frivole. Something like panic sweeps over him. He writhes; from the cavern within a groan wells up and bursts from his throat.

"Pain bad?" says a voice. "Hold still." The prick of a needle. An instant later the pain is washed away, then the panic, then consciousness itself.

He awakes in a cocoon of dead air. He tries to sit up but cannot; it is as if he were encased in concrete. Around him whiteness unrelieved: white ceiling, white sheets, white light; also a grainy whiteness like old toothpaste in which his mind seems to be coated, so that he cannot think straight

3

and grows quite desperate. "What is this?" he mouths or perhaps even shouts, meaning *What is this that is being done to me?* or *What is this place where I find myself?* or even *What is this fate that has befallen me?*

From nowhere a young woman in white appears, pauses, regards him watchfully. Out of the muddle in his head he tries to create an interrogative. Too late! With a smile and a reassuring pat on the arm that he seems strangely to hear but not feel, she moves on.

Is it serious?: if there is time for only one question, then that is what the question ought to be, though what the word *serious* might mean he prefers not to dwell on. But even more urgent than the question of seriousness, more urgent than the lurking question of what exactly it was that happened on Magill Road to blast him into this dead place, is the need to find his way home, shut the door behind him, sit down in familiar surroundings, recover himself.

He tries to touch the right leg, the leg that keeps sending obscure signals that it is now the wrong leg, but his hand will not budge, nothing will budge.

My clothes: perhaps that should be the innocuous preparatory question. *Where are my clothes? Where are my clothes, and how serious is my situation?*

The young woman floats back into his field of vision. "Clothes," he says, with an immense effort, raising his eyebrows as high as he can to signify urgency.

4

"No worries," says the young woman, and blesses him with another of her smiles, her positively angelic smiles. "Everything is safe, everything is taken care of. The doctor will be with you in a minute." And indeed before a minute has passed a young man who must be the doctor referred to has materialised at her side and is murmuring in her ear.

"Paul?" says the young doctor. "Can you hear me? Do I have the name right, Paul Rayment?"

"Yes," he says carefully.

"Good day, Paul. You will be feeling a little fuzzy right now. That's because you have had a shot of morphine. We will be going into surgery in a short while. You took a whack, I don't know how much you remember, and it has left your leg a bit of a mess. We are going to have a look and see how much of it we can save."

Again he arches his eyebrows. "Save?" he tries to say.

"Save your leg," repeats the doctor. "We are going to have to amputate, but we will save what we can."

Something must happen to his face at this point, because the young man does a surprising thing. He reaches out to touch his cheek, and then lets his hand rest there, cradling his old-man's head. It is the kind of thing a woman might do, a woman who loved one. The gesture embarrasses him but he cannot decently pull away.

"Will you trust me in this?" says the doctor.

Dumbly he blinks his eyes.

"Good." He pauses. "We don't have a choice, Paul," he says. "It is not one of those situations where we have a choice. Do you understand that? Do I have your consent? I am not going to ask you to sign on the dotted line, but do we have your consent to proceed? We will save what we can, but you took quite a blow, there has been a lot of damage, I can't say right now whether we can save the knee, for example. The knee has been pretty thoroughly mashed, and some of the tibia too."

As if it knows it is being spoken of, as if these terrible words have roused it from its troubled sleep, the right leg sends him a shaft of jagged white pain. He hears his own gasp, and then the thudding of blood in his ears.

"Right," says the young man, and pats him lightly on the cheek. "Time to get moving."

He awakes very much more at ease with himself. His head is clear, he is his old self (*full of beans!* he thinks), though pleasantly drowsy too, he could settle back into a nap at any moment. The leg that took the whack feels enormous, positively elephantine, but there is no pain.

The door opens and a nurse appears, a new, fresh face. "Feeling better?" she says, and then quickly, "Don't try to talk yet. Dr. Hansen will be along in a while to have a chat. In the meantime there is something we need to do. So could I ask you just to relax while . . ."

What she needs to do while he relaxes is, it

transpires, to insert a catheter. It is a nasty thing to have done to one; he is glad it is a stranger who is doing it. *This is what it leads to!* he berates himself. *This is what it leads to if you let your attention wander for one moment! And the bicycle: what has become of the bicycle? How am I going to do the shopping now? All my fault for taking Magill Road!* And he curses Magill Road, though in fact he has been cycling Magill Road for years without mishap.

What young Dr. Hansen has to present to him, when he arrives, is first a quick overview of his case, to *bring him up to speed,* and then more specific news about his leg, some of it good, some not so good.

First, as regards his condition in general, considering what can and does happen to the human body when it is hit by a car going at speed, he can congratulate himself that it is *not serious.* In fact, it is so much the reverse of serious that he can count himself lucky, fortunate, blessed. The crash left him concussed, yes, but he was saved by the helmet he was wearing. Monitoring will continue, but there is no sign of intracranial bleeding. As for motor functions, the preliminary indication is that they are unimpaired. He lost some blood, but that has been replaced. If he is wondering about the stiffness of his jaw, the jaw is not broken, merely bruised. The abrasions on his back and arm look worse than they are, they will heal in a week or two.

7

Turning to the leg now, the leg that took the blow, he (Dr. Hansen) and his colleagues were not, it turned out, able to save the knee. They had a thorough discussion, and the decision was unanimous. The impact—he will show him later on the X-ray—was directly to the knee, and there was an added component of rotation, so the joint was shattered and twisted at the same time. In a younger person they might perhaps have gone for a reconstruction, but a reconstruction of the required order would entail a whole series of operations, one after another, extending over a year, even two years, with a success rate of less than fifty per cent, so all in all, considering his age, it was thought best to take the leg off cleanly above the knee, leaving a good length of bone for a prosthesis. He (Dr. Hansen) hopes he (Paul Rayment) will come to accept the wisdom of that decision.

"I am sure you have plenty of questions," he concludes, "and I will be happy to try to answer them, but perhaps not now, better in the morning, after you have had some sleep."

"Prosthesis," he says, another difficult word, though now that he understands about the jaw that is not broken, merely bruised, he is less embarrassed about difficult words.

"Prosthesis. Artificial limb. Once the surgical wound has healed we will be fitting a prosthesis. Four weeks, maybe even sooner. In no time at all you will be walking again. Riding your bicycle too, if you like. After some training. Other questions?"

He shakes his head. *Why did you not ask me first?* he wants to say; but if he utters the words he will lose control, he will start shouting.

"Then I'll speak to you in the morning," says Dr. Hansen. "Chin up!"

That is not all, however. That is not the end of it. First the violation, then consent to the violation. There are papers to sign before he will be left alone, and the papers prove surprisingly difficult.

Family, for instance. Who and where are his family, the papers ask, and how should they be informed? And insurance. Who are his insurers? What cover does his policy provide?

Insurance is no problem. He is insured to the hilt, there is a card in his wallet to prove it, he is nothing if not prudent (*but where is his wallet, where are his clothes?*). Family is a less straightforward matter. Who are his family? What is the right answer? He has a sister. She passed on twelve years ago, but she still lives in him or with him, just as he has a mother who, at the times when she is not in or with him, awaits the angels' clarion from her plot in the cemetery in Ballarat. A father too, doing his waiting farther away, in the cemetery in Pau, from where he rarely pays visits. Are they his family, the three of them? *Those into whose lives you are born do not pass away,* he would like to inform whoever composed the question. *You bear them with you, as you hope to be borne by those who come after you.* But there is no space on the form for extended answers.

9

What he can be altogether more definite about is that he has neither wife nor offspring. He was married once, certainly; but the partner in that enterprise is no longer part of him. She has escaped him, wholly escaped. How she managed the trick he has yet to grasp, but it is so: she has escaped into a life of her own. For all practical purposes, therefore, and certainly for the purposes of the form, he is unmarried: unmarried, single, solitary, alone.

Family: *NONE*, he writes in block letters, the nurse overseeing, and draws lines through the other questions, and signs the forms, both of them. "Date?" he demands of the nurse. "Second of July," she says. He writes the date. Motor functions unimpaired.

The pills he accepts are meant to blunt the pain and make him sleep, but he does not sleep. *This*—this strange bed, this bare room, this smell both antiseptic and faintly urinous—this is clearly no dream, it is the real thing, as real as things get. Yet the whole of today, if it is all the same day, if time still means anything, has the feel of a dream. Certainly this *thing*, which now for the first time he inspects under the sheet, this monstrous object swathed in white and attached to his hip, comes straight out of the land of dreams. And what about the other thing, the thing that the young man with the madly flashing glasses spoke of with such enthusiasm—when will that make its appearance? Not in all his days has he seen a naked prosthesis.

The picture that comes to mind is of a wooden shaft with a barb at its head like a harpoon and rubber suckers on its three little feet. It is out of Surrealism. It is out of Dali.

He reaches out a hand (the three middle fingers are strapped together, he notices for the first time) and presses the thing in white. It gives back no sensation at all. It is like a block of wood. *Just a dream*, he says to himself, and falls into the deepest sleep.

"Today we're going to have you walking," says young Dr. Hansen. "This afternoon. Not a long walk, just a few steps to give you the feel of it. Elaine and I will be there to lend a hand." He nods to the nurse. Nurse Elaine. "Elaine, can you set it up with Orthopaedics?"

"I don't want to walk today," he says. He is learning to talk through clenched teeth. It is not just that the jaw is bruised, the molars on that side have been loosened too, he cannot chew. "I don't want to be rushed. I don't want a prosthesis."

"That's fine," says Dr. Hansen. "It's not a pros-thesis we are talking about anyway, that is still down the line, this is just rehabilitation, the first step in rehabilitation. But we can start tomorrow or next day. Just so you can see it isn't the end of the world, losing a leg."

"Let me say it again: *I don't want a prosthesis.*"

Dr. Hansen and Nurse Elaine exchange glances.

11

"If you don't want a prosthesis, what would you prefer?"

"I would prefer to take care of myself."

"All right, end of subject, we won't rush you into anything, I promise. Now can I talk to you about your leg? Can I tell you about care of the leg?"

Care of my leg? He is smouldering with anger— can they not see it? *You anaesthetised me and hacked off my leg and dropped it in the refuse for someone to collect and toss into the fire. How can you stand there talking about care of my leg?*

"We have brought the remaining muscle over the end of the bone," Dr. Hansen is saying, demonstrating with cupped hands how they did it, "and sewn it there. Once the wound heals we want that muscle to form a pad over the bone. During the next few days, from the trauma and from the bed rest, there will be a tendency to oedema and swelling. We need to do something about that. There will also be a tendency for the muscle to retract towards the hip, like this." He stands sideways, pokes out his behind. "We counteract that by stretching. Stretching is very important. Elaine will show you some stretching exercises and help you if you need help."

Nurse Elaine nods.

"Who did this to me?" he says. He cannot shout because he cannot open his jaws, but that suits him, suits his teeth-grinding rage. "Who hit me?" There are tears in his eyes.

★   ★   ★

The nights are endless. He is too hot, he is too cold; the leg, closed in its swaddling, itches and cannot be reached. If he holds his breath he can hear the ghostly creeping of his assaulted flesh as it tries to knit itself together again. Outside the sealed window a cricket chants to itself. When sleep comes it is sudden and brief, as if gusts of leftover anaesthetic were coming up from his lungs to overwhelm him.

Night or day, time drags. There is a television set facing the bed, but he has no interest in television or in the magazines some kind agency has provided (*Who. Vanity Fair. Australian Homes & Gardens*). He stares at his watch face, imprinting the position of the hands on his mind. Then he closes his eyes, tries to think of other things—his own breathing, his grandmother sitting at the kitchen table plucking a chicken, bees among the flowers, anything. He opens his eyes. The hands have not stirred. It is as though they have to push their way through glue.

The clock stands still yet time does not. Even as he lies here he can feel time at work on him like a wasting disease, like the quicklime they pour on corpses. Time is gnawing away at him, devouring one by one the cells that make him up. His cells are going out like lights.

The pills he is given every sixth hour wash away the worst of the pain, which is good, and sometimes send him to sleep, which is better; but they also confuse his mind and bring such panic and terror to his dreams that he baulks at taking them. *Pain is nothing*, he tells himself, *just a warning signal from the body to the brain. Pain is no more the real thing than an X-ray photograph is the real thing.* But of course he is wrong. Pain is the real thing, it does not have to press hard to persuade him of that, it does not have to press at all, merely to send a flash or two; after which he quickly settles for the confusion, the bad dreams.

Someone else has been moved into his room, a man older than himself come back from hip surgery. The man lies all day with his eyes shut. Now and again a pair of nurses close the curtains around his bed and, under cover, attend to his body's needs.

Two oldsters; two old fellows in the same boat. The nurses are good, they are kind and cheery, but beneath their brisk efficiency he can detect— he is not wrong, he has seen it too often in the past—a final indifference to their fate, his and his companion's. From young Dr. Hansen he feels, beneath the kindly concern, the same indifference. It is as though at some unconscious level these young people who have been assigned to care for them know they have nothing left to give to the tribe and therefore do not count. *So young and yet so heartless!* he cries to himself. *How did I come to fall into their hands? Better for the old to tend the old, the dying the dying! And what folly to be so alone in the world!*

They talk about his future, they nag him to do

the exercises that will prepare him for that future, they chivvy him out of bed; but to him there is no future, the door to the future has been closed and locked. If there were a way of putting an end to himself by some purely mental act he would put an end to himself at once, without further ado. His mind is full of stories of people who bring about their own end—who methodically pay bills, write goodbye notes, burn old love letters, label keys, and then, once everything is in order, don their Sunday best and swallow down the pills they have hoarded for the occasion and settle themselves on their neatly made beds and compose their features for oblivion. Heroes all of them, unsung, unlauded. *I am resolved not to be any trouble.* The only matter they cannot take care of is the body they leave behind, the mound of flesh that, after a day or two, will begin to stink. If only it were possible, if only it were permitted, they would take a taxi to the crematorium, set themselves down before the fatal door, swallow their dose, then before consciousness dwindles press the button that will precipitate them into the flames and allow them to emerge on the other side as nothing but a shovelful of ash, almost weightless.

He is convinced that he would put an end to himself if he could, right now. Yet at the same time that he thinks this thought he knows he will do no such thing. It is only the pain, and the dragging, sleepless nights in this hospital, this zone of humiliation with no place to hide from the pitiless gaze of the young, that make him wish for death.

The implications of being single, solitary and alone are brought home to him most pointedly at the end of the second week of his stay in the land of whiteness.

"You don't have family?" says the night nurse, Janet, the one who allows herself banter with him. "You don't have friends?" She screws up her nose as she speaks, as though it is a joke he is playing on them all.

"I have all the friends I could wish for," he replies. "I am not Robinson Crusoe. I just do not want to see any of them."

"Seeing your friends would make you feel better," she says. "Give you a lift. I am sure."

"I will receive visitors when I feel like it, thank you," he says.

He is not irascible by nature, but in this place he allows himself spells of peevishness, tetchiness, choler, since that seems to make it easier for his minders to leave him alone. *He's not so bad under the surface*, he imagines Janet protesting to her colleagues. *That old fart!* he imagines her colleagues reply, snorting with derision.

He knows it is expected of him *now that he is improving* to experience gross desires towards these young women, desires which, because male patients, no matter their age, cannot help themselves, will surface at inconvenient times and must be deflected as quickly and decisively as possible.

The truth is that he has no such desires. His heart is as pure as a babe's. It wins him no credit among the nurses, of course, this purity of heart, nor does he expect it to. Being a lecherous old goat is part of the game, a game he is declining to play.

If he refuses to contact friends, it is simply because he does not want to be seen in his new, curtailed, humiliating, and humiliated state. But of course, one way or another, people get to hear of what happened. They send good wishes, they even call in person. On the telephone it is easy enough to make up a story. *It's only a leg*, he says, with a bitterness that he hopes does not come across on the line. *I will be on crutches for a while, then on a prosthesis.* In person the act is more difficult to bring off, since his detestation of the lumpish thing he will henceforth have to lug around with him is all too plainly written on his face.

From the opening of the chapter, from the incident on Magill Road to the present, he has not behaved well, has not risen to the occasion: that much is clear to him. A golden opportunity was presented to him to set an example of how one accepts with good cheer one of the bitterer blows of fate, and he has spurned it. *Who did this to me?*: when he recalls how he shouted at the no doubt perfectly competent though rather ordinary young Dr. Hansen, seeming to mean *Who drove into me?* but really meaning *Who had the impudence to cut off my leg?*, he is suffused with shame. He is not the first person in the world to suffer an unpleasant accident, not the first old man to find himself in hospital with well-intentioned but ultimately indifferent young people going through the motions of caring for him. A leg gone: what is losing a leg, in the larger perspective? In the larger perspective, losing a leg is no more than a rehearsal for losing everything. Whom is he going to shout at when that day arrives? Whom is he going to blame?

Margaret McCord pays a visit. The McCords are his oldest friends in Adelaide; Margaret is upset at having heard so late, and full of righteous indignation against whoever did this to him. "I hope you are going to sue," she says. "I have no intention of suing," he replies. "Too many openings for comedy. *I want my leg back, failing which* . . . I leave that side of things to the insurance people." "You are making a mistake," she says: "people who drive recklessly should be taught a lesson. I suppose they will fit you out with a prosthesis. They make such wonderful prostheses nowadays, you will soon be riding your bicycle again." "I don't think so," he replies. "That part of my life is over." Margaret shakes her head. "What a pity!" she says. "What a pity!"

Sweet of her to say so, he reflects afterwards. *Poor Paul, poor dear, how difficult, what you are having to go through!*: that was what she meant, what she knew he would understand her to mean. *We all have to go through something of this sort,* he would like to remind her, *in the end.*

What surprises him about the whole hospital business is how swiftly concern passes from patching up his leg ("Excellent!" says Dr. Hansen, probing the stump with a handsomely manicured finger. "It is coming together beautifully. You will soon be yourself again.") to the question of how he will (their word) *cope* once he is set loose in the world again.

Indecently early, or so it seems to him, a social worker, Mrs. Putts or Putz, is brought into the picture. "You're still a young man, Mr. Rayment, Paul," she informs him in the cheery manner she must have been taught to employ upon the old. "You will want to remain independent, and of course that's good, but for quite some time you are going to need nursing, specialised nursing, which we can help to arrange. In the longer term, even once you are mobile, you are going to need someone to be there for you, to give you a hand, to do the shopping and cooking and cleaning and so forth. Is there no one?"

He thinks it over, shakes his head. "No, there is no one," he says; by which he means—and believes Mrs. Putts understands—that there is no one who will conceive it as his or her Confucian duty to devote himself or herself to caring for his wants, his cooking and cleaning and so forth.

What interests him in the question is what it reveals about his condition as viewed by Mrs. Putts, who must have had franker exchanges with the medical people than have yet been afforded him, franker and more down-to-earth. From these down-to-earth exchanges she has evidently concluded that even *in the longer term* he will not get by without being *given a hand.*

In his own vision of the longer term, the vision he has been fashioning in his more equable moments, his crippled self (stark word, but why equivocate?) will somehow, with the aid of a crutch or some other support, get by in the world, more slowly than before, perhaps, but what do slow and fast matter any more? But that does not appear to be their vision. In their vision, it would seem, he is not the kind of amputee who masters his new, changed circumstances and generally *copes,* but the crepuscular kind, the kind who, in the absence of professional support, will end up in an institution for the aged and infirm.

If Mrs. Putts were prepared to be straight with him he would be straight with her. *I have given plenty of thought to coping,* he would tell her. *I made my preparations long ago; even if the worst comes to the very worst, I will be able to take care of myself.* But the rules of the game make it hard for either of them to be straight. If he told Mrs. Putts about the cache of Somnex in the cabinet in the bathroom of his flat, for instance, she might feel bound by the rules of the game to consign him to counselling to protect him from himself.

He sighs. "From your point of view, from a professional point of view, Mrs. Putts, Dorianne," he says, "what steps would you suggest?"

20

"You will need to engage a care-giver, that's for sure," says Mrs. Putts, "preferably a private nurse, someone with experience of frail care. Not that you are frail, of course. But until you are mobile again we would not want to take chances, would we?"

"No, we would not," he says.

Frail care. Care of the frail. He had never thought of himself as frail until he saw the X-rays. He found it hard to believe that the spider-bones revealed in the plates could keep him upright, that he could totter around without them snapping. The taller the frailer. Too tall for his own good. *I've never operated on such a tall man*, Dr. Hansen had said, *with such long legs*. And had then flushed at his gaffe.

"Do you know offhand, Paul," says Mrs. Putts, "whether your insurance stretches to frail care?"

A nurse, yet another nurse. A woman with a little white cap and sensible shoes bustling about his flat, calling out in jolly tones, *Time for your pills, Mr. R!* "No, I do not think my insurance will run to that," he replies.

"Well then you'll have to budget for it, won't you?" says Mrs. Putts.

CHAPTER 3

*F*rivolous. How he had strained, that day on Magill Road, to attend the word of the gods, tapped out on their occult typewriter! Looking back, he can only smile. How quaint, how positively antique, to believe one will be advised, when the time comes, to put one's soul in order. What beings could possibly be left, in what corner of the universe, interested in checking all the deathbed accountings that ascend the skies, debits in the one column, credits in the other?

Yet *frivolous* is not a bad word to sum him up, as he was before the event and may still be. If in the course of a lifetime he has done no significant harm, he has done no good either. He will leave no trace behind, not even an heir to carry on his name. *Sliding through the world*: that is how, in a bygone age, they used to designate lives like his: looking after his interests, quietly prospering, attracting no attention. If none is left who will pronounce judgment on such a life, if the Great Judge of All has given up judging and withdrawn to pare his nails, then he will pronounce it himself: *A wasted chance.*

He had never thought he would have a good word to say for war, but here in his hospital bed, consuming time and being consumed, he seems to be revising his opinions. In the razing of cities, the pillage of treasure, the slaughter of innocents, in all that reckless destruction, he begins to detect a certain wisdom, as though at its deepest level history knows what it is doing. Down with the old, make way for the new! What could be more selfish, more miserly—this in specific is what gnaws at him—than dying childless, terminating the line, subtracting oneself from the great work of generation? Worse than miserly, in fact: unnatural.

The day before his discharge he has a surprise visitor: the boy who hit him, Wayne something-or-other, Bright or Blight. Wayne is calling to see how he is getting on, though not, it emerges, to admit to any fault. "Thought I'd see how you are getting on, Mr. Rayment," says Wayne. "I'm really sorry for what happened. Real bad luck." Not an artist in words, young Wayne; yet his every utterance is carefully evasive, as though he has been told the room is bugged. And indeed, as he later learns, Wayne's father was in the corridor throughout the visit, eavesdropping. No doubt he had coached Wayne beforehand: "Be respectful to the old bugger, say you're sorry, but at all costs don't admit you did anything wrong."

What son and father say to each other in private concerning the riding of pushbikes on busy streets he can imagine all too well. But the law is the law:

even stupid old buggers on pushbikes have the right not to be ridden down, and Wayne and his father know that. They must be trembling at the thought of a suit, from him or his insurance company. That must be why Wayne picks his words so judiciously.

Real bad luck. There is a range of replies he can think of, starting with *Nothing to do with luck, Wayne, just real bad driving*. But what use is there in scoring points off a boy who does not have it in his power to fix what he has smashed? *Go, and sin no more*: that is the best he can think of right now. Just the kind of sententious, old-geezerish pronouncement that the Blights, father and son, would chortle over on the way home. He closes his eyes, wishing Wayne to go away.

An accident: something that befalls one, something unintended, unexpected. By that definition he, Paul Rayment, certainly had an accident. What of Wayne Blight? Did Wayne have an accident too? How did it feel to Wayne, the instant when the missile he was piloting in a haze of loud music dug into the sweet softness of human flesh? A surprise, no doubt, unexpected, unintended; yet not unpleasurable in its way. Could what occurred at the ill-starred crossroads truly be said to have *befallen* Wayne? If there was any befalling done, it was, in his view, Wayne who befell him.

He opens his eyes. Wayne is still by the bedside, sweat pearling on his upper lip. Of course! At school Wayne would have had it drummed into him that you do not leave the room until the teacher signals the session is over. What a relief it must have been to Wayne when at last he was free of school and teachers and all that, when he could put his foot down flat on the accelerator, wind down the window and feel the wind on his face, chew gum, turn up the music as loud as he liked, shout "Fuck you, mate!" at old geezers as he ripped past them! And now here he is, constrained again, having to put on a dutiful face, to grope for apologetic-sounding words.

So the puzzle resolves itself. Wayne is waiting for a signal, and he wants Wayne out of his life. "Good of you to come, lad," he says, "but I have a headache and I need to sleep. So goodbye."

CHAPTER 4

The day nurse recommended by Mrs. Putts is named Sheena. Sheena looks nineteen, but her papers attest she is twenty-nine. She is fat, with a hard, lardy, confident fatness, and under all questioning unshakeably good-humoured. He takes an immediate dislike to her, he does not want her, but Mrs. Putts presses him. "It's specialised work, private nursing," says Mrs. Putts. "Sheena has worked with amputees before. You would be a fool to turn her down." So he yields. In turn Mrs. Putts concedes that he need not engage a night nurse, as long as he registers himself with an emergency service and keeps a pager handy at all times.

He takes care to stay on the right side of Mrs. Putts because he has what he believes to be an accurate idea of Mrs. Putts's powers. Mrs. Putts is part of the welfare system. Welfare means caring for people who cannot care for themselves. If, somewhere down the line, Mrs. Putts were to decide that he is incapable of caring for himself, that he needs to be protected from his own incompetence, what recourse would he have? He has no allies to do battle on his behalf. He has only himself.

It is possible, of course, that he overestimates Mrs. Putts's concern. When it comes to welfare, when it comes to care and the caring professions, he is almost certainly out of date. In the brave new world into which both he and Mrs. Putts have been reborn, whose watchword is *Laissez faire!*, perhaps Mrs. Putts regards herself as neither his keeper nor her brother's keeper nor anyone else's. If in this new world the crippled or the infirm or the indigent or the homeless wish to eat from rubbish bins and spread their bedroll in the nearest entranceway, let them do so: let them huddle tight, and if they wake up alive the next morning, good on them.

When the ambulancemen bring him home, Sheena is ready and waiting. It is she who re-organises his bedroom for him, supervises the cleaning woman, instructs the handyman where to install rails, and generally takes over. She has already drafted a day-by-day schedule for the two of them covering meals, exercises, and what she calls SC, stump care, which she tapes to the wall above his head. It includes three blocks, one in mid-morning, one at noon, one in the afternoon, labelled "SD PRIVATE TIME," time during which she retires to the kitchen to refresh herself. She keeps her supplies in the fridge on a shelf that she labels "SD PRIVATE." So that she will not perish of boredom she keeps the radio on in the kitchen, on a station that alternates clamouring advertisements with thudding music. When he asks her to turn the sound lower she turns the sound lower; nevertheless, without straining, he can still hear it.

The first test of his physical powers comes when, with Sheena supporting his elbow, he attempts to use the toilet. The sitting-down manoeuvre defeats him: the left leg, the leg left to him, is as weak as putty. Sheena purses her lips. "Back to bed at once," she says. "I'll fetch you the potty."

She calls the bedpan the potty; she calls his penis his willie. Halfway through a sponge bath, before dealing with the stump, she pauses and puts on a baby voice. "Now if he wants Sheena to wash his willie, he must ask very nicely," she says. "Otherwise he will think Sheena is one of those naughty girls. Those naughty naughty girls." And she gives him a playful slap on the arm to show it is just a joke.

He puts up with Sheena until the end of the week, then telephones Mrs. Putts. "I am going to ask Sheena not to come back," he says. "I cannot abide her. You will have to find me someone else."

Getting rid of Sheena turns out to be by no means as simple as that. By the time her professional pride has been mollified he has had to fork out two months' wages. He wonders how often in her nursing career she has brought off coups on a similar scale. Perhaps the radio was just a trick to madden him, and the baby-talk too.

After Sheena he is tended by a succession of nurses from the agency, nurses who call themselves *temps* and come for a day or two at a time. "Can't you find me someone regular?" he asks Mrs. Putts on the telephone. "I am stretched to the limit," says Mrs. Putts. "There's a huge demand for frail-care nursing. Be patient, you are on my A list."

His elation at having escaped the hospital does not last long. He slumps into a bad mood, and the mood does not leave him. He does not like any of the temps—does not like being treated as a child or an idiot, does not like the bouncy, cheerful voice they put on for him. "How are we today?" they say. "That's good," they say, even when he has not bothered to reply.

"When are we having our leg fitted?" they say. "So much better than crutches, a new leg, it really is, once you get the hang of it. You'll see."

From being irascible he becomes sullen. He wants to be left alone; he does not want to speak to anyone; he suffers fits of what he thinks of as dry weeping. *If only real tears would come!* he thinks. *If only I could be washed away in tears!* He welcomes those days when for one reason or another no one arrives to take care of him, even if it means he has to get by on biscuits and orange juice.

He blames his gloom on the painkillers. Which is worse, the cloud of gloom in the head or the ache in the bone that keeps him awake all night? He tries doing without the pills and ignoring the pain. But the gloom does not lift. The gloom seems to have settled in, to be part of the climate.

In the old days, the days before the accident, he did not have what he would call a gloomy temperament. He might have been solitary, but only as certain male animals are solitary. There was always more than enough to keep him occupied. He took out books from the library, he went to the cinema; he cooked for himself, he even baked his own bread; he did not own a car but rode a bicycle or walked. If such a way of life made him eccentric, it was eccentricity within the mildest Australian limits. He was tall, he was rangy, he had preserved a certain wiry strength; he was the kind of man who might last into his nineties, eccentricities and all.

Well, he may still live to be ninety, but if that happens it will not be by choice. He has lost the freedom of movement and it would be foolish to think it will ever be restored to him, with or without artificial limbs. He will never stride up Black Hill again, never pedal off to the market to do his shopping, much less come swooping on his bicycle down the curves of Montacute. The universe has contracted to this flat and the block or two around, and it will not expand again.

A circumscribed life. What would Socrates say about that? May a life become so circumscribed that it is no longer worth living? Men come out of prison, out of years of staring at the same blank wall, without gloom taking possession of their souls. What is so special about losing a limb? A giraffe that loses a leg will surely perish; but giraffes do not have the agencies of the modern state, embodied in Mrs. Putts, watching over their welfare. Why should he not settle for a modestly circumscribed life in a city that is not inhospitable to the frail aged?

He cannot give answers to questions like these. He cannot give answers because he is not in the mood for answers. That is what it means to be gloomy: at a level far below the play and flicker of the intellect (*Why not this? Why not that?*) he, *he*, the *he* he calls sometimes *you*, sometimes *I*, is all too ready to embrace darkness, stillness, extinction. *He*: not the one whose mind used to dart this way and that but the one who aches all night.

Of course he is not a special case. People lose limbs or the use of limbs every day. History is full of one-armed sailors and chairbound inventors; of blind poets and mad kings too. But in his case the cut seems to have marked off past from future with such uncommon cleanness that it gives new meaning to the word *new*. By the sign of this cut let a new life commence. If you have hitherto been a man, with a man's life, may you henceforth be a dog, with a dog's life. That is what the voice says, the voice out of the dark cloud.

Has he given up? Does he want to die? Is that what it comes down to? No. The question is false. He does not *want* to slash his wrists, does not *want* to swallow down four and twenty Somnex, does not *want* to hurl himself off the balcony. He does not *want* death because he does not *want* anything. But if it so happens that Wayne Blight bumps into him a second time and sends him

31

flying through the air with the greatest of ease, he will make sure he does not save himself. No rolling with the blow, no springing to his feet. If he has a last thought, if there is time for a last thought, it will simply be, *So this is what a last thought is like.*

Unstrung: that is the word that comes back to him from Homer. The spear shatters the breastbone, blood spurts, the limbs are unstrung, the body topples like a wooden puppet. Well, his limbs have been unstrung and now his spirit is unstrung too. His spirit is ready to topple.

Mrs. Putts's second full candidate is named Marijana. By origin she is Croatian, so she informs him during their interview. She left the land of her birth behind twelve years ago. Her training was done in Germany, in Bielefeld; since coming to Australia she has acquired South Australian certification. Besides private nursing she does housekeeping for, as she puts it, "extra money." Her husband works in a car assembly plant; they live in Munno Para, north of Elizabeth, a half-hour drive from the city. They have a son in high school, a daughter in middle school, a third child not yet of school-going age.

Marijana Jokić is a sallow-faced woman who, if not quite middle-aged, exhibits a thickening about the waist that is quite matronly. She wears a sky-blue uniform that he finds a relief after all the whiteness, with patches of dampness under the arms;

she speaks a rapid, approximate Australian English with Slavic liquids and an uncertain command of *a* and *the*, coloured by slang she must pick up from her children, who must pick it up from their class-mates. It is a variety of the language he is not familiar with; he rather likes it.

The agreement arrived at between himself and Mrs. Jokić, Mrs. Putts mediating, is that she will attend him six days of the week, Monday to Saturday, deploying upon him for those days the full range of her caring skills. On Sundays he will fall back on the emergency service. For as long as his powers of ambulation remain restricted, she will not only nurse him but attend to his everyday needs, that is to say, shop for him, cook his meals, and do the lighter cleaning.

After the misadventure of Sheena he has no great hopes for the lady from the Balkans. In the days that follow, however, he finds himself grudgingly thankful for her advent. Mrs. Jokić—Marijana—seems able to intuit what he is ready for and what he is not. She treats him not as a doddering old fool but as a man hampered in his movements by injury. Patiently, without baby-talk, she helps him through his ablutions. When he tells her he wants to be left alone, she absents herself.

He reclines; she unwraps the thing, the stump, and runs a finger along its naked face. "Nice sutures," she says. "Who put in sutures?"

"Dr. Hansen."

"Hansen. Don't know Hansen. But is good.

Good surgeon." She hefts the stump judiciously in one hand, as if it were a watermelon. "Good job."

She soaps it, washes it. The warm water brings out a pink-and-white flush. It begins to look less like a cured ham than like some sightless deep-water fish; he averts his eyes.

"Do you see many bad jobs?" he asks.

She puckers her lips, draws her hands apart in a gesture that reminds him of his mother. *Maybe,* says the gesture; *it depends.*

"Do you see many of . . . these?" With the lightest of fingertips he touches himself.

"Sure."

He is interested to note how devoid of double entendre the exchange is.

To himself he does not call it a stump. He would like not to call it anything; he would like not to think about it, but that is not possible. If he has a name for it, it is *le jambon.* *Le jambon* keeps it at a nice, contemptuous distance.

He divides people with whom he has contact into two classes: those few who have seen it, and the rest, those who thankfully never will. It strikes him as a pity that Marijana should fall so early and so decisively into the first class.

"I have never understood why they could not leave the knee," he complains to her. "Bone grows together. Even if the joint was shattered, they could have made an attempt to reconstruct it. If I had known what a difference losing a knee makes I would never have consented. They told me nothing."

Marijana shakes her head. "Reconstruction," she says, "very difficult surgery, very difficult. For years, in and out hospital. For, you know, old patients they don't like it to make reconstruction. Only for young. What's the point, eh? What's the point?"

She puts him among the old, those whom there is no point in saving—saving the knee-joint, saving the life. Where, he wonders, would she put herself: among the young? the not-old? the neither young nor old? the never-to-be-old?

Rarely has he seen anyone throw herself as fully into her duties as Marijana does. The list with which she goes off to the shops comes back with the till receipts clipped to it, each item ticked off or, where she has had to vary it, annotated in her neat old-world hand with its barbed 1s and crossed 7s and looped 9s. From the tempests of her cooking emerge meals that are unfailingly appetising.

To friends who telephone to ask how he is getting on, he refers to Marijana simply as *the day nurse*. "I have hired a very competent day nurse," he says. "She does the shopping and the cooking too." He does not refer to her as *Marijana* in case it sounds too familiar; in conversation with her, he continues to call her *Mrs.* Jokić, as she calls him *Mr. Rayment*. But to himself he has no reservation about calling her *Marijana*. He likes the name, with its four full, uncompromising syllables. *Marijana will be here in the morning*, he tells himself when he feels the cloud of gloom descending again. *Pull yourself together!*

Whether he likes Marijana the woman as much as he likes her name he does not yet know. Objectively she is not unattractive. But in his company she seems to have the ability to annul sex. She is brisk, she is efficient, she is cheerful: that is the face she presents to him, her employer, that is the face he pays for and must be content with. So he gives up being irascible and takes pains to meet her with a smile. He would like her to think he bears his mishap gamely; he would like her to think well of him in all respects. If she does not flirt, he does not mind. It is better than coy talk about his willie.

Some mornings she brings her youngest child with her, the one who is not yet at school. Though born in Australia, the child's name is Ljuba, Ljubica. He likes the name, approves of it. In Russian, if he is not mistaken, *lyubov* means love. It is like calling a girl Aimée or, even better, Amour.

Her son and first-born has, she informs him, just turned sixteen. Sixteen: she must have married young. He is in the process of revising his estimate of her. More than not unattractive, she is on occasion a positively handsome woman, well built, sturdy, with nut-brown hair, dark eyes, a complexion olive rather than sallow; a woman who carries herself well, shoulders squared, breasts thrust forward. *Prideful*, he thinks, hunting for an English word that will capture her. Her teeth, stained yellow with nicotine, are the only objective flaw. She smokes in an unreconstructed old-European way, though for his sake she retires to the balcony.

As for the little girl, she is a true beauty, with dark curls and a perfect skin and eyes that glint with what can only be intelligence. Side by side the two make a pretty picture. Get on well together too. While she is cooking, Marijana helps the child to bake cupcakes or gingerbread biscuits. From the kitchen comes the even murmur of their voices. Mother and daughter: the protocols of womanhood being passed on, generation to generation.

CHAPTER 5

Weeks pass: He settles into Marijana's regimen of care. Each morning she takes him through his exercises, massages his wasted and wasting muscles; discreetly she helps him in what he cannot do without a helping hand, what he may never learn to do unaided. When he is in the mood to listen, she is ready to talk—about her work, her experience of Australia. When he withdraws, she seems content to be silent too.

Whatever love he might once have had for his body is long gone. He has no interest in fixing it up, returning it to some ideal efficiency. The man he used to be is just a memory, and a memory fading fast. He still has a sense of being a soul with an undiminished soul-life; as for the rest of him, it is just a sack of blood and bones that he is forced to carry around.

In such a state, it is tempting to let go of all modesty. But he resists the temptation. He does what he can to maintain the decencies, and Marijana backs him. When nakedness cannot be helped, he averts his eyes so that she will see he does not see her seeing him. What has to be done in private she does her best to ensure is done in private.

In all of this he is trying to remain a man, albeit a diminished man; and it could not be clearer that Marijana understands and sympathises. Where did she acquire this delicacy, he wonders, a delicacy her predecessors so signally lacked? In Bielefeld, at nursing college? Perhaps; but his guess is that it comes from deeper wells. *A decent woman*, he thinks to himself, *decent through and through*. One of the better things that has happened to him, having Marijana Jokić come into his life.

"Tell me if it hurts," she says as she bears down with her thumbs on the obscenely curtailed thigh muscles. But it never hurts; or if it does, the hurt is so much like pleasure that he cannot tell the difference. *An intuitive*, he thinks. By intuition pure and simple she seems to know how he feels, how his body will respond.

A man and a woman on a warm afternoon behind locked doors. They might as well be performing a sex act. But it is nothing like that. It is just nursing, just care.

A phrase from catechism class a half-century ago floats into his mind: *There shall be no more man and woman, but* . . . But what—what shall we be when we are beyond man and woman? Impossible for the mortal mind to conceive. One of the mysteries.

The words are St. Paul's, he is sure of that— St. Paul his namesake, his name-saint, explaining what the afterlife will be like, when all shall love all with a pure love, as God loves, only not as fiercely, as consumingly.

He, alas, is no spirit being as yet, but a man of some kind, the kind that fails to perform what man is brought into the world to perform: seek out his other half, cleave to her, and bless her with his seed—seed which, in the allegory or perhaps the anagogy unfolded by Brother Aloysius, he forgets which is which, represents God's word. A man not wholly a man, then: a half-man, an after-man, like an after-image; the ghost of a man looking back in regret on time not well used.

His grandparents Rayment had six children. His parents had two. He has none. Six, two, one or none: all around him he sees the miserable sequence repeated. He used to think it made sense: in an overpopulated world, childlessness was surely a virtue, like peaceableness, like forbearance. Now, on the contrary, childlessness looks to him like madness, a herd madness, even a sin. What greater good can there be than more life, more souls? How will heaven be filled if the earth ceases to send its cargoes?

When he arrives at the gate, St. Paul (for other new souls it may be Peter but for him it will be Paul) will be waiting. "Bless me father for I have sinned," he will say. "And how have you sinned, my child?" Then he will have no words to say, save to show his empty hands. "You sorry fellow," Paul will say, "you sorry, sorry fellow. Did you not understand why you were given life, the greatest gift of all?" "When I was living I did not understand, father, but now I understand, now that it is too late; and believe me, father, I repent, I repent me, *je me repens*, and bitterly too." "Then pass," Paul will say, and stand aside: "in the house of your Father there is room for all, even for the stupid lonely sheep."

Marijana would have set him right, had he only met her in time, Marijana from Catholic Croatia. From the loins of two, Marijana and her spouse, there have issued three—three souls for heaven. A woman built for motherhood. Marijana would have helped him out of childlessness. Marijana could mother six, ten, twelve and still have love left over, mother-love. But too late now: how sad, how sorry!

CHAPTER 6

He came away from the hospital with a pair of forearm crutches and something they called a Zimmer frame, a four-footed aluminium stand for use around the flat. The equipment comes on loan, to be returned when no longer needed, that is to say, when he has graduated to higher forms of mobility or else passed on.

There are other aids to be had (he gets to see the brochure), from a device that adds wheels and a safety brake to the quadrangular Zimmer frame, to a vehicle with a battery-powered motor and a steering bar and a retractable rain-hood, intended for advanced cripples. If he wants one of these fancier aids, however, he will have to buy it himself.

Under Marijana's ministrations, what she likes to call his leg is day by day losing its angry colour and swollen look. The crutches are becoming second nature, though he feels more secure leaning on the frame. When he is by himself he roams on his crutches from room to room, thinking of it as exercise when it is really only restlessness.

He visits the hospital for weekly checkups. On

one of these visits he shares the lift with an old woman, stooped, with a hawklike nose and a dark, Mediterranean skin. By the hand she holds a younger version of herself, small-boned, almost as dark, wearing a wide-brimmed hat and a pair of sunglasses huge enough to hide the upper half of her face. Pressed up against the younger woman, he has time, before they exit, to take in a lungful of rather overpowering gardenia perfume and to notice that, oddly, she is wearing her dress inside out, with the dry-cleaning instructions protruding like a bold little flag.

An hour later, on his way out of the building, he remarks the couple again, having a hard time with the swing door. By the time he himself reaches the street he can see only the wide black hat bobbing in the crowd.

Their image stays with him: the crone leading the hastily clad princess in an enchanted sleep-walk. Not quite young enough for the role of princess, perhaps, but attractive nonetheless: soft-fleshed, petite, big-bosomed, the kind of woman he imagines slumbering till noon and then break-fasting on bonbons served on a silver platter by a little slave-boy in a turban. What can she have done to her face that she needs to hide it?

She is the first woman to provoke his sexual interest since the accident. He has a dream in which she is somehow present though she does not reveal herself. In utter silence a crack in the earth opens and races towards him. Two vast waves

43

of dust rise in the air. He tries to run but his legs will not move. *Help!* he whispers. With black unseeing eyes the old woman, the crone, stares at him and through him. Over and over she mutters a word that he cannot quite catch, something like *Toomderoom.* The earth beneath his feet gives way, he plunges.

Margaret McCord telephones. She is sorry she has not been in touch, she has been out of town. Can she take him to lunch, perhaps on Sunday? They could drive out to the Barossa Valley. Unfortunately her husband will not be able to join them: he is overseas.

He would love to come, he replies, but alas, he finds long car rides a bit of a calvary.

"Then shall I just drop by?" she says.

Years ago, after his divorce, he and Margaret had a brief fling. According to Margaret, whom he does not necessarily trust, her husband knows nothing of those intimacies.

"Why not?" he says. "Come on Sunday. Come to dinner. I have some excellent cannelloni that my house help has prepared."

They eat on the balcony, on a rather cool evening, amid the valedictory calls of birds, with citronella candles flickering on the table. There is a certain constraint: what once passed between them is by no means forgotten. Margaret does not mention the absent husband.

He tells Margaret about his time under the rule of Sheena; he tells her about Mrs. Putts the social worker, who prepared him for the afterlife in all respects save sex, a topic she found herself too modest to broach, or perhaps thought inappropriate to a man of his age.

"And is it inappropriate?" asks Margaret. "Candidly?"

Candidly, he replies, he cannot yet tell. He is not incapacitated, if that is what she is asking. His spine is unharmed, as are the relevant nerve connections. The as yet unanswered question is whether he would be able to perform the motions required of the active member in a sexual couple. A second and related question is whether embarrassment and shame might not outweigh pleasure.

"I would have thought," says Margaret, "that given the circumstances you might be excused from playing the role of active member. As for your second question, how will you ever know until you have tried? But why should you be embarrassed? It's not as though you have leprosy. You are just an amputee. Amputees can be rather romantic. Think of all those war films: men coming home from the front with eye-patches or empty sleeves pinned across their chests or on crutches. Women swooned over them."

"Just an amputee," he says.

"Yes. You were the victim of an accident, a crash. Nothing shameful in that, nothing blameworthy. After which you had a leg amputated. Part of a leg. Part of a stupid body-part. That's all. You still have your health. You are still yourself. You are the

same handsome, healthy man you always were."
She gives him a smile.

They could test it out in the bedroom right now,
the two of them, test whether he is the same man
he always was, test whether even with a body-
part missing pleasure can outweigh its opposite.
Margaret would not be averse, he is sure of that.
But the moment passes and they do not grasp
it, for which, looking back later, he is thankful.
He does not care to become the object of any
woman's sexual charity, however good-natured.
Nor does he care to expose to the gaze of an
outsider, even if she is a friend from the old days,
even if she does claim to find amputees romantic,
this unlovely new body of his, that is to say, not
only the hectically curtailed thigh but the flaccid
muscles and the obscene little paunch that has
ballooned on his abdomen. If he ever goes to bed
with a woman again, he will make sure it is in the
dark.

"I have had a visitor," he tells Marijana the next
day.

"Yes?" says Marijana.

"There may be other visitors," he plunges on
grimly. "I mean women."

"To live with you?" says Marijana.

To live with him? The thought has never crossed
his mind. "Of course not," he says. "Just friends,
women friends."

"That's good," she says, and switches on the
vacuum cleaner.

46

Marijana, it would appear, could not care less whether he has women in the flat. What he gets up to in his own time is none of her business. And what could he get up to anyway?

Unlike Margaret, Marijana has never seen him as he used to be. To her he is simply her latest client, a pale-skinned, slack-thewed old man on crutches. Even so, he feels shame before Marijana, and before her daughter too, as if the ruddy good health of the mother and the angelic clarity of the child were pronouncing a joint judgment on him. He finds himself avoiding the child's gaze, hiding out in his armchair in a corner of the living-room as if the flat belonged to the two women and he were some pest, some rodent that had found its way in.

Margaret's visit sparks a series of day-dreams about women. All of the dreams are sexually coloured; in some he and the woman get as far as going to bed. In these dreams his new and altered body is not spoken of, is not even seen; all is well, all is as it was before. But the woman he is with is not Margaret. It is, most of the time, the woman he saw in the lift, the one with the dark glasses and the inside-out clothes. *Your dress*, he says to her: *let me help you adjust it*. She raises a hand to take off her glasses. *All right*, she says. Her voice is low, her eyes are dark pools into which he plunges.

CHAPTER 7

On the job Marijana wears not a nurse's cap but a head-scarf, like any good Balkan housewife. He approves of the scarf, as he approves of any token that she has not wholly cast off the old world in favour of the new.

Aside from assorted war criminals and the tall tennis player with the big serve whose name escapes him (Ilja? Ilic? Roman Ilic?), Croats are an unknown quantity to him. Yugoslavs are another matter. He must have crossed paths with dozens of Yugoslavs in the days when there were still Yugoslavs; but of course it never occurred to him to ask what variety of Yugoslav they were.

Where does Marijana fit into the Yugoslav picture, Marijana and the husband who assembles cars? What were they fleeing when they fled the old country? Or was it simply the case that, growing sick and tired of strife, they packed their goods and crossed the border in quest of a better, more peaceable life? And if a better, more peaceable life is not to be found in Australia, where is it to be found?

Marijana is telling him about her son, whose name

is Drago but who is known to his mates as Jag. For his just-passed sixteenth birthday, her husband bought Drago a motorcycle. A big mistake, in Marijana's opinion. Now Drago stays out every evening, neglecting his homework, missing meals. He and his friends hang out on the back roads, racing each other, practising skids and God knows what else. She is afraid he is going to break a limb, or worse.

"Your son is a young man," he tells Marijana. "He is testing himself. You cannot stop young men from exploring their limits. They want to be the fastest. They want to be the strongest. They want to be admired."

He has never met Drago, probably never will. But he enjoys Marijana's performance, enjoys its transparency: too well-mannered to boast about her boy, she complains instead about his un-ruliness, his recklessness, his *joie de vivre*, about how he will be her ruin.

"If you want to give Drago a fright," he suggests not entirely seriously, "bring him here one day. I'll show him my leg."

"You think he will listen, Mr. Rayment? He will say is nothing, is just bicycle accident."

"I'll show him what's left of the bicycle too."

He still has the bicycle in the store room down-stairs, the back wheel folded in two, the stays jammed into the spokes. No one bothered to steal it after all, that day on Magill Road, though it lay by the roadside till evening. Then the police took

49

it in. They rescued the plastic box too that had been strapped to the carrier, along with a fraction of the morning's purchases: a can of chickpeas with a dent in it, a quarter kilo of Brie that had melted in the sun and then congealed. He has kept the can as a memento, a memento mori. It is on a shelf in the kitchen. He will show Drago the can, he tells Marijana. *Imagine if that was your skull*, he will say to him. And then: *Spare a thought for your mum. She worries about you. She's a good woman. She wishes you to have a long and happy life.* Or perhaps he will not say the bit about her being a good woman. If her son does not know, who is he, a stranger, to tell him?

The next day Marijana brings a photograph: Drago standing beside the motorcycle in question, wearing boots and tight jeans, in the crook of his arm a helmet emblazoned with a lightning bolt. He is tall and husky for a sixteen-year-old, with a winning smile. *A dreamboat*, as girls used to say in the old days, just as his mother must have been *a peach*. No doubt he will break many hearts.

"What are your son's plans?" he asks.

"He wants to go to Defence Force Academy. He wants to join navy. He can get bursary for that."

"And your daughter, your older daughter?"

"Ah, she is too young for plans, her head is in sky."

Now she has a question for him, one that has taken surprisingly long in coming. "You have no children, Mr. Rayment?"

"No, alas not. We did not get around to it, my wife and I. We had other things on our minds, other ambitions. And then, before we knew it, we were divorced."

"And you never worry about it after?"

"On the contrary, I worried about it more and more, particularly as I grew older."

"And your wife? She worry about it?"

"My wife remarried. She married a divorcé with children of his own. They had a child together and became one of those complicated modern families where everyone calls everyone else by the first name. So no, my wife does not worry about our childlessness, my childlessness. My ex-wife. I do not have much contact with her. It was not a happy marriage."

It is all within bounds, what is passing between them, within the bounds of the impersonal personal. A conversation between a man and a woman, a woman who happens to be the man's nurse and shopping assistant and cleaning woman and general help, getting to know each other better in a country where all persons are equal, and all faiths. Marijana is a Catholic. He is no longer anything. But in this country the one is as good as the other, Catholicism and nothing. Marijana may disapprove of people who marry and unmarry and never get around to having children, but she knows enough to keep her disapproval to herself.

"So who is going to take care of you?"

An odd question to ask. The obvious answer is,

You are: you are going to take care of me, for the immediate future, you or whoever else I employ for that purpose. But presumably there is a more charitable way of interpreting the question—as *Who is going to be your stay and support?*, for instance.

"Oh, I'll take care of myself," he replies. "I do not expect a lengthy old age."

"You have family in Adelaide?"

"No, not in Adelaide. I have family in Europe, I suppose, but I long ago lost touch with them. I was born in France. Didn't I tell you? I was brought to Australia when I was a child, by my mother and my stepfather. I and my sister. I was six. My sister was nine. She is dead now. She died early, of cancer. So no, I have no family to take care of me."

They leave it at that, he and Marijana, their exchange of particulars. But her question echoes in his mind. *Who is going to take care of you?* The more he stares at the words *take care of*, the more inscrutable they seem. He remembers a dog they had when he was a child in Lourdes, lying in its basket in the last stages of canine distemper, whimpering without cease, its muzzle hot and dry, its limbs jerking. "*Bon, je m'en occupe,*" his father said at a certain point, and picked the dog up, basket and all, and walked out of the house. Five minutes later, from the woods, he heard the flat report of a shotgun, and that was that, he never saw the dog again. *Je m'en occupe*: I'll take charge of it; I'll take care of it; I'll do what has to be done. That kind of caring, with a shotgun, was certainly not what Marijana had in mind. Nevertheless, it lay englobed in the phrase, waiting to leak out. If so, what of his reply: *I'll take care of myself?* What did his words mean, objectively? Did the taking care, the care-taking he spoke of extend to donning his best suit and swallowing down his cache of pills, two at a time, with a glass of hot milk, and lying down in bed with his hands folded across his breast?

He has many regrets, he is full of regrets, they come back nightly like roosting birds. Chief among them is regret that he does not have a son. It would be nice to have a daughter, girls have an appeal of their own, but the son he does not have is the one he truly misses. If he and Henriette had had a son right away, while they still loved each other, or were enamoured of each other, or cared for each other, that son would be thirty years old by now, a man in his own right. Unimaginable perhaps; but the unimaginable is there to be imagined. Imagine the two of them, then, out for a stroll, father and son, chatting about this and that, men's talk, nothing serious. In the course of that chat he could let fall a remark, one of those oblique remarks that people make at moments when the real words are too difficult to bring out, about it being *time to pass on.* His son, his imaginary but imagined son, would understand at once: pass on the burden, pass on the succession, call it a day. "Mm," his son would say, William or Robert or whatever, meaning *Yes, I accept. You have done your duty, taken care of me, now it is my turn. I will take care of you.*

It is not beyond the bounds of the possible to acquire a son, even at this late juncture. He could, for instance, locate (but how?) some wayward orphan, some Wayne Blight in embryo, and put in an offer to adopt him, and hope to be accepted; though the chances that the welfare system, as represented by Mrs. Putts, would ever consign a child to the care of a maimed and solitary old man would be zero, less than zero. Or he could locate (but how?) some fertile young woman, and marry her or pay her or otherwise induce her to permit him to engender, or try to engender, a male child in her womb.

But it is not a baby he wants. What he wants is a son, a proper son, a son and heir, a younger, stronger, better version of himself.

His willie. *If you want me to wash your willie,* said Sheena in her private time with him, *you will have to ask.* Does he have it in his willie, in his exhausted loins, to father a child? Does he have the seed, and enough animal passion to drive the seed to the right place? The record would not seem to indicate so. The record would seem to indicate that passionate outpourings are not part of his nature. A pleasant affectionateness, a mild if gratifying sensuality— that is what Margaret McCord will recall about him, she and half a dozen other women, not including his wife. As a lover rather *doggy,* in fact: not a word he is fond of but an apt one. A

54

nice man to cuddle up to on a chilly evening; the kind of male friend you rather absent-mindedly go to bed with, then wonder later whether it really happened.

All in all, not a man of passion. He is not sure he has ever liked passion, or approved of it. Passion: foreign territory; a comical but unavoidable affliction like mumps, that one hopes to undergo while still young, in one of its milder, less ruinous varieties, so as not to catch it more seriously later on. Dogs in the grip of passion coupling, hapless grins on their faces, their tongues hanging out.

CHAPTER 8

"**Y**ou want I dust your books?"

Eleven in the morning, and Marijana would seem to have run out of tasks.

"All right, if you like. You can run the vacuum cleaner over them with that nozzle attachment."

She shakes her head, "No, I clean them good. You are book saver, don't want dust on books. You are book saver, yes?"

A book saver: is that what they call people like him in Croatia? What could it mean, book saver? A man who saves books from oblivion? A man who clings to books that he never reads? His study is lined from floor to ceiling with books he will never open again, not because they are not worth reading but because he is going to run out of days.

"A book collector, that's what we say here. Just those three shelves, from there to there, are a collection properly speaking. Those are my books on photography. The rest are just common or garden books. No, if I have saved anything it has been photographs, not books. I keep them in those cabinets. Would you like to see?"

In two old-fashioned cedarwood cabinets he has

hundreds of photographs and postcards of life in the early mining camps of Victoria and New South Wales. There is a handful from South Australia too. Since the field is not a popular or even a properly defined one, his collection may be the best in the country, even in the world.

"I began saving them in the 1970s, when first-generation photographs were still affordable. And when I still had the heart to go to auctions. Deceased estates. It would depress me too much now."

For her eyes he takes out the group photographs that are the core of his collection. For the photographer's visit some of the miners have put on their Sunday best. Others are content with a clean shirt, the sleeves rolled high to show off their brawny arms, and perhaps a clean neckerchief. They confront the camera with the look of grave confidence that came naturally to men in Victoria's day, but seems now to have vanished from the face of the earth.

He lays out two of his Faucherys. "Look at these," he says. "They are by Antoine Fauchery. He died young, otherwise he might have become one of the great photographers." By their side he lays out a few of the naughty postcards: Lil displaying a length of thigh as she snaps a garter; Flora, in déshabillé, smiling coyly over a plump naked shoulder. Girls whom Tom and Jack, fresh from the diggings, flush with cash, would visit on Saturday nights for a bit of you-know-what.

"So this is what you do," says Marijana when

the show is over. "Is good, is good. Is good you save history. So people don't think Australia is country without history, just bush and then mob of immigrants. Like me. Like us." She has taken off the head-scarf: she shakes her hair free, smoothes it back, gives him a smile.

Like us. Who are these *us?* Marijana and the Jokić family; or Marijana and he?

"It was not just bush, Marijana," he says cautiously.

"No, of course, is not bush, is Aboriginal people. But I talk about Europe, what they say in Europe. Bush, then Captain Cook, then immigrants— where is history, they say?"

"You mean, where are the castles and cathedrals? Don't immigrants have a history of their own? Do you cease to have a history when you move from one point on the globe to another?"

She brushes aside the rebuke, if that is what it is. "In Europe people say Australia have no history because in Australia everybody is new. Don't mind if you come with this history or that history, in Australia you start zero. Zero history, you understand? That's what people say in my country, in Germany too, in all Europe. Why you want to go to Australia, they say? Is like you go to desert, to Qatar, to Arab countries, oil countries. You only do it for money, they say. So is good somebody save old photographs, show Australia has history, too. But they worth lots of money, these photographs, eh?"

"Yes, they are worth money."

"So who gets them, you know, after you?"

"After my decease, do you mean? They are going to the State Library. It is all arranged. The State Library here in Adelaide."

"You don't sell them?"

"No, I won't sell them, it will be a bequest."

"But they put your name on, eh?"

"They will put my name on the collection indeed. The Rayment Bequest. So that in future days children will whisper to each other, 'Who was he, Rayment of the Rayment Bequest? Was he someone famous?'"

"But photograph too, maybe, eh, not just name? Photograph of Mr. Rayment. Photograph is not the same as just name, is more living. Otherwise why save photographs?"

No doubt about it, she has a point. If names are as good as images, why bother to save images? Why save the light-images of these dead miners, why not just type out their names and display the list in a glass case?

"I'll ask the people at the library," he says, "I'll see how they feel about the idea. But not a picture of me as I am now, God spare us that. As I used to be."

The dusting of the books, a chore that cleaning women in the past disposed of by running a feather duster over the spines, is attacked by Marijana as a major operation. Desk and cabinets are covered with newspaper; then, half a shelf at a time, the

59

books are carried out to the balcony and individually dusted, and the emptied shelves wiped immaculately clean.

"Just be sure," he intervenes nervously, "that the books go back in the same order."

She treats him to a look of such scorn that he quails.

Where does the woman get the energy? Does she run her home on the same lines? How does Mr. J cope with it? Or is it for his eyes alone, her Australian boss's: to show how much of herself she is prepared to give to her new country?

It is on the day of the book-dusting that what had been a mild interest in Marijana, an interest that had not amounted to more than curiosity, turns into something else. In her he begins to see if not beauty then at least the perfection of a certain feminine type. *Strong as a horse*, he thinks, eyeing the sturdy calves and well-knit haunches that ripple as she reaches for the upper shelves. *Strong as a mare.*

Has whatever it is that had been floating in the air these past weeks begun to settle, *faute de mieux*, on Marijana? And what is its name, this sediment, this sentiment? It does not feel like desire. If he had to pick a word for it, he would say it was admiration. Can desire grow out of admiration, or are the two quite distinct species? What would it be like to lie side by side, naked, breast to breast, with a woman one principally admires?

Not just a woman: a married woman too, he

must not forget that. Not too far away there lives and breathes a Mr. Marijana Jokić. Would Mr. Jokić or Pan Jokić or Gospodin Jokić or whatever he calls himself fly into a rage if he found out that his wife's employer indulged in daytime reveries about lying breast to breast with her—fly into one of those elemental Balkan rages that give birth to clan feuds and epic poems? Would Mr. Jokić come after him with a knife?

He makes jokes about Jokić because he envies him. When the chips are down, Jokić has this admirable woman and he does not. Not only does Jokić have her, he also has the children who come with her, come out of her: Ljubica the love-child; the distracted but no doubt equally pretty middle daughter whose name he cannot recall; and the dashing boy with the motorcycle. Jokić has them all and he has—what? A flat full of books and furniture. A collection of photographs, images of the dead, which after his own death will gather dust in the basement of a library along with other minor bequests more trouble to the cataloguers than they are worth.

Among the Faucherys he did not bring out for Marijana is the one that haunts him most deeply. It is of a woman and six children grouped in the doorway of a mud and wattle cabin. That is to say, it could be a woman and six children, or the eldest girl could be not a child at all but a second woman, a second wife, brought in to take the place of the first, who looks drained of life, exhausted of loins.

All of them wear the same expression: not hostile to the stranger with the newfangled picture-machine who a moment before this moment plunged his head under the dark cloth, but frightened, frozen, like oxen at the portal of a slaughterhouse. The light hits them flat in the face, picks out every smudge on their skin and their clothes. On the hand that the smallest child brings to her mouth the light exposes what might be jam but was more likely mud. How the whole thing could have been brought off with the long exposures required in those days he cannot even guess.

Not just bush, he would like to tell Marijana. Not just blackfellows either. Not zero history. Look, that is where we come from: from the cold and damp and smoke of that wretched cabin, from those women with their black helpless eyes, from that poverty and that grinding labour on hollow sto-machs. A people with a story of their own, a past. *Our* story, *our* past.

But is that the truth? Would the woman in the picture accept him as one of her tribe—the boy from Lourdes in the French Pyrenees with the mother who played Fauré on the piano? Is the history that he wants to claim as his not finally just an affair for the English and the Irish, foreigners keep out?

Despite Marijana's bracing presence, he seems to be on the brink of one of his bad spells again, one of the fits of lugubrious self-pity that turn into black gloom. He likes to think they come from elsewhere, episodes of bad weather that cross the sky and pass on. He prefers not to think they come from inside him and are his, part of him.

Fate deals you a hand, and you play the hand you are dealt. You do not whine, you do not complain. That, he used to believe, was his philosophy. Why then can he not resist these plunges into darkness?

The answer is that he is running down. Never is he going to be his old self again. Never is he going to have his old resilience. Whatever inside him was given the task of mending the organism after it was so terribly assaulted, first on the road, then in the operating theatre, has grown too tired for the job, too over-burdened. And the same holds for the rest of the team, the heart, the lungs, the muscles, the brain. They did for him what they could as long as they could; now they want to rest.

A memory comes back to him of the cover of a book he used to own, a popular edition of Plato. It showed a chariot drawn by two steeds, a black steed with flashing eyes and distended nostrils representing the base appetites, and a white steed of calmer mien representing the less easily identifiable nobler passions. Standing in the chariot, gripping the reins, was a young man with a half-bared torso and a Grecian nose and a fillet around his brow, representing presumably the self, that which calls itself *I*. Well, in his book, the book of him, the book of his life, if that ever comes to be written, the picture will be more humdrum than in Plato. Himself, the one he calls Paul Rayment, will be seated on a wagon hitched to a mob of nags and drays that huff and puff, some barely pulling their weight. After sixty years of waking up every blessed morning, munching their ration of oats, pissing and shitting, then being harnessed for the day's haul, Paul Rayment's team will have had enough. Time to rest, they will say, time to be put out to pasture. And if rest is denied them, well, they will just fold their limbs and settle down in their traces; and if the whip starts to whistle around their rumps, let it whistle.

Sick at heart, sick in the head, sick to the bone, and, if the truth be told, sick of himself—sick even before the wrath of God, transmitted through his angel Wayne Blight, struck him down. He would never want to diminish that event, that blow. It was nothing less than a calamity. It has shrunk his world, turned him into a prisoner. But escaping death ought to have shaken him up, opened windows inside him, renewed his sense of the preciousness of life. It has done nothing of the sort. He is trapped with the same old self as before, only greyer and drearier. Enough to drive one to drink.

One o'clock and Marijana has not finished with the books. Ljuba, usually a good child—if it is still permitted to divide children into the good and the bad—is beginning to whine.

"Leave the cleaning. Finish it off tomorrow," he tells Marijana.

"I am finished in flesh of lightning," she replies. "Maybe you give her something to eat."

"Flash. A flash of lightning. Flesh is what we are made of, flesh and bone."

She does not reply. Sometimes he thinks she does not bother to listen to him.

He should give Ljuba something to eat, but what? What do small children eat other than popcorn and cookies and toasted cereal flakes encrusted in sugar, none of which he has in his pantry?

He tries stirring a spoonful of plum jam into a pot of yoghurt. Ljuba accepts it, seems to like it.

She sits at the kitchen table, he stands by her leaning on Zimmer's invention. "Your mum is a great help to me," he says. "I don't know what I would do without her."

"Is it true you've got a artificial leg?" She produces the long word casually, as though she uses it every day.

"No, it's the same leg I always had, just a bit shorter."

"But in your cupboard in your bedroom. Do you got a artificial leg in your cupboard?"

"No, I'm afraid not, there is nothing of the sort in my cupboard."

"Do you got a screw in your leg?"

"A screw? No, no screws. My leg is all natural. It has a bone inside, just like your legs and your Mommy's legs."

"Doesn't it got a screw, to screw on your artificial leg?"

"No, not as far as I know. Because I have no artificial leg. Why do you ask?"

"Because." And she will say no more.

A screw in his leg. Perhaps in the past Marijana nursed a man with screws in his leg, screws and bolts and pins and struts and braces, all made of gold or titanium—a man with a reconstructed leg of the kind that was not awarded to him because he was too old for it, not worth the trouble and expense. Perhaps that is the explanation.

As a child, he remembers, he was told the story of a woman who in a moment of absent-mindedness stuck a tiny sewing-needle into the palm of her hand. Unnoticed, the needle climbed up the woman's veins and in the fullness of time pierced her heart and killed her. The story was presented to him as a caution against treating needles carelessly, but in retrospect it reads more like a fairytale. Is steel really antipathetic to life? Can needles really enter the bloodstream? How could the woman in the story have been unaware of the tiny metallic weapon cruising up her arm towards her armpit, rounding the axillar curve, and heading south towards its help-less, thudding prey? Should he be re-telling the story to Ljuba, passing on its cryptic wisdom, whatever that may be?

"No," he repeats, "I have no screws in me. If I had screws I would be a mechanical man. Which I am not."

But Ljuba has lost interest in the leg that is not a mechanical leg. With a smack of the lips she finishes off the yoghurt and draws the sleeve of her jumper across her mouth. He reaches for a tissue and wipes her lips, which she allows him to do. After that he wipes her sleeve clean too.

It is the first time he has laid a finger on the child. For a moment her wrist lies limp in his hand. *Perfect:* no other word will do. They arrive from the womb with everything new, everything in perfect order. Even in the ones who arrive damaged, with funny limbs or a brain that sends out sparks, each cell is as fresh, as clean, as new as on creation day. Each new birth a new miracle.

CHAPTER 9

Margaret pays a second visit, this time unannounced. It is a Sunday, he is alone in the flat. He offers her tea, which she declines. She circles the room, comes up behind him where he sits, strokes his hair. He is still as a stone.

"So is this the end of it, Paul?" she asks.

"The end of what?"

"You know what I mean. Have you decided this is the end of your sexual life? Tell me straight so that I will know how to conduct myself in future."

Not someone to beat about the bush, Margaret. He has always liked that about her. But how should he respond? *Yes, I have come to the end of my sexual life, from now on treat me like a eunuch?* How can he say that when it may not even be true? Yet what if it is indeed true? What if the snorting black steed of passion has given up the ghost? The twilight of his manhood. What a let-down; but what a relief too!

"Margaret," he says, "give me time."

"And your day help?" says Margaret, going for

the weak spot. "How are you and your day help getting on?"

"My day help and I get on well, thank you. But for her I might not bother to get out of bed in the mornings. But for her I might end up as one of those cases one reads about, where the neighbours smell a bad smell and call in the police to break down the door."

"Don't be melodramatic, Paul. Nobody dies of an amputated leg."

"No, but people do die of indifference to the future."

"So your day help has saved your life. That's good. She deserves a medal. She deserves a bonus. When am I going to meet her?"

"Don't take it personally, Margaret. You asked me a question, I am trying to give a truthful answer."

But Margaret does take it personally. "I'll be on my way now," she says. "Don't get up, I'll let myself out. Give me a call when you are ready for human society again."

In his sessions with the physiotherapist he was warned about the tendency of the severed thigh muscles to retract, pulling the hip and pelvis backward. He props himself on the frame and with a free hand explores his lower back. Can he feel the beginnings of a backward jut? Is this ugly half-limb becoming even uglier?

If he were to give in and accept a prosthesis there would be a stronger reason for exercising the stump. As it is, the stump is of no use to him at all. All he can do with it is carry it around like an unwanted child. No wonder it wants to shrink, retract, withdraw.

But if this fleshly object is repulsive, how much more so a leg moulded out of pink plastic with a hinge at the top and a shoe at the bottom, an apparatus that you strap yourself to in the morning and unstrap yourself from at night and drop on the floor, shoe and all! He shudders at the thought of it; he wants nothing to do with it. Crutches are better. Crutches are at least honest.

Nevertheless, once a week he allows a ferry vehicle to call for him and convey him to George Street in Norwood, to a rehabilitation class run by a woman named Madeleine Martin. There are half a dozen other amputees in the class, all of them on the wrong side of sixty. He is not the only one without a prosthesis, but he is the only one to have refused one.

Madeleine cannot understand what she calls his attitude. "There are people all around in the street," she says, "who you could not even tell they are wearing prostheses, it's so natural the way they walk."

"I don't want to look natural," he says. "I prefer to feel natural."

She shakes her head in smiling incredulity. "It's a new chapter in your life," she says. "The old chapter is closed, you must say goodbye to it and accept the new one. Accept: that's all you need to do. Then all the doors that you think are closed will open. You'll see."

He does not reply.

Does he really want to feel natural? Did he feel natural before the occurrence on Magil Road? He has no idea. But perhaps that is what it means to feel natural: to have no idea. Does the Venus of Milo feel natural? Despite having no arms the Venus of Milo is held up as an ideal of feminine beauty. Once she had arms, the story goes, then her arms were broken off; their loss only makes her beauty more poignant. Yet if it were discovered tomorrow that the Venus was in fact modelled on an amputee, she would be removed at once to a basement store. Why? Why can the fragmentary image of a woman be admired but not the image of a fragmentary woman, no matter how neatly sewn up the stumps?

He would give a great deal to be pedalling his bicycle down Magill Road again, with the wind on his face. He would give a great deal for the chapter that is now closed to be opened again. He wishes Wayne Blight had never been born. That is all. Easy enough to say. But he keeps his mouth shut.

Limbs have memories, Madeleine tells the class, and she is right. When he takes a step on his crutches his right side still swings through the arc that the old leg would have swung through; at night his cold foot still seeks its cold ghostly brother.

Her job, Madeleine tells them, is to re-program old and now obsolete memory systems that dictate

71

to us how we balance, how we walk, how we run. "Of course we want to hold on to our old memory systems," she says. "Otherwise we would not be human. But we must not hold on to them when they hinder our progress. Not when they get in our way. Are you with me? Of course you are."

Like all the health professionals he has met of late, Madeleine treats the old people consigned to her care as if they were children—not very clever, somewhat morose, somewhat sluggish children in need of being bucked up. Madeleine herself is the right side of sixty, the right side of fifty, even the right side of forty-five; she runs no doubt like a gazelle.

To re-program the body's memories, Madeleine uses dance. She shows them videotapes of ice-skaters in skin-tight scarlet or golden suits gliding in loops and circles, first the left foot, then the right; in the background, Delibes. "Listen, and let the rhythm take charge of you," says Madeleine. "Let the music run through your body, let it dance inside you." Around him those of his team mates who have already acquired their artificial limbs imitate as best they can the movements of the skaters. Since he cannot do that—cannot skate, cannot dance, cannot walk, cannot even stand up straight unaided—he closes his eyes, clings to the rails, and sways in time with the music. Somewhere, in an ideal world, he glides around the ice hand in hand with his attractive instructress. *Hypnotism, that's all it is!* he thinks to himself. *How quaint; how old-fashioned!*

His personal programme (they each have a personal programme) consists largely of balancing exercises. "We will have to learn to balance all over again," Madeleine explains, "with our new body." That is what she calls it: our new body, not our truncated old body.

There is also what in the hospital was called hydrotherapy and what Madeleine calls water-work. In the narrow pool in the back room he grips the rails and walks in the water. "Keep the legs straight," says Madeleine. "Both of them. Like scissors. Snip snip snip."

In the old days he would have been sceptical of people like Madeleine Martin. But, for the time being, Madeleine Martin is all that is offered him to believe in. So at home, sometimes under the eye of Marijana, sometimes not, he goes through his personal exercise programme, even the swaying-to-music part of it.

"Is good, is good for you," says Marijana, nodding. "Is good you get some rhythm." But she does not bother to hide the note of professional derision in her voice.

Good?, he would like to say to her. *Really? I am not so sure it is good for me. How can it be, when I find it humiliating, all of it, the whole business from beginning to end?* But he does not speak the words. He holds himself back. He has entered the zone of humiliation; it is his new home; he will never leave it; best to shut up, best to accept.

Marijana collects all his trousers and takes them

home with her. She brings them back two days later with the right legs neatly folded and sewn. "I don't cut them," she says. "Maybe you change your mind and wear, you know, *prosthese*. We see."

Prosthese: she pronounces it as if it were a German word. Thesis, antithesis, then prosthesis.

The surgical wound, which has given no trouble hitherto and which he thought had healed for good, starts to itch. Marijana dusts it with anti-biotic powder and winds it in fresh bandages, but the itching continues. It is worst at night. He has to stay awake to keep himself from scratching. The wound feels to him like a great inflamed jewel glowing in the dark; both guard and prisoner, he is condemned to crouch over it, protecting it.

The itching abates, but Marijana continues to wash the stump with particular care, powder it, tend it.

"You think your leg grow again, Mr. Rayment?" she asks one day, out of the blue.

"No, I have never thought so."

"Still, maybe you think so sometimes. Like baby. Baby think, you cut it off, it grow again. Know what I mean? But you are not baby, Mr. Rayment. So why don't you want this *prosthese*? Maybe you shy like a girl, eh? Maybe you think, you walk in street, everybody look at you. *That Mr. Rayment, he got only one leg!* Isn't true. Isn't true. Nobody look at you. You wear *prosthese*, nobody look at you. Nobody know. Nobody care."

"I'll think about it," he says. "There's lots of time. All the time in the world."

After six weeks of water-work and swaying and being re-programmed he gives up on Madeleine Martin. He telephones her studio after hours and leaves a message on the answer machine. He telephones the ferry service and tells them not to come again. He even thinks of telephoning Mrs. Putts. But what would he say to Mrs. Putts? For six weeks he was prepared to believe in Madeleine Martin and the cure she offered, the cure for old memory systems. Now he has stopped believing in her. That is all, there is no more to it than that. If there is any residue of belief left in him, it has been shifted to Marijana Jokić, who has no studio and promises no cure, just care.

Perching on his bedside, pressing down on his groin with her left hand, Marijana watches, nodding, as he flexes, extends, and rotates the stump. With the lightest of pressure she helps him extend the flexion. She massages the aching muscle; she turns him over and massages his lower back.

From the touch of her hand he learns all he needs to know: that Marijana does not find this wasted and increasingly flabby body distasteful; that she is prepared, if she can, and if he will permit it, to transmit to him through her fingertips a fair quantum of her own ruddy good health.

It is not a cure, it is not done with love, it is probably no more than orthodox nursing practice,

75

but it is enough. What love there is is all on his side.

"Thank you," he says when their time is over, speaking with such feeling that she gives him a quizzical look.

"No worries," she replies.

One evening after Marijana has left he rings for a taxi, then embarks alone on the slow sideways descent of the stairs, holding tight to the banister, sweating with fear that a crutch will slip. By the time the taxi arrives he has reached the street.

In the public library—where thankfully he does not have to leave ground level—he finds two books on Croatia: a guidebook to Illyria and the Dalmatian coast and a guidebook to Zagreb and its churches; also a number of books on the Yugoslav Federation and on the recent Balkan wars. On what he has come to enlighten himself about, however—the character of Croatia and its people—there is nothing.

He checks out a book called *Peoples of the Balkans*. When the taxi returns he is ready and waiting.

Peoples of the Balkans: Between East and West, so runs the full title. Is that how the Jokićs felt back home: caught between Orthodox East and Catholic West? If so, how do they feel in Australia, where east and west have quite new meanings? The book has pages of black-and-white photographs. In one of them, a pair of peasant girls in head-scarves conduct a donkey laden with firewood

76

along a rocky mountain path. The younger girl smiles shyly at the camera, revealing a gap in her teeth. *Peoples of the Balkans* dates from 1962, before Marijana was even conceived. The pictures date from who knows when. The two girls could be grandmothers by now, they could be dead and buried. The donkey too. Was this the world Marijana was born into, an immemorial world of donkeys and goats and chickens and water-buckets sheeted in ice in the mornings, or was she a child of the workers' paradise?

More than likely the Jovićs brought with them from the old country their own picture collection: baptisms, confirmations, weddings, family get-togethers. A pity he will not get to see it. He tends to trust pictures more than he trusts words. Not because pictures cannot lie but because, once they leave the darkroom, they are fixed, immutable. Whereas stories—the story of the needle in the bloodstream, for instance, or the story of how he and Wayne Blight came to meet on Magill Road—seem to change shape all the time.

The camera, with its power of taking in light and turning it into substance, has always seemed to him more a metaphysical than a mechanical device. His first real job was as a darkroom technician; his greatest pleasure was always in darkroom work. As the ghostly image emerged beneath the surface of the liquid, as veins of darkness on the paper began to knit together and grow visible, he would sometimes experience a little shiver of ecstasy, as though he were present at the day of creation.

That was why, later on, he began to lose interest in photography: first when colour took over, then when it became plain that the old magic of light-sensitive emulsions was waning, that to the rising generation the enchantment lay in a *techne* of images without substance, images that could flash through the ether without residing anywhere, that could be sucked into a machine and emerge from it doctored, untrue. He gave up recording the world in photographs then, and transferred his energies to saving the past.

Does it say something about him, that native preference for black and white and shades of grey, that lack of interest in the new? Is that what women missed in him, his wife in particular: colour, openness?

The story he told Marijana was that he saved old pictures out of fidelity to their subjects, the men and women and children who offered their bodies up to the stranger's lens. But that is not the whole truth. He saves them too out of fidelity to the photo-graphs themselves, the photographic prints, most of them last survivors, unique. He gives them a good home and sees to it, as far as he is able, as far as anyone is able, that they will have a good home after he is gone. Perhaps, in turn, some as yet unborn stranger will reach back and save a picture of him, of the extinct Rayment of the Rayment Bequest.

As for the politics of the Jokić family, as for what

niche they might have occupied in the mosaic of Balkan loyalties and enmities, he has never quizzed Marijana and he has no intention of doing so. As with most immigrants, their feelings towards the old country are probably mixed. The Dutchman who married his mother and brought her and her children from Lourdes to Ballarat kept a framed photograph of Queen Wilhelmina side by side with a plaster statuette of the Virgin Mary in the living-room. On the monarch's birthday he lit a candle before her image as if she were a saint. *Infidèle Europe*, he used to say of Europe; the queen's picture bore the motto *Trouw*, faith fidelity. In the evenings he would huddle over the short-wave radio trying to catch through the crackle a word here and a word there from Radio Hilversum. At the same time he was desperate for the country of his new allegiance to live up to the idea of it he had formed from afar. In the face of a dubious wife and two unhappy stepchildren, Australia had to be the sunny land of opportunity. If the natives were un-welcoming, if they fell silent in their presence or mocked their faltering English, no matter: time and hard work would wear down that hostility. A faith the man still held to when he last saw him, aged ninety, pale as a mushroom, shuffling among the pot-plants in his ramshackle greenhouse. The Jokics, man and wife, must hold to some variant of the Dutchman's faith. Whereas their children, Drago and Ljuba and the other one, will have formed their own picture of Australia, clearer and cooler.

CHAPTER 10

One morning Marijana turns up in the company of a tall youth. It is the boy in the picture, unmistakably: Drago.

"My son come look at your bicycle," says Marijana. "He can fix it maybe."

"Yes. Of course." (But, he asks himself, whatever gave her the idea he wants the wreck of a bicycle fixed?) "Hello, Drago, good to meet you, thanks for coming." He fishes out the key to the store from a mess of keys in a drawer and gives it to the boy. "See what you think. In my opinion the bike is beyond help. The frame is bent. Ten to one the tubing is cracked. But have a look."

"OK," says the boy.

"I bring him to talk to you," says Marijana when they are alone. "Like you said."

Like he said? What could he have said? That he would give Drago a lesson in road safety?

The yarn that Marijana has spun her son to get him to give up his morning emerges only piece by piece: that Mr. Rayment has a bicycle that he wants fixed so that he can sell it, but that, being not only crippled but maladroit too, he cannot do the fixing himself.

Drago returns from his inspection and delivers his report. Whether the frame is cracked or not he cannot say offhand. He and his mates, one of whom has access to a machine shop, could probably bend it back into shape and respray it. But even so, a new wheel and hub and derailleur and brakes would probably set him, Mr. Rayment, back as much as a good second-hand bike.

It is perfectly sensible advice. It is what he would have said himself.

"Thanks for looking at it anyway," he says. "Your mother tells me you are into motorcycles."

"Yeah, my dad bought me a Yamaha, 250 c.c."

"That's good." He casts Marijana a glance which the boy pretends not to pick up. What more does she want him to say?

"Mum says you had a pretty bad accident," offers the boy.

"Yes. I was in hospital for a while."

"What happened?"

"I was hit by a car as I was turning. The driver said he didn't see me. Said I didn't signal my intentions. Said he was dazzled by the sun."

"That's bad."

A silence. Is the boy absorbing the lesson he is supposed to be absorbing? Is Marijana getting what she wants? He suspects not. She wants him to be more voluble—to warn the boy how perilous the lot of cyclists is, and by analogy the lot of motorcyclists; to bring home to him the agonies of injury and the humiliations of the crippled state. But his sense of this youth is that he prefers laconism, that he will not take kindly to being preached to. In fact, if Drago were to sympathise with anyone in the story of the encounter on Magill Road, it would more likely be with Wayne Blight, the speedy youngster behind the wheel, than with Paul Rayment, the absent-minded old geezer on the pushbike.

And what sea-change does Marijana want him to bring about anyway? Does she really expect this handsome youth, bursting with good health, to spend his evenings at home curled up with a book while his mates are out having fun? To leave the gleaming new Yamaha in the garage and catch a bus? Drago Jokić: a name from folk-epic. *The Ballad of Drago Jokić.*

He clears his throat. "Drago, your mother has asked me to have a word with you in private."

Marijana leaves the room. He turns to the boy. "Look, I'm nothing to you, just the man your mother looks after and very grateful to her for that. But she asked me to speak to you and I agreed I would. What I want to tell you is, if I could turn back the clock to before my accident, believe me, I would. You may not think it, looking at me, but I used to lead an active life. Now I can't even go to the shops. I have to depend on other people for the smallest thing. And it happened in a split second, out of nowhere. Well, it could happen to you just as easily. Don't take risks with your life, son, it's not worth it. Your mother wants you to be careful on your bike. I think you should listen to her. That's all I'm going to say. Your mother is a good person, she loves you. Do you understand?"

If he had been asked to predict, he would have said that young Drago would sit through a lecture of this kind with his eyes cast down, picking at his cuticles, wishing the old geezer would get it over with, cursing his mother for bringing him. But it is not like that at all. Throughout his speech Drago regards him candidly, a faint, not unfriendly smile on his well-shaped lips. "OK," he says at the end. "Message received. I'll be careful." Then, after a pause: "You like my mum, don't you?"

He nods. He could say more, but a nod is enough for the present.

"She likes you too."

She likes him too. His heart swells unreasonably. *I don't just like her, I love her!*: those are the words he is on the point of bursting out with. "I'm trying to be of assistance, that's all," he says instead. "That's why I've spoken to you. Not because I think I can save you by talking, since something like this"—he slaps the bad hip lightly, jocularly— "just happens, you can't foresee it, you can't prevent it. But it may help your mother. It may help her to know that you know she loves you and wants you to be safe, wants it enough to ask a stranger, namely me, to put in a word. OK?"

There are the words themselves, and then, behind or around or beneath the words, there is the intention. As he speaks he is aware of the boy watching his lips, brushing aside the word-strings as if they were cobwebs, tuning his ear to the intention. His respect for the boy is growing, growing by leaps and bounds. No ordinary boy, this one! The envy of the gods he must be. *The Ballad of Drago Jokić*. No wonder his mother is fearful. A telephone call in the early hours of the morning: "Is that Mrs. Jokić? Do you have a son named Dragon? This is the hospital in Gumeracha." Like a needle in the heart, or a sword. Her first-born.

Marijana returns, Drago rises. "I'll be getting along now," he says. "Bye Mum." From his lofty height he stoops and touches his lips to her forehead. "Bye Mr. Rayment. Sorry about the bike." And he is gone.

"Very good tennis player," says Marijana. "Very good swimmer. Very good at everything. Very clever." She gives a wan smile.

"My dear Marijana," he says—*heightened emotion, he tells himself, in a moment of heightened emotion one can be forgiven for slipping in the odd term of endearment*—"I am sure he will be all right. I am sure he will have a long and happy life and rise to be an admiral, if that is what he wants to be."

"You think so?" The smile has not left her lips, but now it speaks pure joy: despite the fact that he is useless with his hands and a cripple to boot, she believes he has powers of foretelling the future. "That's good."

CHAPTER 11

It is Marijana's smile, lingering in his memory, that brings about the longed-for, the long-needed change. At once all gloom is gone, all dark clouds. He is Marijana's employer, her boss, the one whose wishes she is paid to carry out, yet before she arrives each day he fusses around the flat, doing his best to make things spick and span for her. He even has flowers delivered, to brighten the drabness.

The situation is absurd. What does he want of the woman? He wants her to smile again, certainly, to smile on him. He wants to win a place in her heart, however tiny. Does he want to become her lover too? Yes, he does, in a sense, fervently. He wants to love and cherish her and her children, Drago and Ljuba and the third one, the one whom he has yet to clap eyes on. As for the husband, he has not the slightest malign intent towards him, he will swear to that. He wishes the husband all happiness and good fortune. Nevertheless, he will give anything to be father to these excellent, beautiful children and husband to Marijana—co-father if need be, co-husband if need be, platonic if need be. He wants to take care of them, all of them, protect them and save them.

Save them from what? He cannot say, not yet. But Drago above all he wants to save. Between Drago and the lightning-bolt of the envious gods he is ready to interpose himself, bare his own breast.

He is like a woman who, having never borne a child, having grown too old for it, now hungers suddenly and urgently for motherhood. Hungry enough to steal another's child: it is as mad as that.

CHAPTER 12

"How is Drago getting on?" he asks Marijana, as casually as he can.

She shrugs despondently. "This weekend he will go with his friends to Tunkalooloo beach. You say it like that—Tunkalooloo?"

"Tunkalilla."

"They go by bike. Wild friends, wild boys. I'm frighted. Is like gang. Girls too, you can't believe it so young. I'm glad you speak to him last week. Spoke."

"It was nothing. Just a few fatherly words."

"Yes, he don't get enough fatherly words, like you say, that's his problem."

It is the first criticism she has voiced of the absent husband. He waits for more, but there is no more.

"This is not an easy country for a boy to grow up in," he replies cautiously. "A climate of manliness prevails. A lot of pressure on a boy to excel in manly deeds, manly sports. Be a daredevil. Take risks. It is probably different back where you come from."

Back where you come from. Now that he hears

them, the words sound condescending. Why should boys not also be boys where the Jokićs come from? What does he know about the forms that manliness takes in south-eastern Europe? He waits for Marijana to set him right. But her mind is elsewhere.

"What you think of boarding school, Mr. Rayment?"

"What do I think of boarding school? I think it can be very expensive. I also think it is a mistake, a bad mistake, to believe that in boarding schools young people are watched over night and day to make sure they come to no harm. But you can get a good education at a boarding school, no doubt about that, or at the better boarding schools. Is that what you are thinking of for Drago? Have you checked into their fees? You should do that first. Their fees can be high, absurdly high, in fact astronomical."

What he refrains from saying is: *So high as to exclude children whose fathers assemble cars for a living. Or whose mothers nurse the aged.*

"But if you are serious about it," he plunges on, and even as he speaks he feels the recklessness of what he is saying, but he cannot stop himself, will not stop himself, "and if Drago himself really wants to go, I could help financially. We could treat it as a loan."

There is a moment's silence. *So,* he thinks, *it is out. No going back.*

"We are thinking, maybe he can get scholarship,

with his tennis and all that," says Marijana, who has perhaps not absorbed his words and what must lie behind them.

"Yes, a scholarship is certainly a possibility, you can investigate that."

"Or we can get loan." Now the echo of his words seems to reach her, and her brow furrows. "You can loan us money, Mr. Rayment?"

"I can make you a loan. Interest-free. You can pay it back when Drago is earning."

"Why?"

"It is an investment in his future. In the future of all of us."

She shakes her head. "Why?" she repeats, "I don't understand."

It is one of the days when she has brought Ljuba with her. In her scarlet pinafore, with her legs, one in a scarlet stocking, one in a purple, stretched out on the sofa, her arms slack at her sides, the child could be mistaken for a doll, were it not for the searching black eyes.

"Surely you must know, Marijana," he whispers. His mouth is dry, his heart is thudding, it is as awful and as thrilling as when he was sixteen. "Surely a woman always knows."

Again she shakes her head. She seems genuinely puzzled. "Don't understand."

"I will tell you in private."

She murmurs to the child. Obediently Ljuba picks up her little pink backpack and trots off to the kitchen.

"There," says Marijana. "Now say."

"I love you. That is all. I love you and I want to give you something. Let me."

In the books that his mother used to order from Paris when he was still a child, that used to arrive in brown pasteboard packets with the Librairie Hachette crest and a row of stamps bearing the head of stern Marianne decked in her Phrygian cap, books that his mother would sigh over in the living-room in Ballarat where the shutters were always closed, either against the heat or against the cold, and that he would secretly read after her, skipping the words he did not know, as part of his sempiternal quest to find what it was that would please her, it would have been written that Marijana's lip curled with scorn, perhaps even that her lip curled with scorn while her eye gleamed with secret triumph. But when he left his childhood behind he lost faith in the world of Hachette. If there ever was—which he doubts—a code of looks that, once mastered, would allow one to read infallibly the transient motions of the human lips and eyes, it has gone now, gone with the wind.

A silence falls, and Marijana does nothing to help. But at least she does not turn on her heel. Whether or not her lip curls, she does seem prepared to hear more of this extraordinary, irregular declaration.

What he ought to do, of course, is embrace the woman. Breast to breast she could not mistake him. But to embrace her he must put aside the absurd crutches that allow him to stand up; and once he does that he will totter, perhaps fall. For the first time he sees the sense of an artificial leg, a leg with a mechanism that locks the knee and thus frees the arms.

Marijana waves a hand as if wiping a window-pane or flapping a dishcloth. "You want to pay so Drago can go to boarding school?" she says, and the spell is broken.

Is that what he wants: to pay for Drago's schooling? Yes. He wants Drago to have a good education, and then, after that, if he holds to his ambition, if the sea is indeed his heart's desire, to qualify as a naval officer. He wants Ljuba and her elder sister to grow up happy too, and have their own hearts' desire. Over the whole brood he wants to extend the shield of his benevolent protection. And he wants to love this excellent woman, their mother. That above all. For which he will pay anything.

"Yes," he says. "That is what I am offering."

She meets his gaze squarely. Though he can-not swear to it, he believes she is blushing. Then, swiftly, she leaves the room. A moment later she is back. The red kerchief is gone, her hair is shaken free. On one arm she has Ljuba, on the other the pink satchel. She is murmuring into the child's ear. The child, thumb in mouth, turns and inspects him curiously.

"We must go," Marijana says. "Thank you." And in a whisk they are gone.

He has done it. He, an old man with knobbly

fingers, has confessed his love. But dare he even for a moment hope that this woman, in whom he has without forethought, without hesitation sunk all his hopes, will love him back?

CHAPTER 13

The next day Marijana does not arrive. Nor does she come on Friday. The shadows that he had thought gone for ever return. He telephones the Jokic home, gets a female voice, not Marijana's (whose? the other daughter's?), on an answering machine. "Paul Rayment here, for Marijana," he says. "Could she give me a call?" There is no call.

He sits down to write a letter. *Dear Marijana,* he writes, *I fear you may have misunderstood me.* He deletes *me* and writes *my meaning*. But what is the meaning she may have misunderstood? *When I first met you,* he writes, beginning a new paragraph, *I was in a shattered state.* Which is not true. His knee might have been shattered, and his prospects, but not his state. If he knew the word to describe his state as it was when he met Marijana, he would know his meaning too, as it is today. He deletes *shattered*. But what to put in its place?

While he is dithering the doorbell rings. His heart gives a leap. Will the troublesome word, and the troublesome letter, not after all be needed?

"Mr. Rayment?" says the voice on the entryphone. "Elizabeth Costello here. May I speak with you?"

Elizabeth Costello, whoever she is, takes her time climbing the stairs. By the time she gets to the door she is panting: a woman in her sixties, he would say, the later rather than the earlier sixties, wearing a floral silk dress cut low behind to reveal unattractively freckled, somewhat fleshy shoulders.

"Bad heart," she says, fanning herself. "Nearly as much of an impediment as" (she pauses to catch her breath) "a bad leg."

Coming from a stranger the remark strikes him as inappropriate, unseemly.

He invites her in, offers her a seat. She accepts a glass of water.

"I was going to say I was from the State Library," she says. "I was going to introduce myself as one of the Library's volunteers, come to assess the scale of your donation, the physical scale, I mean, the dimensions, so that we could plan ahead. Later it would have come out who I actually am."

"You are not from the Library?"

"No. That would have been a fib."

"Then you are—?"

She glances around his living-room with what seems to be approval. "My name is Elizabeth Costello," she says. "As I mentioned."

"Ah, are you *that* Elizabeth Costello? I am sorry, I was not thinking. Forgive me."

"No need." From the depths of the sofa she

struggles to her feet. "Shall we come to the point? This is not something I have done before, Mr. Rayment. Will you give me your hand?"

For an instant he is confused. Give her his hand? She reaches out her own right hand and he takes it. For a moment the plump and rather cool feminine hand rests in his own, which he notices with distaste has taken on the livid hue it does when he has been inactive too long.

"So," she says. "I am rather a doubting Thomas, as you see." And when he looks puzzled: "I mean, wanting to explore for myself what kind of being you are. Wanting to be sure," she proceeds, and now he is really losing her, "that our two bodies would not just pass through each other. Naïve, of course. We are not ghosts, either of us—why should I have thought so? Shall we proceed?"

Heavily she seats herself again, squares her shoulders, and begins to recite. "*The blow catches him from the right, sharp and surprising and painful, like a bolt of electricity, lifting him up off the bicycle. Relax!* he tells himself as he tumbles through the air, and so forth."

She pauses and inspects his face, as if to measure the effect she is having.

"Do you know what I asked myself when I heard those words for the first time, Mr. Rayment? I asked myself, *Why do I need this man?* Why not let him be, coasting along peacefully on his bicycle, oblivious of Wayne Bright or Blight, let us call him Blight, roaring up from behind to blight his life

95

and land him first in hospital and then back in this flat with its inconvenient stairs? Who is Paul Rayment to me?"

Who is this madwoman I have let into my home? How am I going to rid myself of her?

"And what is the answer to your question?" he replies cautiously. "Who am I to you?"

"You came to me," she says. "In certain respects I am not in command of what comes to me. You came, along with the pallor and the stoop and the crutches and the flat that you hold on to so doggedly and the photograph collection and all the rest. Also along with Miroslav Jokić the Croatian refugee—yes, that is his name, Miroslav, his friends call him Mel—and your inchoate attachment to his wife."

"It is not inchoate."

"Yes it is. To whom you blurt out your feelings, instead of keeping them to yourself, though you have no idea *and you know you have no idea* what the consequences will be. Reflect, Paul. Do you seriously mean to seduce your employee into abandoning her family and coming to live with you? Do you think you will bring her happiness? Her children will be angered and confused; they will stop speaking to her; she will lie in your bed all day, sobbing and inconsolable. How will you enjoy that? Or do you have other plans? Do you plan for Mel to walk into the surf and disappear, leaving his wife and children to you?

"I return to my first question. Who are you, Paul

Rayment, and what is so special about your amorous inclinations? Do you think you are the only man who in the autumn of his years, the late autumn, I may say, thinks he has found what he has never known heretofore, true love? Two a penny, Mr. Rayment, stories like that are two a penny. You will have to make a stronger case for yourself."

Elizabeth Costello: it is coming back to him who she is. He tried once to read a book by her, a novel, but gave up on it, it did not hold his attention. Now and then he has come across articles by her in the press, about ecology or animal rights, which he passes over because the subjects do not interest him. Once upon a time (he is dredging his memory now) she was notorious for something or other, but that seems to have gone away, or perhaps it was just another media storm. Grey-haired; grey-faced too, with, as she says, a bad heart. Breathing fast. And here she is preaching to him, telling him how to run his life!

"What case would you prefer me to make?" he says. "What story would make me worthy of your attention?"

"How must I know? Think of something."

Idiot woman! He ought to throw her out.

"Push!" she urges.

Push? Push what? *Push!* is what you say to a woman in labour.

"Push the mortal envelope," she says. "Magill Road, the very portal to the abode of the dead: how did you feel as you tumbled through the air?

Did the whole of your life flash before you? How did it seem to you in retrospect, the life you were about to depart?"

Is that true? Did he nearly die? Surely there is a distinction between being at risk of dying and being on the brink of death. Is this woman privy to something that he is not? Soaring through the air that day, he thought—what? That he had not felt so free since he was a boy, when he would leap without fear out of trees, once even off a rooftop. And then the gasp when he hit the road, the breath going out of him in a whoosh. Could a mere gasp be interpreted as a last thought, a last word?

"I felt sad," he says. "My life seemed frivolous. What a waste, I thought."

"Sad. He flies through the air with the greatest of ease, this daring young man on his flying trapeze, and he feels sad. His life seems frivolous, in retrospect. What else?"

What else? Nothing else. What is the woman fishing for?

But the woman seems to have lost interest in her question. "I'm sorry, all of a sudden I'm not feeling well," she says, mumbling, straining to get to her feet. And indeed she is distinctly white about the gills.

"Would you like to lie down? There's a bed in my study. Can I make you a cup of tea?"

She flutters a hand. "It's just dizziness, from the heat, from climbing the stairs, from who knows what. Yes, thank you, I'll lie down for a moment." She makes a gesture to push the cushions off the sofa.

"Let me help you." He gets up and, leaning on a crutch, takes her arm. *The halt leading the halt*, he thinks. Her skin is noticeably clammy.

The bed in the study is in fact quite comfortable. He does what he can to clear the clutter off it; she slips off her shoes and stretches out. Through her stockings he notes blue-veined, rather wasted calves.

"Pay no attention to me," she says, an arm over her eyes. "Isn't that what we say, we unwelcome guests? Carry on as though I were not here."

"I'll leave you to rest," he replies. "When you are feeling better I'll phone for a taxi."

"No, no, no," she says, "it's not like that, I'm afraid. I'll be with you a while yet."

"I think not."

"Oh yes, Mr. Rayment, I'm afraid so. For the foreseeable future I am to accompany you." She raises the arm that has been shielding her eyes, and he sees she is smiling faintly. "Bear up," she says. "It's not the end of the world."

Half an hour later he looks in again. She is asleep. Her lower denture bulges out, a faint rasp like the stirring of gravel comes from the back of her throat. It does not sound healthy to him.

He tries to return to the book he is reading, but he cannot concentrate. Moodily he stares out of the window.

There is a cough. She is standing in the doorway in her stockinged feet. "Do you have aspirin?" she says.

"In the bathroom, in the cabinet, you will find paracetamol. It is all I have."

"No good pulling faces at me, Mr. Rayment," she says. "I did not ask for this any more than you did."

"Ask for *what*?" He cannot keep the irritation from his voice.

"I did not ask for *you*. I did not ask to spend a perfectly good afternoon in this gloomy flat of yours."

"Then go! Leave the flat, if it so offends you. I still have not the faintest idea why you came. What do you want with me?"

"You came to me. You—"

"*I* came to *you*? *You* came to *me*!"

"Shush, don't shout, the neighbours will think you are beating me." She slumps into a chair. "I'm sorry. I am intruding, I know. You came to me, that is all I can say. You occurred to me—a man with a bad leg and no future and an unsuitable passion. That was where it started. Where we go from there I have no idea. Have you any proposal?"

He is silent.

"You may not see the point of it, Mr. Rayment, the pursuit of intuitions, but this is what I do. This is how I have built my life: by following up intuitions, including those I cannot at first make sense of. Above all those I cannot at first make sense of."

Following up intuitions: what does that mean, in the concrete? How can she have intuitions about a complete stranger, someone she has never laid eyes on?

"You got my name out of the telephone directory," he says. "You are just chancing your arm. You have no conception of who I really am."

She shakes her head. "Would that it were as simple as that," she says, so softly that he barely catches the words.

The sun is going down. They fall silent and, like an old married couple declaring truce, sit for a while giving ear to the birds screeching their vespers in the trees.

"You mentioned the Jokićs," he says at last. "What do you know about them?"

"Marijana Jokić, who looks after you, is an educated woman. Hasn't she told you? She spent two years at the Art Institute in Dubrovnik and came away with a diploma in restoration. Her husband worked at the Institute too. That was where they met. He was a technician, specialising in antique technology. He reassembled, for instance, a mechanical duck that had lain in parts in the basement of the Institute for two hundred years, rusting. Now it quacks like a regular duck, it waddles, it lays eggs. It is one of the *pièces de résistance* of their collection. But alas, his are skills for which there is no call in Australia. No mechanical ducks here. Hence the job in the car plant.

"What else can I tell you that you might find

useful? Marijana was born in Zadar, she is a city girl, she would not know one end of a donkey from the other. And she is chaste. In all her years of marriage she has never been unfaithful. Never fallen into temptation."

"I am not tempting her."

"I understand. As you said, you want merely to pour out your love upon her. You want to give. But being loved comes at a price, unless we are utterly without conscience. Marijana will not pay that price. She has been in this situation before, with patients who fall for her, who cannot help themselves, so they say. She finds it tiresome. *Now I will have to find another job*: that is what she thinks to herself. Do I make myself clear?"

He is silent.

"You are in the grip of something, aren't you?" she says. "Some quality in her draws you. As I conceive it, that quality is her burstingness, the burstingness of fruit at its ripest. Let me suggest to you why Marijana leaves that impression, on you and on other men too. She is bursting because she is loved, loved as much as one can expect to be in this world. You will not want to hear the details, so I will not supply them. But the reason why the children too make such an impression on you, the boy and the little girl, is that they have grown up drenched in love. They are at home in the world. It is, to them, a good place."

"And yet . . ."

"Yes, and yet the boy has the mark of death

on him. We both see it. Too handsome. Too luminous."

"One wants to cry."

They are growing lugubrious, the two of them, lugubrious and drowsy. He rouses himself. "There is the last of Marijana's cannelloni in the freezer, with ricotta and spinach," he says. "Would you like some? After that I do not know what your plans are. If you want to stay the night, you are welcome, but that must be the end of it, in the morning you will have to leave."

Slowly, decisively, Elizabeth Costello shakes her head. "Not possible, I am afraid, Paul. Like it or not, I will be with you a while yet. I will be a model guest, I promise. I won't hang my undies in your bathroom. I'll keep out of your way. I barely eat. Most of the time you won't notice I am here. Just a touch on the shoulder, now and then, left or right, to keep you on the path."

"And why should I put up with that? What if I refuse?"

"You must put up with it. It is not for you to say."

CHAPTER 14

It is indeed true, Elizabeth Costello is a model guest. Bent over the coffee table in the corner of the living-room that she has annexed as her own, she spends the weekend absorbed in a hefty typescript, which she seems to be annotating. He does not offer her meals, and she does not ask. Now and again, without a word, she disappears from the flat. What she does with herself he can only guess: perhaps wander the streets of North Adelaide, perhaps sit in a café and nibble a croissant and watch the traffic.

During one of her absences he hunts for the typescript, merely to see what it is, but cannot find it.

"Am I to infer," he says to her on the Sunday evening, "that you have come knocking on my door in order to study me so that you can use me in a book?"

She smiles. "Would that it were so simple, Mr. Rayment."

"Why is it not simple? It sounds simple enough to me. Are you writing a book and putting me in it? Is that what you are doing? If so, what sort of book is it, and don't you think you need my consent first?"

She sighs. "If I were going to *put you in a book*, as you phrase it, I would simply do so. I would change your name and one or two of the circumstances of your life, to get around the law of libel, and that would be that. I would certainly not need to take up residence with you. No, you came to me, as I told you: the man with the bad leg."

He is getting tired of being told he *came to* this woman. "Wouldn't you find it easier to use someone who came to you more willingly?" he remarks as dryly as he can. "Give up on me. I am not an amenable subject, as you will discover before long. Walk away. I won't detain you. You will find it a relief to be rid of me. And vice versa."

"And your unsuitable passion? Where would I find another such?"

"My passion, as you call it, is none of your business, Mrs. Costello."

She gives a wintry smile, shakes her head. "It is not for you to tell me my business," she replies softly.

His hand tightens on his crutch. If it were a proper, old-fashioned crutch of ash or jarrah, with some weight to it, instead of aluminium, he would bring it down on the old hag's skull, again and again, as often as might be necessary, till she lay dead at his feet and her blood soaked the carpet, let them do with him afterwards what they will.

The telephone rings. "Mr. Rayment? This is

Marijana. How are you? Sorry I missed my days. I was crook. I come tomorrow, OK?"

So that is to be the fiction between them: she was crook. "Yes, of course it is OK, Marijana. I hope you are feeling better. I will see you as usual tomorrow."

"Marijana will be back on the job tomorrow," he informs his guest as matter-of-factly as he can. *Time for you to bugger off*: he hopes she gets the message.

"That's all right. I'll keep out of her way." And when he glares at her angrily: "Are you worried she will think I am one of your lady friends from the old days?" She gives him a smile that is nothing less than merry. "Don't take everything so seriously, Paul."

Why Marijana has decided to come back emerges as soon as she steps through the front door. Before even taking off her coat—it is raining, a warm steamy rain that carries a tang of eucalyptus—she slaps down on the table a glossy brochure. On the cover, mock-Gothic buildings against acres of greensward; in a panel, a well-scrubbed boy in shirtsleeves and tie at a computer keyboard, with an equally well-scrubbed chum peering over his shoulder. *Wellington College: Five Decades of Excellence*. He has never heard of Wellington College.

"Drago say he will go here," says Marijana. "Look like good school, don't you think?"

He pages through the brochure. "Sister institution to Wellington College in Pembrokeshire," he reads aloud. "Preparing young men for the challenges of

106

a new century . . . Careers in business, science and technology, the armed forces. Where is this place? How did you find out about it?"

"In Canberra. In Canberra he find new friends. His friends in Adelaide no good, just pull him down." She pronounces *Adelaide* in the Italian way, rhyming with *spider*. From Dubrovnik, just a stone's throw from Venice.

"And where did you hear about Wellington College?"

"Drago know all about it. Is food school for Defence Force Academy."

"Feeder school."

"Feeder school. They get, you know, preference."

He returns to the brochure. Application form. Schedule of fees. He knew that boarding school fees were high; nevertheless, in black and white the figures give him a jolt.

"How many years would he be there?"

"If he start January, two years. In two years he can get year twelve, then he can get bursary. Is just fee for two years he need."

"And Drago is enthusiastic about the school? He has agreed to go?"

"Very enthusiastic. He want to go."

"It's normal, you know, for the parents to take a look at a school first before committing themselves. Make a tour of the premises, speak to the headmaster, get a feel of the place. Are you sure you and your husband and Drago don't want to pay a visit to Wellington College first?"

Marijana takes off the raincoat—it is made of some clear plastic material, purely functional—and drapes it over a chair. Her skin is warm, ruddy. No trace of the tension of their last encounter. "Wellington College," she says. "You think Wellington College wants that Mr. and Mrs. Jokić from Munno Para come visit, see if maybe Wellington College is OK for their boy?"

Her tone is good-natured enough. If anyone is embarrassed, it is he.

"In Croatia, you know, Mr. Rayment, my husband was famous man, sort of. You don't believe me? In all newspapers photographs of him. Miroslav Jokić and mechanical duck. On television"—with two fingers she makes walking motions in the air—"pictures of mechanical duck. Only man who can make mechanical duck walk, make noise like how you say *kwaak*, eat"—she pats her bosom—"other things too. Old, old duck. Come from Sweden. Come to Dubrovnik 1680, from Sweden. Nobody know how to fix it. Then Miroslav Jokić fix it perfect. One week, two week he is famous man in Croatia. But here"—she casts her eyes up to the heavens—"who cares? In Australia nobody hear of mechanical duck. Don't know what is it. Miroslav Jokić, nobody hear of him. Just auto worker. Is nothing, auto worker."

"I am not sure I agree," he says. "An auto worker is not nothing. Nobody is nothing. Anyhow, whether you visit them or not, whether you are from Munno Para or Timbuctoo, my guess is that

Wellington College will be only too glad to take your money. Go ahead and apply. I'll pay. I'll give you a cheque right now for the application fee."

So there it is. As easy as that. He is committed. He has become a godfather. A godfather: one who leads a child to God. Does he have it in him to lead Drago to God?

"Is good," says Marijana. "I tell Drago. You make him very happy." A pause. "And you? Leg is OK? No pain? You do your exercises?"

"The leg is OK, no pain," he says. What he does not say is: *But why did you walk off the job, Marijana? Why did you abandon me? Hardly professional conduct, was it? I bet you would not want Mrs. Putz to hear of it.*

He is still full of aggrievement, he wants some sign of contrition from Marijana. At the same time he is drunk with the pleasure of having her back, excited too by the money he is about to give away. Giving always bucks him up, he knows that about himself. Spurs him to give more. Like gambling. The thrill all in the losing. Loss upon loss. The reckless, heedless falling.

In her usual busy fashion Marijana has already set to work. Beginning in the bedroom, she is stripping the bed and fitting clean sheets. But she can feel his eyes on her, he is sure of that, can feel the warmth coming from him, caressing her thighs, her breasts. Eros always ran strong for him in the mornings. If by some miracle he could embrace Marijana right now, in this mood, taking the tide while it is high, he would overcome all that rectitude of hers, he is prepared to bet. But impossible, of course. Imprudent. Worse than imprudent, crazy. He should not even think of it.

Then the bathroom door opens and the Costello woman, wearing his dressing gown and slippers, makes her entry on the scene. She is drying her hair with a towel, showing patches of pink scalp. Cursorily he introduces her. "Marijana, this is Mrs. Costello. She is staying here briefly. Mrs. Jokić."

Marijana offers her hand and with solemn mummery the Costello woman takes it. "I promise not to get in your way," she says.

"No worries."

Minutes later he hears the front doorlock click. From a window he watches the Costello woman recede down the street towards the river. She is wearing a straw hat he recognises as his own, one he has not worn for years. Where did she find it? Has she been rooting in his cupboards?

"Nice lady," says Marijana. "She is friend?"

"A friend? No, not at all, just an associate. She has business in town, she is staying here for the duration."

"That's good."

Marijana is in a hurry, so it seems. Normally, first thing in the morning, she attends to the leg and conducts him through his exercises. But today there is no mention of exercises. "I must go, is special day, must pick up Ljubica from play group," she says. From her bag she brings out a frozen quiche. "I come back this afternoon, maybe. Here is something little I buy for your lunch. I leave slip, you pay me later."

"A little something," he corrects her.

"Little something," she says.

She is barely gone when the key scrapes in the lock and Elizabeth Costello is back. "I bought some fruit," she announces. She sets down a plastic bag on the table. "There will be an interview, I would guess. Do you think Marijana will be up to it?"

"Interview?"

"For this college. They will want to interview the boy and his parents, but mainly the parents, to make sure they are the right sort."

"It is Drago who is applying for admission, not his parents. If the Wellington College people have any sense, they will jump to take Drago."

"But what if they ask the parents straight out how they are going to pay those outrageous fees?"

"I will write them a letter. I will lodge guarantees. I will do whatever is required."

She is building a little pyramid of fruit—apricots, nectarines, grapes—in the bowl on the coffee table. "That's admirable," she says. "I'm so glad to have this chance to get to know you better. You give me faith."

"I give you faith? No one has said that to me before."

"You, you give me faith again. You must not take seriously what I said about yourself and Mrs. Jokić. One is embarrassed, that is all, to find oneself in the presence of true, old-fashioned love. I bow before you."

She pauses in what she is doing and offers, not without irony, the lightest of inclinations of the head.

"However," she continues, "do remember that there is still the hurdle of Miroslav to overcome. We cannot take it for granted that Miroslav will agree to have his son go off to a fancy boarding school a thousand miles away. Or that he will want his pecuniary obligations to be taken over by the man his wife visits six days a week, the man with the missing leg. Have you thought what you will do about Miroslav?"

"He would be stupid to refuse. It doesn't affect him. It affects his son, his son's future."

"No, Paul, that is not right," she says softly. "From the son to the wife, from the wife to him: that is how the thread runs. You touch his pride, his manly honour. Sooner or later you are going to have to face Miroslav. What will you say when that day comes? 'I am just trying to help'? Is that what you will say? That won't be good enough. Only the truth will be good enough. And the truth is that you are not trying to help. On the contrary, you are trying to throw a spanner into the Jokić family works. You are trying to get into Mrs. J's pants. Also to seduce Mr. J's children away from him and make them your own, one, two and even three. Not what I would call a friendly agenda, all in all. No, you are not Miroslav's friend, not in any way I can see. Miroslav is not going to take kindly to you; and can you blame him? Therefore what are you going to do about Miroslav? You must think. You must *think*." With the tip of a finger she taps her forehead. "And if your thinking leads you where I think it will, namely to a blank wall, I have an alternative to propose."

"An alternative to what?"

"An alternative to this entire imbroglio of yours with the Jokićs. Forget about Mrs. Jokić and your fixation on her. Cast your mind back. Do you remember the last time you visited the osteopathy department at the hospital? Do you remember the woman in the lift with the dark glasses? In the company of an older woman? Of course you remember. She made an impression on you. Even I could see that.

"Nothing that happens in our lives is without a meaning, Paul, as any child can tell you. That is one of the lessons stories teach us, one of the many lessons. Have you given up reading stories? A mistake. You shouldn't.

"Let me fill you in on the woman with the dark glasses. She is, alas, blind. She lost her sight a year ago, as the result of a malignancy, a tumour. Lost one whole eye, surgically excised, and the use of the other too. Before the calamity she was beautiful, or at least highly attractive; today, alas, she is unsightly in the way that all blind people are unsightly. One prefers not to look on her face. Or rather, one finds oneself staring and then withdraws one's gaze, repelled. This repulsion is of course invisible to her, but she feels it nevertheless. She is conscious of the gaze of others like fingers groping at her, groping and retreating.

"Being blind is worse than she was warned it would be, worse than she had ever imagined. She is in despair. In a matter of months she has become an object of horror. She cannot bear being in the open, where she can be looked at. She wants to hide herself. She wants to die. And at the same time—she cannot help herself—she is full of unhappy lust. She is in the summer of her womanly life; she moans aloud with lust, day after day, like a cow or a sow in heat.

"What I say surprises you? You think this is just a story I am making up? It is not. The woman exists, you have seen her with your own two eyes, her name is Marianna. This tranquil-seeming world we inhabit contains horrors, Paul, such as you could not dream up for yourself in a month of Sundays. The ocean depths, for instance, the floor of the sea—what goes on there exceeds all imagining.

"What Marianna aches for is not consolation, much less worship, but love in its most physical expression. She wants to be, no matter how briefly, as she was before, as you in your way want to be as you were before. I say to you: Why not see what you can achieve together, you and Marianna, she blind, you halt?

"Let me tell you one more thing about Marianna. Marianna knows you. Yes, she knows you. You and she are acquainted. Are you aware of that?"

It is as if she were reading his diary. It is as if

114

he kept a diary, and this woman crept nightly into the flat and read his secrets. But there is no diary, unless he writes in his sleep.

"You are mistaken, Mrs Costello," he says. "The woman you refer to, whom you call Marianna— I saw her only on the one occasion, at the hospital, where she could not have seen me, by definition. So she cannot be acquainted with me, not even in the most trivial sense."

"Yes, perhaps I am mistaken, that is possible. Or perhaps you are the one who is mistaken. Perhaps Marianna comes out of an earlier part of your life, when both of you were young and whole and good to look at, and you have simply forgotten about it. You were a photographer by profession, were you not? Perhaps once upon a time you took her photograph, and it happened that all your attention was concentrated on the image you were making, not on her, the source of the image."

"Perhaps. But there is nothing wrong with my memory, and I have no recollection of such an experience."

"Well, old friends or not, why not see what you can achieve together, you and Marianna? Given the extraordinary circumstances of the case, I will take it on myself to arrange a meeting. You need merely wait and prepare yourself. Be assured, if there is any proposal I will put it to her in a way that will allow her to come without losing self-respect.

"A final word. Let me suggest that, whatever you and she get up to, you get up to it in the dark. As a kindness to her. Think of your bed as a cave. A storm is raging, a maiden huntress enters seeking shelter. She stretches out a hand and meets another hand, yours. And so forth."

He ought to say something sharp, but he cannot, it is as if he is drugged or bemused.

"Of the episode of which you claim to have no recollection," Costello goes on, "—the day when you might or might not have taken her photograph—I would only say, be a little less sure of yourself. Stir the memory and you will be surprised at what images rise to the surface. But let me not press you. Let us build your side of the story on the premise that you have had only that single glimpse of her, in the lift. A single glimpse, but enough to ignite desire. From your desire and her need, what will be born? Passion on the grandest of scales? One last great autumnal conflagration? Let us see. The issue is in your hands, yours and hers. Is my proposal acceptable? If so, say yes. Or if you are too abashed, just nod. Yes?

"Her name is Marianna, as I said, with two *ns*. I cannot help that. It is not in my power to change names. You can give her some interim other name if you wish, some pet name, Darling or Kitten or whatever. She was married, but after the stroke of fate I described her marriage broke up, as all else broke up. Her life is in disarray. For the present she lives with her mother, the woman you saw with her, the crone.

"That is sufficient background for the time

being. You can get the rest from her own lips. Two ns. Once upon a time a pig-farmer's daughter. Her toilette is in disarray as is everything else in her life, but that can be forgiven, who would not make the occasional mistake, dressing in the dark?

"Agitated but clean. Since her surgery, her extremely delicate surgery, quite unlike the gross butchery of amputation, she has become morbidly scrupulous about cleanliness, about the way she smells. That happens with some blind people. You had better be clean for her too. If I speak crudely, forgive me. Wash yourself well. Wash everywhere. And put away that sad face. Losing a leg is not a tragedy. On the contrary, losing a leg is comic. Losing any part of the body that sticks out is comic. Otherwise we would not have so many jokes on the subject. There was an old man with one leg / Who stood with his hat out to beg. And so forth.

"Be advised, Paul: The years go by as quickly as a wink. So enjoy yourself while you're still in the pink. It's always later than you think.

"And no, the other Marijana, the nurse woman, was not my idea, if that is what you are wondering. There is no system for these things. Marijana of Dubrovnik, your unsuitable passion, arrived via your friend Mrs. Putts. Nothing to do with me.

"You don't know what to make of me, do you? You think of me as a trial. Much of the time you think I am talking rubbish, making things up as I go. Yet you have not rebelled, I notice, not yet. You tolerate me in the hope that I will give up

117

and go away. Don't deny it, it is written on your face, plain for all to see. You are Job, I am one of your unmerited afflictions, the woman who goes on and on, full of plans for saving you from yourself, gab gab gab, when all you crave is peace.

"It does not have to be this way, Paul. I say it again: this is your story, not mine. The moment you decide to take charge, I will fade away. You will hear no more from me; it will be as if I had never existed. That promise extends to your new friend Marianna as well. I will retire; you and she will be free to work out your respective salvations.

"Think how well you started. What could be better calculated to engage one's attention than the incident on Magill Road, when young Wayne collided with you and sent you flying through the air *like a cat*. What a sad decline ever since! Slower and slower, till by now you are almost at a halt, trapped in a stuffy flat with a caretaker who could not care less about you. But be of good heart. Marianna has possibilities, with her devastated face and the remorseful lust that grips her. Marianna is quite a woman. The question is, are you man enough for her?

"Answer me, Paul. *Say* something."

It is like a sea beating against his skull. Indeed, for all he knows he could already be lost overboard, tugged to and fro by the currents of the deep. The slap of water that will in time strip his bones of the last sliver of flesh. Pearls of his eyes; coral of his bones.

CHAPTER 15

Marijana calls. Even before she speaks he knows what she is going to say: that she is sorry, but she cannot come today. A problem with her daughter. No, not Ljubica: Blanka.

"Can I help?" he asks.

"No, nobody can help." She sighs. "I come tomorrow for sure, OK?"

"Trouble with her daughter," muses Elizabeth Costello. "I wonder what kind of trouble that might be. Still, no cloud without a silver lining. The woman I mentioned, Marianna, the blind one—you can't keep her from your thoughts, can you? Don't dissemble, Paul, I can read you like a book. It so happens that Marianna is at a loose end today. Does not know what to do with herself. Be in the café on the corner, Alfredo's I think it is called, at five this afternoon, and I will bring her to you. Dress up, even if she can't see. I will bring her, then I will bid adieu. Don't ask me how I do these things, it's not magic, I just do them."

Costello stays away all afternoon. At four-thirty, as he is about to leave the flat, she reappears, breathless. "A change of plan," she says. "Marianna is waiting downstairs. She does not like the idea of Alfredo's. She is being"—she gives an exasperated snort—"she is being difficult. May I use your kitchen?"

She returns from the kitchen bearing a little bowl of what looks like cream. "Just a paste of flour and water. It goes over your eyes. Have no fear, it will not hurt you. Why must you wear it? Because Marianna does not want you to see her. She insists. Here, bend down. Keep still. Don't blink. To hold it in place, a lemon leaf over each eye. And to hold the leaves in place, a nylon stocking, freshly washed, I promise, knotted behind your head. You can slip it off at any time you wish. But I would not recommend that, truly I would not.

"So. All done. I am sorry it is so complicated, but that is how we human beings are, complicated, each in our own unique way. Now, if you will settle down and wait, I will fetch your Marianna. Do you feel you are ready? Do you feel up to it? Yes? Good. Remember, you must pay her. That is the arrangement, that is how she keeps her self-respect. A topsy-turvy world, isn't it? But it's the only one we have.

"As soon as I have delivered her I will slip away and allow the two of you to get to know each other better. I won't be back until tomorrow or even the next day. Goodbye. Do not worry about me. I'm a tough old bird."

She is gone. He stands facing the door, leaning

on his frame. There is a murmur of voices from the stairwell. The door-latch clicks again.

"I am here," he says into the dark. Despite his unbelief, his heart seems to be hammering.

A gliding, a rustling. The scent of the damp leaves over his eyes overpowers every other smell. A pressure on the frame, which he feels through his hands. "My eyes are shut, sealed," he says. "I am not used to being blind, bear with me."

A hand, small, light, touches his face, rests there. *What the hell*, he thinks: he turns towards the hand and kisses it. *Let us play this to the end.*

Fingers explore his lips, the nails cut back. Through the veil of lemon he smells, faintly, wool. The fingers trace the line of his chin; they cross the blindfold, run through his hair.

"Let me hear your voice," he says.

She clears her throat, and already in the high, clear tone he can hear that she is not Marijana Jokić: lighter, more a creature of air.

"If you would sing, that would be best of all," he says. "We are on stage, in a certain sense, even if we are not being watched."

Even if we are not being watched. But in a certain sense they are being watched, he is sure of that, on the back of his neck he can feel it.

"What is this?" says the light voice, and ever so gently he feels the frame being rocked. The accent not Australian, not English either. Croatian? Another Croatian? Surely not; surely Croatians are not so thick on the ground. Besides, what meaning could a string of Croatians have, one after another?

"It is an aluminium frame, known colloquially as a walker. I have lost a leg. I find a frame less tiring than crutches." Then it occurs to him that the frame might be taken for a barrier. "Let me put it aside." He puts it aside and lowers himself onto the sofa. "Will you sit down beside me? This is a sofa, one or two paces in front of you. I am afraid I cannot assist you, because of a blindfold that our mutual friend Mrs. Costello has made me wear. She has a lot to answer for, Mrs. Costello."

He blames Mrs. Costello for the blindfold as he blames her for much else, but he will not take it off, not yet, will not strip his vision bare.

With a rustle (what can she be wearing that makes so much noise?) the woman sits down at his side— sits on his hand, in fact. For a moment, until she lifts herself and he can withdraw it, his hand is under her bottom in the most vulgar of ways. Not a large woman but a large bottom nevertheless, large and soft. But then the blind are inactive, do not walk, do not run, do not ride bicycles. All that energy pent up with nowhere to vent itself. No wonder she is restless. No wonder she is ready to visit a strange man all alone.

Now that his hands are free, he can touch her as she touched him. But is that what he wants to do? Does he want to explore those eyes or anywhere near them? Does he want to be—what is the word?—*appalled*? The appalling: that which turns one's stomach, unmans one, leaves one pale and shaking. Can one be appalled by what one cannot see but what the fingertips report, even the fingertips of a novice like himself in the land of the blind?

Uncertainly he stretches out a hand. He meets a hard cluster of something or other, bubbles, baubles, berries sewn up in sheaths. Her throat or her bodice, it must be. An inch higher, her chin. The chin firm, pointed; then a short jaw, then the beginning of furze or hair that feels dark to him, just as her skin feels dark; then something hard, an earpiece. She is wearing glasses, glasses that curve back across her cheekbones, perhaps the same dark glasses she wore in the lift.

"Your name is Marianna, Mrs. Costello tells me."

"Marianna."

He says *Marianna*, she says *Marianna*, but it is not the same name. His *Marianna* is still coloured by *Marijana*: it is heavier than hers, more solid. Of her *Marianna* he can say only that it is liquid, silver: not as quick as quicksilver, more like running water, a furling stream. And is this what it is like, being blind: having to weigh each word in one's hand, weigh each tone, fumble for equivalents that sound all too much (*a furling stream*) like bad poetry?

"Not the French *Marianne*?"

"No."

No. Not French. A pity. France would be

something in common, like a blanket to deploy over the pair of them.

The flour-and-water paste does its work surprisingly well. Even though his pupils must have dilated to their fullest, he is in a world of utter blackness. Where did Costello get the idea from? From a book? A recipe handed down from the ancients?

With his fingers still in her somewhat curly hair he draws her towards him, and she comes. Her face is pressed to his, the dark glasses too, though her fists are raised, two knobs keeping her breast apart from him.

"Thank you for your visit," he says. "Mrs. Costello mentioned your present troubles. I am sorry."

She says nothing. He can feel a light trembling run through her.

"There is no need," he goes on, but then does not know what comes next. What is there need of, what is there no need of? Something to do with their being man and woman; something to do with yielding to, to resort to the Costello woman's term, lust. But between where they are, man and woman, and the exercise of lust a veritable chasm yawns. "There is no need," he begins again, "for us to adhere to any script. No need to do anything we do not wish. We are free agents."

She is still shivering, shivering or trembling like a bird. "Come to me," he says, and obediently she sidles closer. It must be difficult for her. He must aid her, they are in this together.

The strings and berries and baubles at her throat turn out to be purely decorative. The dress opens via a zip at the back, which helpfully goes all the way down to the waist. His fingers are slow and clumsy. If she had consented to sit on his hand a while longer his fingers would have warmed up. Animal heat. As for the brassière, it is well constructed, sturdy, the sort of thing he imagines Carmelites would wear. Big breasts, a big bottom, yet slight for the rest. Marianna. Who is here, says the Costello woman, not out of solicitude for him, but for her own sake. Because there is a thirst in her that cannot be slaked. Because of her visage, her devastated face, that he is warned not to look upon and perhaps not even touch, because it would turn him to ice.

"I suggest we don't talk too much," he says. "Nevertheless there is one circumstance I should mention, for practical reasons. I have had no experience of this sort of thing since my accident. I may require a little help."

"I know that. Mrs. Costello told me."

"Mrs. Costello does not know everything. She cannot know what I do not know."

"Yes."

Yes? What does it mean, *yes*?

He doubts profoundly that he ever photographed this woman solo. If he had, he would not have forgotten her. Perhaps she was part of a group, in the days when he visited schools to take group photographs, that is possible; but not alone. The image he has of her comes only from the lift and from what his fingers tell him now. To her he must be even more of a jumble of sense-data: the cold of his hands; the roughness of his skin; the rasp of his voice; and an odour probably unpleasing to her supersensitive nostrils. Is that enough for her to construct the image of a man from? Is it an image she would be prepared to give herself to? Why did she agree to come, sight unseen? It is like a primitive experiment in biology—like bringing different species together to see if they will mate, fox and whale, cricket and marmoset.

"Your money," he says. "I am putting it on this side table, in an envelope. Four hundred and fifty dollars. Is that acceptable?"

He feels her nod.

A minute passes. Nothing more happens. A one-legged man and a partially disrobed woman waiting for what? For the click of a camera shutter? Australian Gothic. Matilda and her bloke, worn down by a lifetime of waltzing, parts of their bodies falling off or falling out, face the photographer one last time.

The woman's trembling has not ceased. He can swear it has infected him too: a light trilling of the hand that might be put down to age but is in fact something else, fear or anticipation (but which?).

If they are to proceed with the act for which she has been paid, for which she has accepted payment, she must overcome her present embarrassment and move on to the next step. She has been forewarned of his bad leg, of his untrustworthy undercarriage in general. Since he would find it hard to straddle a woman, it would be best if she were to straddle him. While she is negotiating that passage, he will have problems of his own to wrestle with, problems of quite another order. Perhaps, among the blind, there grow up intuitions of beauty based solely on touch. In the realm of the unseen, however, he is still groping his way. Beauty without the sight of beauty is not yet, to him, imaginable. The episode in the lift, during which his attention was held as much by the old woman as by her, has left behind in his memory only the sketchiest of outlines. When to a wide-brimmed hat, dark glasses, the curve of an averted face he tries to add heavy breasts and spreading, unnaturally soft buttocks, like volumes of liquid trapped in silk balloons, he cannot make the parts cohere. How can he even be sure they belong to the same woman?

Gently he tries to draw the woman to him. Though not resisting, she turns her face away, either because she is unwilling to yield her lips or because she does not want to give him a chance to lift off her glasses and explore what lies beneath—does not want it because where mutilation is concerned men are notoriously queasy.

How long since she lost her sight? Can he decently ask? And can he then decently go on to the next question: Has she been loved since it happened? Is it experience that has taught her her devastated eyes will kill off a man's desire?

Eros. Why does the sight of the beautiful call eros into life? Why does the spectacle of the hideous strangle desire? Does intercourse with the beautiful elevate us, make better people of us, or is it by embracing the diseased, the mutilated, the repulsive that we improve ourselves? What questions! Is that why the Costello woman has brought the two of them together: not for the vulgar comedy of a man and a woman with parts of their bodies missing doing their best to interlock, but in order that, once the sexual business has been got out of the way, they can hold a philosophy class, lying in each other's arms discoursing about beauty, love, and goodness?

And somehow or other, in the midst of all of this—the fretting, the embarrassment, the averting, the philosophising, to say nothing of an attempt on his part to loosen his tie, which has begun to choke him (why on earth is he wearing a tie?)—somehow, clumsily yet not as clumsily as might have been, shamefacedly yet not so shamefacedly as to paralyse them, they manage to slip into it, into the physical act to which they have willy-nilly contracted themselves, an act which while not *the* act of sex as generally understood is nevertheless *an* act of sex, and which, despite the truncated haunch on the one hand and the blasted eyes on the other, proceeds with some dispatch from beginning to middle to end, that is to say in all its natural parts.

What disquieted him most in Costello's account of Marianna was what she said about the hunger or thirst raging in her body. He has never been fond of immoderacy, immodesty, wild motions, grunts and shouts and cries. But Marianna seems to know how to contain herself. Whatever is going on inside her she keeps to herself; and, once they have concluded, she swiftly makes everything decent again, more or less. The sole intimation he has of either raging thirst or raging hunger comes in the form of an unusual but not unpleasing heat at the core of her body, as though her womb or perhaps her heart were glowing with a fire of its own.

Though the sofa was built neither for sexual coupling nor for subsequent philosophic languor, and though, without a covering, they are soon going to be chilled, there is no question yet of groping their way to a proper bed in a proper bedroom.

"Marianna," he says, testing the name on his tongue, tasting the two *ns:* "I know that is your name, but is it what people call you? There isn't another name you use?"

"Marianna. That is it. That is all."

"Very well," he says. "Marianna, Mrs. Costello says we have met before. When was that?"

"A long time ago. You took my photograph. It was for my birthday. You don't remember?"

"I don't and can't remember because I don't know what you look like. And it can't be that you

129

remember me because you don't know what I look like. Where did it take place, this portrait session?"

"In your studio."

"And where was the studio?"

She is silent. "It is too long ago," she says at last. "I can't remember."

"On the other hand, our paths did cross much more recently. We shared a lift at the Royal Hospital. An elevator. Did Mrs. Costello mention that?"

"Yes."

"What else did she say?"

"Just that you were lonely."

"Lonely. How interesting. Mrs. Costello is a close friend of yours?"

"No, not close."

"What then?"

There is a long silence. He strokes her through her clothes, up and down, thigh, side, breast. What a pleasure, and how unexpected, to have the freedom of a woman's body again, even if the woman is invisible!

"Did she just walk in on you?" he says. "She just walked in on me."

He feels her shake her head slowly from side to side.

"Does she intend, do you think, that you and I should become a couple? For her entertainment perhaps? The halt leading the blind?"

The remark is meant lightly, but he can feel her stiffen. He hears the lips part, hears her swallow, and all of a sudden she is crying.

"I am sorry," he says. He reaches out to touch her cheek. It is bathed in wetness. At least, he thinks, she has tear ducts left. "I am sorry, truly. But we are grown people, so why are we letting someone we barely know dictate our lives? That is what I ask myself."

She gives a gasp that is presumably a laugh, and the laugh brings on sobs. She sits up beside him, half dressed, sobbing freely, shaking her head from side to side. Now is surely the time to slip off the blindfold, wipe the muck from his eyes, behold her as she is. But he does not. He waits. He tarries. He delays.

She blows her nose on a tissue she seems to have brought with her, clears her throat. "I thought," she says, "this was what you wanted."

"It is, make no mistake about it, it is. Nevertheless, the idea came from our friend Elizabeth. The first impulse. She issues instructions, we follow. Even when there is no one to see that we obey."

See. Not the right word, but he lets it stand. She must be used to it by now, to people who say "see" when they mean something else.

"Unless," he goes on, "she is still in the room, observing, checking up."

"No," Marianna says, "there is no one here."

There is no one here. Being blind, and therefore attuned to the subtler emanations of living beings, she must be right. Nevertheless, the feeling has not left him that he need only reach down and his fingers will encounter Elizabeth Costello, stretched out on the carpet like a dog, watching and waiting.

"Our friend advocated this"—he waves a vague hand—"because in her eyes it represents the crossing of a threshold. She is of the opinion that until I have crossed a certain threshold I am caught in limbo, unable to grow. That is the hypothesis she is testing out in my case. She probably has another hypothesis to cover you."

Even as he speaks he knows it is a lie. Elizabeth Costello has never used the word *growth* in his hearing. *Growth* comes out of the self-help manuals. God knows what Elizabeth Costello really wants, for him or for herself or for this Marianna; God knows to what theory of life or love she really holds; God knows what will happen next.

"Anyway, having crossed her threshold, we are now free to proceed to higher and better things."

He is just talking, making the best of an uncomfortable situation, trying to cheer up a woman suffering the *tristesse* that descends after coitus with a stranger. From his envelope of darkness, not yet giving up hope of forming a picture of her, he reaches out again to touch her face; and in the act plunges into a dark gulf of his own. All his larkiness deserts him. Why, why did he put enough trust in the Costello woman to go through with this performance, which seems to him now less rash than simply stupid? And what on earth is this poor blind unlucky woman going to do with herself in these less than welcoming surroundings while she waits for her mentor in her mercy to return and release her? Did Costello really believe that a few minutes of inflamed physical congress could like a gas expand to fill up a whole night? Did she believe she could throw two strangers together, neither of them young, one positively old, old and cold, and expect them to behave like Romeo and Juliet? How naïve! And she a noted literary artist too! And this damned paste which, though she swore it was harmless, is beginning to irritate his eyes as it dries out: how could she have imagined that being blinded with flour and water would change his character, make a new man of him? Blindness is a handicap pure and simple. A man without sight is a lesser man, as a man with one leg is a lesser man, not a new man. This poor woman she has sent him is a lesser woman too, less than she must have been before. Two lesser beings, handicapped, diminished: how could she have imagined a spark of the divine would be struck between them, or any spark at all?

As for the woman herself, growing colder minute by minute at his side, what can be running through her mind? What a load of poppycock she must have been told to persuade her to come knocking at the door of a strange man and offering herself to him! Just as in his case there was a long preamble to this lamentable encounter, a preamble stretching far enough back into the past to constitute a book in its own right, beginning with Wayne Blight and Paul Rayment setting off

133

from their respective homes that fatal winter morning, oblivious as yet of each other's existence, so in her case there must be a prelude beginning with the virus or the sunspot or the bad gene or the needle or whatever else is to blame for her blinding, and proceeding step by step to a meeting with a plausible old woman (all the more plausible if you have only the voice to go by) telling you she has the means to quench your burning thirst if only you will take a taxi to a café called Alfredo's in North Adelaide, here is the fare, I am putting it in your hand, no need to be nervous, the man in question is quite harmless, merely lonely, he will treat you as a callgirl and pay you for your time, and I will be there anyway, hovering in the background, watching over you—if you have only the voice to go by and cannot see the mad glint in the eye.

An experiment, that is what it amounts to, an idle, biologico-literary experiment. Cricket and marmoset. And they fell for it, both of them, he in his way, she in hers!

"I must leave," says the woman, the marmoset. "The taxi will be waiting."

"If you say so," he says. "How do you know about the taxi?"

"Mrs. Costello ordered it."

"Mrs. Costello?"

"Yes, Mrs. Costello."

"How does Mrs. Costello know when you will need a taxi?"

She shrugs.

"Well, Mrs. Costello takes good care of you. Can I pay for the taxi?"

"No, no, it's all included."

"Well then, give my greetings to Mrs. Costello. And be careful on the way down. The stairs can be slippery."

He sits still, containing himself, while she dresses. The instant the door closes behind her, however, he whips off the blindfold and claws at his eyes. But the paste has caked and hardened. If he tears at it too hard he will lose his eyelashes. He curses: he will have to soak it off.

CHAPTER 16

"She came to me as you came to me," says Costello. "A woman of darkness, a woman in darkness. *Take up the story of such a one*: words in my sleeping ear, spoken by what in the old days we would have called an angel calling me out to a wrestling match. Therefore no, I have no idea where she lives, your Marianna. All my dealings with her have been on the telephone. If you would like her to repeat her visit, I can give you her number."

A repeat visit. That is not what he wants. Sometime in the future, perhaps, but not now. What he wants right now is an assurance that the story he has been presented with is the true story: that the woman who came to his flat was truly the woman he saw in the lift; that her name is truly Marianna; that she truly lives with her crookbacked mother, her husband having abandoned her because of her affliction; and so forth. What he wants is assurance that he has not been duped.

For there is an alternative story, one that he finds all too easy to make up for himself. In the alternative story the Costello woman would have located big-bottomed Marianna, known otherwise as Natasha, known also as Tanya, and hailing from Moldavia via Dubai and Nicosia, in the Yellow Pages. On the telephone she would have coached her in a charade. "My brother-in-law, you will need to know," she would have told her, "has certain eccentricities. But then, what man does not have his little eccentricities, and what can a woman do, if she wants to get by, but find ways of accommodating them? My brother-in-law's chief eccentricity is that he prefers not to see the woman he is engaged with. He prefers the realm of the imaginary; he prefers to keep his head in the clouds. Once upon a time he was head over heels in love with a woman named Marianna, an actress. What he wants from you, and has in an indirect way asked me to convey to you, is that you should present yourself as Marianna the actress, wearing certain accoutrements or properties which I shall provide. That is to be your role; and for enacting that role he will pay you. Do you understand?" "Sure," Natasha or Tanya would have said, "but outcalls is extra." "Outcalls is extra," Costello would have agreed: "I'll be sure to remind him of that. One last word. Be nice to him. He lost a leg recently, in a road accident, and is not what he used to be."

Might that be the real story, give or take a detail here and there, behind the visit of the so-called Marianna? Were the dark glasses worn to hide not the fact that she was blind but the fact that she was not blind? When she trembled, was it less with nervousness than with the effort of holding back her giggles as the man with the stocking around his head fumbled at her underwear? *We have crossed the threshold. Now we can proceed to higher and better things.* What a solemn fool! She must have laughed in the taxi all the way home.

Was Marianna Marianna or was Marianna Natasha? That is what he must find out in the first instance; that is what he must squeeze out of Costello. Only when he has his answer may he turn to the deeper question: Does it matter who the woman really was; does it matter if he has been duped?

"You treat me like a puppet," he complains. "You treat everyone like a puppet. You make up stories and bully us into playing them out for you. You should open a puppet theatre, or a zoo. There must be plenty of old zoos for sale, now that they have fallen out of fashion. Buy one, and put us in cages with our names on them. *Paul Rayment: canis infelix. Marianna Popova: pseudocaeca (migratory).* And so forth. Rows and rows of cages holding the people who have, as you put it, *come to you* in the course of your career as a liar and fabulator. You could charge admission. You could make a living out of it. Parents could bring their children at weekends to gawp at us and throw peanuts. Easier than writing books that no one reads."

He pauses, waiting for her to rise to the bait. She is silent.

"What I don't understand," he goes on—he was

not angry when he began this tirade, he is not angry now, but there is certainly a pleasure in letting himself go—"what I don't understand is, seeing that I am so dull, so unresponsive to your schemes, why you persist with me. Drop me, I beseech you, let me get on with my life. Write about this blind Marianna of yours instead. She has more potential than I will ever have. I am not a hero, Mrs. Costello. Losing a leg does not qualify one for a dramatic role. Losing a leg is neither tragic nor comic, just unfortunate."

"Don't be bitter, Paul. Drop you, take up Marianna: maybe I won't, maybe I will. Who knows what one may not be driven to."

"I am not bitter."

"Of course you are. I can hear it in your voice. You are bitter, and who can blame you, after all that has happened to you."

He gathers his crutches. "I can do without your sympathy," he says curtly. "I am going out now. I don't know when I will be back. When you leave, lock the door behind you."

"If I do leave I will certainly lock the door. But I don't think that is what I will be doing. I can't tell you how much I have been longing for a hot bath. So that is what I will treat myself to, if you don't mind. Such a luxury these days."

It is not the first time the Costello woman has refused to explain herself. But her latest evasion both irritates and disturbs him. *Maybe I won't, maybe I will.* Is it as provisional as that, her interest in him? May Marianna, rather than he, turn out to be the chosen one? Setting aside the shadowy portrait session, of which he can truly remember nothing, were their two encounters, the first in the lift, the second on the sofa, episodes in the life-story not of Paul Rayment but of Marianna Popova? Of course there is a sense in which he is a passing character in the life of this Marianna or of anyone else whose path he crosses, just as Marianna and everyone else are passing characters in his. But is he a passing character in a more fundamental sense too: someone on whom the light falls all too briefly before it passes on? Will what passed between himself and Marianna turn out to be simply one passage among many in Marianna's quest for love? Or might the Costello woman be writing two stories at once, stories about characters who suffer a loss (sight in the one case, ambulation in the other) which they must learn to live with; and, as an experiment or even as a kind of professional joke, might she have arranged for their two life-lines to intersect? He has no experience of novelists and how they go about their business, but it sounds not implausible.

In the public library, under A823.914, he finds a whole row of books by Elizabeth Costello: *The Fiery Furnace*, *The House on Eccles Street* in several well-thumbed copies, *To the Friendly Isles*, *Tango with Mr. Dunbar*, *The Roots of Time*, *Mannerly*; also a rather severe dark-blue volume with the title *A Constant*

Flame: Intent and Design in the Novels of Elizabeth Costello. He scans the index. No mention of a Marianna or a Marijana; no entry for blindness.

He pages through *The House on Eccles Street.* Leopold Bloom. Hugh Boylan. Marion Bloom. What is wrong with her? Can she not make up characters of her own?

He replaces the book, takes up *The Fiery Furnace,* reads at random.

He rolls the plasticine between his palms until it is warm and supple, then pinches it into little animal figures: birds, toads, cats, dogs with pricked-up ears. On the table top he sets the figures in a half-circle, bending their necks back as if howling at the moon, or baying, or croaking.

It is old plasticine, from his last Christmas stocking. The pristine cakes of brick red, leaf green, sky blue have bled into each other by now and become a leaden purple. Why, he wonders—why does the bright grow dull and the dull never bright? What would it need to make the purple fade away and the red and blue and green emerge again, like chicks from a shell?

Why, why? Why does she ask a question and then not give the answer? The answer is simple: the red and the blue and the green will never return because of entropy, which is irreversible and irrevocable and rules the universe. Even a literary person ought to know that, even a lady novelist. From the multifarious to the uniform and never back again. From the perky chick to the old hen dead in the dust.

He flips to the middle of the book. *She could not stay with a man who was tired all the time. It was hard enough to hold her own tiredness at bay. She had only to stretch out beside him in the too familiar bed to feel the weariness begin to seep out of him and wash over her in a colourless, odourless, inert tide. She had to escape! Now!*

A Marion but no Marianna. No blind folk, as far as he can see, no amputees. He snaps *The Fiery Furnace* shut. He is not going to expose himself to any more of the colourless, odourless, inert, and depressive gas given off by its pages. How on earth did Elizabeth Costello get to be a popular author, if popular is what she is?

There is a photograph on the jacket: a younger Elizabeth Costello wearing a windbreaker, standing against what appears to be the rigging of a yacht. Her eyes are screwed up against the light, her skin is deeply tanned. A seawoman? Is there such a word, or must a seawoman be a mermaid, as a seahorse, *cheval marin*, is a fish? Not exactly handsome, but probably better looking in middle age than in youth. Nonetheless, a certain plainness, even blankness, to her. Not his type. Not any man's type, maybe.

Contemporary World Authors, in the reference section of the library, has a brief biography together with the same nautical photograph. Born Melbourne, Australia, 1928. Lengthy residence in Europe. First book 1957. List of awards, prizes. Bibliography but no plot summaries. Twice married. A son and a daughter.

Seventy-two! As old as that! What is she doing, sleeping on park benches? Has her mind begun to ramble? Is she dotty? Might that explain everything? Ought the son and daughter to be brought into the picture? Is it his duty to track them down? *Please come at once. Your mother has taken up residence with me, a complete stranger, and refuses to leave. I am at my wits' end. Remove her, commit her, do whatever is called for as long as I am liberated.*

He returns to the flat. Costello is not there, but on the coffee table lies her notebook. Quite possibly she has left it out intentionally. If he takes a peek it will be another victory for her. Nevertheless.

She writes in fat black ink, in large free-flowing script, just a few words to a line. He pages to the most recent entry. *Dark dark dark*, he reads. *They all go into the dark, the vacant interlunar spaces.*

He leafs back.

Keening over the body, he reads. *Davening*, the word underlined. *Rocking stiffly back and forth at the bedside, her hands over her ears, her eyes wide open, unblinking, as though afraid she might miss the moment when, like a spurt of gas, the soul will leave the body and rise through the layers of air, one after another, to the stratosphere and beyond. Outside the window, sunshine, birdsong, the usual. She is locked into the rhythm of her grief like a long-distance runner. A marathon of grief. If no one comes to coax her away she will go on thus all day. Yet not once does she touch him ("him," his body). Why not? The horror of cold flesh? Is horror after all stronger than love? Or perhaps,*

143

in among the welter of grief, she has steeled herself not to try to hold him back. She has said her goodbyes, goodbyes are over with. Goodbye: God be with you. And then, over the page: *Dark dark dark . . .*

If he reads back far enough, it will no doubt become clearer who the grieving woman is, whose the corpse. But the imp of curiosity seems to be deserting him. He is not sure he wants to know more. Something unseemly about this writing, the fat ink sprawling carelessly over the tramlines; something impious, provocative, uncovering what does not belong in the light of day.

Is the whole notebook like that: a provocation, an affront to decency? He pages cautiously through it from the beginning. For long stretches he cannot stitch the entries together. She writes as if she were hurrying through some story she had overheard, compressing the narrative, cutting the dialogue short, jumping impatiently from one scene to the next. But then a phrase catches his eye: *One leg blue, one red.* Ljuba? It can only be Ljuba. *Harlequin, crazy-coloured. In Germany, brindle cows are the crazy ones, the moonstruck, the ones that jump over the moon. And the little dog laughs. Bring in a dog, a little mutt that wags its tail to all and sundry, yapping, eager to please? PR's reaction: "I may be doggy, but not to that extent, surely!" Mutt and Jeff.*

He snaps the book shut. If his ears are not burning they might as well be. It is as he feared: she knows everything, every jot and tittle. Damn her! All the time he thought he was his own master he has been in a cage like a rat, darting this way and that, yammering to himself, with the infernal woman standing over him, observing, listening, taking notes, recording his progress.

Or is it worse than that, incomparably worse, so much worse that the mind threatens to buckle? Is this what it is like to be translated to what at present he can only call *the other side*? Is that what has happened to him; is that what happens to everyone?

Gingerly he settles into an armchair. If this does not amount to a big moment, a Copernican moment, then what does? The greatest of all secrets may just have unveiled itself to him. There is a second world that exists side by side with the first, unsuspected. One chugs along in the first for a certain length of time; then the angel of death arrives in the person of Wayne Blight or someone like him. For an instant, for an aeon, time stops; one tumbles down a dark hole. Then, hey presto, one emerges into a second world *identical with the first*, where time resumes and the action proceeds—flying through the air like a cat, the throng of curious onlookers, the ambulance, the hospital, Dr. Hansen, et cetera—except that one now has Elizabeth Costello around one's neck, or someone like her.

Quite a leap to make, from the word *D-O-G* in a notebook to life after death. A wild surmise. He could be wrong. More than likely he is wrong. But whether he is wrong or right, whether what in the most hesitant of spirits he calls *the other side* is truth or delusion, the first epithet that occurs to him, typed out letter by letter behind his eyelids by the celestial typewriter, is *puny*. If dying turns out to be nothing but a trick that might as well be a trick with words, if death is a mere hiccup in time after which life goes on as before, why all the fuss? Is one allowed to refuse it—refuse this deathlessness, this puny fate? *I want my old life back, the one that came to an end on Magill Road.*

He is exhausted, his mind is reeling, he has merely to close his eyes and he will sink into sleep. But he does not want to be lying here inert and exposed when the Costello woman comes back. He has begun to be aware of a certain quality about her, vulpine rather than canine, that has nothing to do with her appearance but that makes him nervous and that he does not trust at all. He can all too easily imagine her prowling from room to room in the dark, sniffing, on the hunt.

He is still sitting in the armchair when he is lightly shaken. Before him stands not the vulpine Mrs. Costello but Marijana Jokic, the woman with the red head-scarf who is in some way (he cannot for the moment remember how, his mind is too befuddled) the root or source or font of all these complications.

"Mr. Rayment, you OK?"

"Marijana! Yes, of course. Of course I am OK." But that is not the truth. He is not OK. His mouth tastes foul, his back is stiff, and he hates being surprised. "What time is it?"

Marijana ignores the question. She sets down an envelope on the coffee table beside him. "Your cheque," she says. "He say give it back, we don't accept money. My husband. He say he don't accept other man's money."

Money. Drago. Another universe of discourse. He must collect his wits. "And what about Drago himself?" he says. "What about Drago's education?"

"Drago can go to school like before, he don't need boarding school, my husband say."

The child Ljuba fingers her mother's skirt absent-mindedly, sucking on her thumb. Behind her the Costello woman glides discreetly into the room. Was she here in the flat while he was sleeping?

"Would you like me to speak to your husband?" he says.

Vigorously Marijana shakes her head. She could not imagine anything worse, more stupid.

"Well, let's give some thought to what to do next. Perhaps Mrs. Costello has a word of advice to offer."

"Hello Ljuba," says Elizabeth Costello, "I'm a friend of your mother's, you can call me Elizabeth or Aunt Elizabeth. Sorry to hear of your problem, Marijana, but I am new on the scene, I don't think I should interfere."

You interfere all the time, he thinks venomously. *Why are you here if not to interfere?*

With a sigh that is almost a cry, Marijana throws herself down on the sofa. She shields her eyes; the tears are coming now. The child takes up her post beside her.

"Such good boy," she says. "Such good boy." Sobs overtake her. "He want to go so much!"

In another world, a world in which he was young and whole and his breath sweet, he would gather Marijana in his arms, kiss away her tears. *Forgive me, forgive me,* he would say. *I have been unfaithful to you, I don't know why! It happened only once and will never happen again! Admit me to your heart and I will take care of you, I swear, until the day I die!*

The child's dark eyes bore into him. *What have you done to my mother?* she seems to say. *It's all your fault!*

And indeed it is his fault. Those dark eyes see into his heart, see his secret desire, see that in his innermost this first glimpse of a rift between man and wife makes him exult, not grieve. *Forgive me too!* he says mutely, looking straight into the child's eyes. *I mean no harm, I am in the grip of a force beyond me!*

"We have plenty of time," he says in his most sober voice. "There is still a week before applications close for next year. I will guarantee the school fees; I will get my solicitor to write a letter guaranteeing them, then it will not seem so personal. Speak to your husband again, once he has calmed down. I am sure you will be able to bring him around, you and Drago together."

Marijana shrugs hopelessly. She says something to the child that he does not understand; the child trots out of the room and comes back with a handful of tissues. Noisily Marijana blows her nose. Tears, mucus, snot: the less romantic side of sorrow, the underside. Like the underside of sex: stains, smells.

Is she aware of what happened here, on the very sofa where she sits? Can she sense it?

"Or," he continues, "if it has become a matter of honour, if your husband finds it impossible to accept a loan from another man, perhaps Mrs. Costello can be persuaded to write the cheque, acting as an intermediary in this good cause."

It is the first time he has put the Costello woman on the spot. He feels a surge of mean triumph.

Mrs. Costello shakes her head. "I do not believe I can interfere," she says. "In addition there are certain practical difficulties, which I prefer not to go into."

"Such as?" he says.

"Which I prefer not to go into," she repeats.

"I don't see any practical difficulties at all," he says. "I write a cheque to you and you write a cheque to the school. Nothing could be simpler. If you will not do that, if you refuse to, as you put it, interfere, then just go away. Go away and leave us alone."

He hopes that his tartness will fluster her. But she is not flustered at all. "Leave you alone?" she says softly, so softly that he can barely hear. "If I left you alone"—her eyes flicker to Marijana—"if I left you both alone, what would become of you?"

Marijana gets up, blows her nose again, stows the tissue in her sleeve. "We must go," she says decisively.

"Help me up, Marijana," he says. "Please."

On the landing, out of earshot of the Costello woman, she faces him. "Elizabeth—she is good friend?"

"Good? No, I don't think so. Not a good friend, not a close friend. I had never laid eyes on her until quite recently. Not a friend at all, in fact. Elizabeth is a professional writer. She writes novels, romances. At present she is hunting around for characters to put in a book she is planning. She seems to be pinning her hopes on me. On you too, at a remove. But I do not fit. That is why she is pestering me. Trying to make me fit."

She is trying to take over my life. That is what he would like to say. But it seems unfair to be making an appeal to Marijana in her present state. *Save me.*

Marijana gives him a faint smile. Though the tears are gone, her eyes are still red, her nose puffy. The bright light from the skylight shows her up cruelly, her skin coarse without make-up, her teeth discoloured. *Who is this woman,* he thinks, *to whom I yearn to give myself? A mystery, all a mystery.* He takes her hand. "I will stand by you," he says. "I will help you, I promise. I will help Drago."

"Mama!" whines the child.

Marijana extracts her hand. "We must go," she says, and is gone.

150

CHAPTER 17

"I am having visitors," he announces to the Costello woman. "It won't be your kind of evening, I'm afraid. You may want to make other arrangements."

"Of course. I'm glad to see you getting back into the social whirl. Let me think . . . What shall I do? Maybe I will go to the cinema. Is there anything worth seeing, do you know?"

"I am not making myself clear. When I say make other arrangements, I mean make arrangements to stay somewhere else."

"Oh! And where else should I stay, do you think?"

"I don't know. It is not my business to say where you go from here. Back to where you came from, perhaps."

There is a silence. "So," she says. "At least you are blunt." And then: "Do you remember, Paul, the story of Sinbad and the old man?"

He does not reply.

"By the bank of a swollen stream," she says, "Sinbad comes upon an old man. 'I am old and weak,' says the old man. 'Carry me to the other

151

side and Allah will bless you.' Being a good-hearted fellow, Sinbad lifts the old man onto his shoulders and wades across the stream. But when they reach the other side, the old man refuses to climb down. Indeed, he tightens his legs around Sinbad's neck until Sinbad feels himself choking. 'Now you are my slave,' says the old man, 'who must do my bidding in all things.'"

He remembers the story. It was in a book called *Légendes dorées*, Golden Legends, in his book-chest in Lourdes. Vividly he remembers the illustration: the skinny old man naked but for a loincloth, his wiry legs hooked around the hero's neck while the hero strides through the waist-deep torrent. What has happened to the book? What has happened to the book-chest and the other remnants of a French childhood that crossed the oceans with them to the new country? If he went back to the Dutchman's house in Ballarat, would he find them in the cellar, Sinbad and the fox and the crow and Jeanne d'Arc and the rest of his story-companions, closed up in cardboard boxes, patiently waiting for their little master to return and rescue them; or did the Dutchman cast them out long ago, after he became a widower?

"Yes, I remember," he says. "Am I to understand that I am Sinbad in the story and you the old man? In that case you face a certain difficulty. You have no means of—how shall I put this delicately—no means of getting onto my shoulders. And I am not going to help you up."

Costello smiles a secretive smile. "Perhaps I am already there," she says, "and you do not know it."

"No, you are not, Mrs. Costello. I am not under your control, not in any sense of the word, and I am going to prove it. I request you to kindly return my key—a key you took without my permission—and leave my flat and not come back."

"That's a hard word to be speaking to an old woman, Mr. Rayment. Are you sure you mean it?"

"This is not a comedy, Mrs. Costello. I am asking you to leave."

She sighs. "Very well then. But I'm sure I don't know what will become of me, with the rain pelting down and the dark coming fast and all."

There is no rain, no dark. It is a pleasant afternoon, warm and still, the kind of afternoon that ought to make one glad to be alive.

"Here," she says: "your key." With exaggerated care she sets down the latchkey on the coffee table. "I will need a brief grace to collect my belongings and put on my face. Then I will be off, and you will be alone again. I am sure you are looking forward to that."

Impatiently he turns away. In a few minutes she is back.

"Goodbye." She transfers a plastic shopping bag from right hand to left, offers him the right hand. "I am leaving a small suitcase. I will send for it in a day or two, when I have found alternative quarters."

"I would prefer it if you took your suitcase with you."

"That is not possible."

"It is possible, and I would prefer it if you did so."

No more words pass between them. From the front door he watches her descend the stairs lingeringly, step by step, bearing the suitcase. If he were a gentleman he would offer to help, bad leg or no. But in this case he is not a gentleman. He just wants her out of his life.

CHAPTER 18

It is true: he is indeed looking forward to being alone. In fact he hungers for solitude. But no sooner has Elizabeth Costello taken her leave than Drago Jokić, with a bulging rucksack on his shoulder, is at the door.

"Hi," Drago greets him. "How's the pushbike?"

"I have not done anything about the pushbike, I'm afraid. I have had other matters to attend to. What can I do for you? Would you like to come in?"

Drago comes in, drops the rucksack on the floor. The self-assured air is no longer so marked; he seems, in fact, embarrassed.

"Have you come about Wellington College?" he asks. "Do you want to talk about that?"

The boy nods.

"Well, fire away. What is the problem?"

"My mum says you will pay my fees."

"That's right. I will guarantee the fees for two years. You can think of it as a loan if you prefer, a long-term loan. It is not important to me how you think of it."

"Mum told me how much it adds up to. I didn't know it was that much."

"I have no use for the money, Drago. If we did not spend it on your education it would just sit in the bank doing nothing."

"Yes," says the boy doggedly, "but why me?"

Why me?—a question on everyone's lips, it seems. He could fob Drago off with some polite form of words, but no, the boy has come in person to inquire, so he will give him an answer, the true answer or part of the true answer.

"In the time your mother has worked here I have developed a soft spot for her, Drago. She has made a huge difference to my life. She does not have an easy time of it, we both know that. I want to help where I can."

Now the evasive air is gone. The boy is looking him straight in the eye, challenging him: *Is that all you can say? Is that as far as you will go?* And his answer? *Yes, that is as far as I will go, for the present.*

"My dad won't allow it," says Drago.

"So I hear. To your dad it is probably a matter of pride. I can understand that. But you should remind him there is no shame in taking a loan from a friend. Because that is how I would like to be thought of: as a friend."

Drago is shaking his head. "It's not that. They had a fight about it, my mum and my dad." His lip begins to quiver. Sixteen years old: still a child. "They had a fight last night," he goes on softly. "Mum has walked out. She has gone to stay with Aunt Lidie."

"And where is that? Where is Aunt Lidie?"

"Just down the road, in Elizabeth. Elizabeth North."

"Drago," he says, "let us be frank with each other. You would not have come here today, I know, if you had not had troubling thoughts about your mother and myself. So let me set your mind at rest. There is nothing dishonourable going on between your mother and me. There is nothing dishonourable in my feelings for her. I honour her as much as any woman on earth."

Nothing dishonourable. What a funny old form of words! Are they not just a fig-leaf to cover something a great deal coarser, something unsayable: *I haven't been fucking your mother?* If fucking is what it is all about, if fucking is what sends Miroslav Jokić into a jealous rage and brings his son to the edge of tears, why is he making speeches about honour? *I haven't been fucking your mother, I haven't even solicited her: go and tell that to your father.* Yet if he does not plan to solicit Marijana, if he does not aspire to fuck her, what in God's name does he plan or aspire to do, in words that make sense to a youth born in the 1980s?

"I am sorry to be a source of trouble between your parents. It is the last thing I want. Your father has quite the wrong idea about me. If he met me in person he would know better."

"He hit her," says Drago, and now control is starting to go—control over his voice, control over his tears, perhaps control over the motions of his heart. "I hate him. He hit my sister too."

157

"He hit Blanka?"

"No, my little sister. Blanka sides with him. She says Mum has affairs. She says Mum is having an affair with you."

Mum has affairs. The Costello woman called her a faithful spouse. He should not waste his time trying his luck with Marijana Jokić, she said, because Marijana Jokić is a faithful spouse. Who is right, the spiteful daughter or the crazy old woman? And what an appalling picture! Miroslav, no doubt a great bear of a man, enraged and drunk, laying into Marijana with his fists, laying into his porcelain-featured daughter too, while the son stands by seething! Balkan passions! How on earth did he get involved with a Balkan, a Balkan mechanic and his mechanical duck!

"Your mother and I are not having an affair," he repeats doggedly. "She would not dream of it, I would not dream of it." *What a lie! I dream of it daily.* "If you don't believe me, that is the end of it, I am not going to try to persuade you. What are your plans now, your immediate plans? Will you be staying at home or with your mother?"

Drago shakes his head. "I'm not going back. I'll crash at a mate's." He gives the rucksack a kick. "I brought my things."

From the look of the rucksack he has brought a great many things.

"You can sleep here if you like. There is a spare bed in my study."

"I don't know. I told my mate I would stay with

158

him. Can I tell you later? Can I leave my bag here?"

"Please yourself."

He stays up past midnight waiting for Drago. But it is not until the next day that Drago comes back. "I've got a friend with me downstairs," he announces on the entryphone. "Can she come up?"

A friend, a girlfriend: so that is where he spent the night! "Yes, come up." But when he opens the door he nearly cries out with exasperation. By the side of a grubby, weary-looking Drago stands Elizabeth Costello. Will he never be rid of the woman?

He and she eye each other warily, like feuding dogs. "Drago and I bumped into each other on Victoria Square," she says. "That's where he was spending the night. In the company of some new mates. Who were inducting him into the fruits of the Barossa."

"I thought you said you were staying with a friend," he says to Drago.

"It didn't work out. I'm OK."

I'm OK. The boy is clearly not OK. He seems sunk in dejection, which a bout of drinking cannot have helped.

"Have you spoken to your mother?"

The boy nods.

"And?"

"I phoned her. I told her I'm not coming back."

"I'm not asking about you, I'm asking about her. How is she?"

"She's OK."

"Take a shower, Drago. Go on. Clean yourself up. Have a nap. Then go home. Make peace with your father. I'm sure he is sorry for what he did."

"He's not sorry. He's never sorry."

"May I put in a word?" says Elizabeth Costello. "Drago's father is unlikely to be sorry as long as he is convinced he is in the right. That, at least, is how I see it. As for Marijana, whatever she may tell her son on the phone, she is certainly not OK. If she has taken refuge with her sister-in-law, that is only because she has nowhere else to go. Her sister-in-law is not sympathetic to her."

"This is Lidie? Lidie is Jokić's sister?"

"Lidija Karadžić. Miroslav's sister, Drago's aunt. Lidie and Marijana do not get on, have never got on. In Lidie's opinion, what is being dished out to Marijana is no more than she deserves. 'Where there is smoke there is fire,' says Lidie. A Croatian proverb."

"How on earth can you know these things? How do you know what Lidie says?"

The Costello woman brushes the question aside. "To Lidie it does not matter whether in truth Marijana is having an extra-marital affair. What matters is that stories are being whispered in the rather narrow circle of the Croatian community. Pay heed, Paul, don't curl your lip with disdain. Gossip, public opinion, *fama* as the Romans called it, makes the world go round—gossip, not truth. You tell us you are *in truth* not having an affair with Drago's mother because you and she have not *in truth* (excuse me, Drago) had sexual intercourse. But what counts as sexual intercourse nowadays? And how do we weigh a quick deed in a dark corner as against months of fevered longing? When love is the subject, how can an outside observer ever be sure of the truth of what has gone on? What we can be a great deal more sure of is that whispers of an affair between Marijana Jokić and one of her clients have been released into the air, who knows by whom. And the air is common, the air is what we breathe and live by; the more loudly the rumour is denied, the more it is in the air.

"You don't like me, Mr. Rayment, you want to be rid of me, you make that quite plain. And I myself am not exactly rejoicing, I assure you, to find myself back in this hideous flat. The sooner you settle on a course of action vis-à-vis Drago's mother, or vis-à-vis the lady in black who called on you the other day, or even vis-à-vis Mrs. McCord, whom you never mention in my hearing, but most likely vis-à-vis Drago's mother, since she seems to be the light of your life—the sooner you settle on a course of action and commit yourself to it, the sooner you and I, to our mutual relief, will be able to part. What that course of action should consist in I cannot advise, that must come from you. If I knew what came next there would be no need for me to be here, I could go back to my own life, which is a great deal more comfortable, I assure you, and more

161

satisfying, than what I have to put up with here. But until you choose to act I must wait upon you. You are, as the saying has it, your own man."

He shakes his head. "I don't understand your meaning. You make no sense at all."

"Of course you understand. And anyway, one does not need to understand before one takes action, not unless one is excessively philosophic. Let me remind you, there is such a thing as acting on impulse, and I would certainly urge it on you if I were only permitted. You say you are in love with Mrs. Jokić, or at least when Drago is not around that is what you say. Well, *do* something with your love. And, by the way, a little more frankness in front of Drago would not hurt—would it, Drago?"

Drago gives a crooked smile.

"Part of a growing boy's education. Better than sending him off to that pretentious college in Canberra. Give him a glimpse of the wilder shores of love. Let him see how one navigates the passions, how one steers by the stars—the Great and Little Bear, the Archer, and so forth. The Southern Cross. He must have passions of his own by now, he is old enough for passions. You do have passions, don't you, Drago?"

Drago is silent, but the smile does not leave his lips. Something is on the go between the woman and the boy. But what?

"Let me ask you, Drago: What would you do if you were in Mr. Rayment's shoes, if you were Mr. Rayment?"

"What would I do?"

"Yes. Imagine: you are sixty years old and suddenly one morning you wake up head over heels in love with a woman who is not only younger than you by a quarter of a century but also married, happily married, more or less. What would you do?"

Slowly Drago shakes his head. "That's not a fair question. If I'm sixteen, how do I know what it is like to be sixty? It's different if you're sixty—then you can remember. But . . . It's Mr. Rayment we are talking about, right? How can I be Mr. Rayment if I can't get inside him?"

They are silent, waiting for more. But that seems to be as far as the boy, who despite his hangover still has the looks of an angel of God, will venture into the hypothetical.

"Then let us rephrase the question," says Mrs. Costello. "Some people say that love makes us youthful again. Makes the heart beat faster. Makes the juices run. Puts a lilt in our voice and a spring in our walk. Let us agree that it is so, for argument's sake, and let us look back over Mr. Rayment's case. Mr. Rayment has an accident as a result of which he loses a leg. He engages a nurse to look after him, and in no time has fallen in love with her. He has intimations that a miraculous, love-born reflorescence of his youth might be around the corner; he even dreams of engendering a son (yes, it is true, a little half-brother to you). But can he trust these intimations? Are they not

163

perhaps a dotard's fantasies? So the question to ponder, given the situation as I have described it, is: What does Mr. Rayment, or someone like Mr. Rayment, do next? Does he blindly follow the promptings of his desire as his desire strives to bring itself to fruition; or, having weighed up the pros and cons, does he conclude that throwing himself heart and soul into a love affair with a married woman would be imprudent, and creep back into his shell?"

"I don't know. I don't know what he does. What do *you* think?"

"I too don't know what he does, Drago, not yet. But let us tackle the question methodically. Let us hypothesise. First, let us presume that Mr. Rayment does not act. For whatever reason, he decides to rein in his passion. What consequences do you think will follow?"

"If he doesn't do anything?"

"Yes, if he sits here in his flat and does nothing."

"Then everything will be like it was before. Boring. He will go on being like he was before."

"Except—?"

"Except what?"

"Except that soon enough regret will start creeping in. His days will be cast over with a grey monotone. By night he will wake with a start, gnashing his teeth and muttering to himself *If only, if only!* Memory will eat away at him like an acid, the memory of his pusillanimity. *Ah, Marijana!* he will grieve. *If only I had not let my Marijana get away!* A man of sorrow,

164

a shadow of himself, that is what he will become. To his dying day."

"OK, he will regret it."

"So what should he do in order not to die full of regret?"

He has had enough. Before Drago can make up an answer he intervenes. "Stop dragging the boy into your games, Elizabeth. And stop talking about me as if I were not in the room. How I conduct my life is my own business, it is not for strangers to say."

"Strangers?" says Elizabeth Costello, raising an eyebrow.

"Yes, strangers. You in particular. You are a stranger to me, one on whom I wish I had never laid eyes."

"Likewise, Paul, likewise. How you and I became coupled God alone knows, for we were certainly not meant for each other. But here we are. You want to be with Marijana but are saddled with me instead. I would prefer a more interesting subject but am saddled with you, the one-legged man who cannot make up his mind. A right mess, wouldn't you agree, Drago? Come on, help us, advise us. What should we do?"

"I reckon you should split up. If you don't like each other. Say goodbye."

"And Paul and your mother? Should they split up too?"

"I don't know about Mr. Rayment. But how come no one asks my mother what *she* wants?

Maybe she wishes she had never taken a job with Mr. Rayment. I don't know. Maybe she just wants everything to be like it was before, when we were . . . a family."

"So you are an enemy of passion, extra-marital passion."

"No, I didn't say that. I am not like you say, an enemy of passion. But—"

"But your mother is a good-looking woman. When she goes out, glances get cast at her, feelings get felt towards her, desire buds in the stranger's heart, and before you can say Jiminy Cricket unforeseen passions have sprung up that you have to contend with. Consider the situation from your mother's viewpoint. Easy enough to resist these passion-filled strangers once they have declared themselves, but less easy to ignore them. For that you need ice in your veins. Given the fact of strange men and their desires, how would you like your mother to behave? Shut herself away at home? Wear a veil?"

Drago gives a strange, barking laugh of delight. "No, but maybe she doesn't feel like having an affair"—he snorts as he utters the phrase, as though it belonged to some curious, probably barbarian, foreign tongue—"with every man that gives her—you know—the eye. That is why I say, why does no one ask her?"

"I would ask her right now if I could," says Elizabeth Costello. "But she is not available. She is not on stage, so to speak. We can only guess.

166

But giving in and having an affair with a sixty-year-old man whom she is contracted to see six times a week, come rain or hail or snow, is, I would expect, pretty far from her thoughts. What would you say, Paul?"

"Far from her thoughts indeed. As far as far could be."

"So there we are. We are all unhappy, it seems. You are unhappy, Drago, because the ructions at home have forced you to pitch your tent on Victoria Square among the winos. Your mother is unhappy because she must take shelter among relatives who disapprove of her. Your father is unhappy because he thinks people are laughing at him. Paul here is unhappy because unhappiness is second nature to him but more particularly because he has not the faintest idea of how to bring about his heart's desire. And I am unhappy because nothing is happening. Four people in four corners, moping, like tramps in Beckett, and myself in the middle, wasting time, being wasted by time."

They are silent, all of them. *Being wasted by time*: it is a plea of a kind that the woman is uttering. Why then is he so signally unmoved?

"Mrs. Costello," he says, "please open your ears to what I am saying. What is going on between myself and Drago's family is none of your business. You do not belong here. This is not your place, not your sphere. I feel for Marijana. I feel for Drago, in a different way, and for his sisters too. I can even feel for Drago's father. But I cannot

167

feel for you. None of us is able to feel for you. You are the one outsider among us. Your involvement, however well-meaning it may be, does not help us, merely confuses us. Can you understand that? Can I not persuade you to leave us alone to work out our own salvation in our own way?"

There is a long, uncomfortable silence. "I've got to go," says Drago.

"No," he says. "You may not go back to the park, if that is what you have in mind. I don't approve. It is dangerous; your parents would be horrified if they knew. Let me give you a key. There is food in the fridge, there is a bed in my study. You can come and go as you wish. Within reason."

Drago seems about to say something, then changes his mind. "Thanks," he says.

"And me?" says Elizabeth Costello. "Am I to be turned out of doors to suffer the heat of the sun and the furious winter's raging, while young Drago is lodged like a prince?"

"You are a grown woman. You can look after yourself."

CHAPTER 19

There is a car parked across the street from his flat, a weathered red Commodore station-wagon. It has been there since noon. The figure behind the wheel is indistinct, but it can only be Miroslav Jokić. What is less certain is what Miroslav is up to. Is he spying on his wife? Is he trying to intimidate the guilty couple?

On his crutches it takes him a full ten minutes to navigate the stairs and entranceway, and almost as long to cross the street. As he approaches the car, the man inside winds down the window and lets out a cloud of stale cigarette smoke.

"Mr. Jokić?" he says.

Jokić is not the burly, shambling creature he had imagined. On the contrary, he is tall and wiry, with a dark, narrow face and an aquiline nose.

"I am Paul Rayment. Can we talk? Can I buy you a beer? There is a pub just around the corner."

Jokić gets out of the car. He is wearing work boots, blue jeans, a black T-shirt, a black leather jacket. His hips are so narrow that he barely seems to have buttocks. *A body like a whip*, he thinks.

Unwilled, a vision comes to him of that body atop Marijana, covering her, pressing itself into her.

Hopping as fast as he can, he leads the way.

The pub is half empty. He slides into a booth and Jokić, tight-lipped, follows. He glances at Jokić's hands. Long fingers with tufts of black hair, clipped fingernails. Hair at his collar too. Does Marijana like all that hair, that bear's pelt?

Of confrontations with aggrieved husbands he has no experience to call on. Is he supposed to feel pity for the man? He feels none.

"May I come to the point? You want to know why I am offering to help with your son's education. I am not a wealthy man, Mr. Jokić, but I am comfortably off and I have no children. I offered your son a loan because I would like to see him do well. I am impressed with Drago. He shows great promise. As for the college he has chosen, I have not heard of it before, but he tells me it has a good reputation and I accept that.

"I am sorry my offer has caused an upset in your household. I should have spoken to you as well as to your wife, I now realise.

"Regarding your wife, let me simply say that my relations with her have always been correct." He hesitates. The man's eyes are like gun-muzzles trained on him. He returns the gaze as directly as he can. "I do not get involved with women, Mr. Jokić, not any more. That part of my life is behind me. If I still practise love, I practise it in a different way. When you know me better you will understand."

Is he lying? He might be, but it does not feel that way. Despite her calves, which he has not forgotten, despite her breasts, which he would give anything to bury his face in, he loves Marijana at this moment with a pure and benevolent heart, as God must love her; it is preposterous that he should be hated in return, by this man or by anyone else.

"I and my wife are married since '82," says Jokić. A deep voice, a bear's voice, at least he has that. "Eighteen years. She was student in Academy Fine Arts Dubrovnik when I meet her. First I was in federal army, then I get a job in Academy, as welder. Welder and craftsman, but mostly welder. That's where we meet. Then we go to Germany, we work hard, we save our money, live poor—you know what I mean?—and apply to come to Australia. My sister too. Four together. Drago still a kid then. First we live in Melbourne, I work in welding shop. Then I go to Coober Pedy with some mates, try our luck with opals. You know Coober Pedy?"

"I know Coober Pedy."

"Very hot place. Later on Marijana come. Three years we stay in Coober Pedy. Very hard for a woman. Opals, you got to be lucky. Me—no luck, you know what I mean? But my mates, they help me, we help each other."

"Yes."

"Very hard for a woman with children. So then I get a job with Holden and we come to Elizabeth.

171

Good job, nice house." He sets down his empty glass. Silence. End of recital. *That's my story*, he seems to be saying, as if laying his cards out on the table. *Beat that, Mr. Coniston Terrace!*

"Do you happen to know a woman named Elizabeth Costello, an elderly woman, a professional writer?"

Jokić shakes his head.

"Because she seems to know you. She told me some of the same history you have just been telling me—how you and Marijana met, what the two of you did in Dubrovnik, and so forth. Nothing about Melbourne or Coober Pedy. Anyway, Elizabeth Costello is at work on a new book, and seems to be using me in it as a character, so to speak. Her interest in me has led her to an interest in Marijana and in you. Evidently she has been ferreting around in your past."

Jokić waits for him to complete the paragraph, but he cannot as yet, it would sound too preposterous. What he hesitates to say is: *This imbroglio in which you and I are caught is Elizabeth Costello's doing. If you want to blame anyone, blame her. She is behind it all. Elizabeth Costello is a mischiefmaker.*

"If you don't mind my saying so," he continues instead, "you should make your peace with Marijana. Also, for Drago's sake, please accept the loan. Drago has set his heart on Wellington College, anyone can see that. We can make the loan as formal or informal as you like. There can be papers or we can dispense with papers, it makes no difference to me."

He ought at this point to offer Jokić another beer. He ought to make it as easy as possible for Jokić to swallow his pride, to become, however reluctantly, a chum. But he does not. He has said enough; now it is Jokić's turn—Jokic's turn to pay for drinks, Jokić's turn to have his say. After which, he hopes, this meeting, this scene, to which he has lent himself so reluctantly, will be over with. Though this man has fathered on Marijana two angelic children, perhaps even three, he can find in himself no curiosity about him. His interest is in Marijana: Marijana and whatever of Marijana has found its way into her children. Is his interest in Marijana an interested or a disinterested interest? Is the God with whose love for Marijana he compares his own an interested or a disinterested God? He does not know. The question is too abstract for his present mood.

Jokić breaks into his thoughts. "You have nice apartment."

A question? A statement? It must be a question, since Jokić has never been into the flat. He nods.

"Comfortable. You say you are comfortable. You are comfortable in your apartment."

"Comfortably off, that's what I said. It has nothing to do with my apartment. 'Comfortably off' is an expression used by people who find money embarrassing to talk about. In my case it means that I have a comfortable income. It means that I have sufficient for my needs and some left over. I can give to charity if I choose, or I can do a good deed like sending your son to college."

"My son go to a fancy college, he get fancy friends, he want all kind of fancy things, you know what I mean?"

"Yes. A fancy college might teach him to look down on his origins. I cannot deny that. Do not mistake me, Mr. Jokić, I am not an enthusiast of fancy colleges. It was not I who came up with the name of Wellington. But if that is where Drago wants to go, I will back him. My guess is that Wellington is not as fancy as it pretends to be. A truly fancy college does not need to advertise."

Jokić ponders. "Maybe," he says, "maybe we can make a trust fund for Drago. Then it is not so, you know, personal like."

A trust fund? Not a bad idea, though an expensive solution to a simple problem. But what does this refugee from state socialism know about trust funds?

"We could think about that," he says. "If you wanted to be very legal, very legally watertight. We could speak to a solicitor."

"Or the bank," says Jokić. "We can make an account for Drago, trust account. You can put money in a trust account. Then it is safe. In case . . . you know."

In case of what? In case he, Paul Rayment, should change his mind, leaving Drago in the lurch? In case he should die? In case he should fall out of love with Miroslav Jokić's wife?

"Yes, we can do that," he says, though with growing misgiving. Is the fiction of a trust fund all that will be needed to salve Jokić's pride?

"And Marijana."

"Yes, Marijana. What do you want to say about Marijana?"

"Marijana is tired all the time, from the nursing. Two jobs she's got, two assignments, you and this other old lady, Mrs. Aiello. Not proper nursing, professional like, more housework. You add it up, fifty hours a week, sixty hours, and the driving, every day driving. A cultured person. It's not good, this housework, for a cultured person. She come home tired all the time. So we think, maybe she give up nursing, find another kind of work."

"I am sorry. I didn't realise Marijana had two jobs. She didn't mention a second job to me."

Jokić is gazing at him pointedly. Is there something he is failing to grasp?

"I will miss her if she moves on," he says. "She is a very capable woman."

"Yes," says Jokić. "Me, I'm just mechanic, you know. Mechanic is nothing, not in Croatia, not in Australia. But Marijana is cultured person. Diploma in restoration—she tell you that? No restoration work in Australia, but still. In Munno Para, who she can talk to? OK, Drago is interested in lot of things, she can talk to him. Then she meet Mr. Rayment."

"My own conversations with Marijana have been

limited," he replies cautiously. "Like the rest of my relationship with her. Very limited. I found out about her background in art only recently, from Mrs. Costello, the woman I mentioned."

Slowly it is beginning to dawn on him why Jokić, having thrashed his wife and driven her from their home, is prepared to take a day off from work and spend it sitting in a car on Coniston Terrace. Jokić must believe that his wife, whether or not she has fallen in the absolute sense, is in the process of being lured from hearth and home by a client with plenty of money and an easy familiarity with the world of art and artists; also that the elegant environment of Coniston Terrace is teaching her to look down on working-class Munno. Jokić is making an appeal, an appeal to his better nature. And if that appeal fails—what? Is Jokić planning to thrash him too?

Look at me, your hated rival! he would like to protest. *You still have the limbs that God gave you, while I have this obscene monstrosity to drag around with me! Half the time I pee, I pee on the floor! I could not seduce your wife away from you if I tried, not in any sense of the word!*

Yet at the same moment memory throws up again the image of Marijana stretching to dust the top shelves, Marijana with her strong, shapely legs. If his love for Marijana is indeed pure, why did it wait to take up residence in his heart until the instant she flashed him her legs? Why does love, even such love as he claims to practise, need the spectacle of beauty to bring it to life? What, in the abstract, do shapely legs have to do with love, or for that matter with desire? Or is that just the nature of nature, about which one does not ask questions? How does love work among the animals? Among foxes? Among spiders? Are there such things as shapely legs among lady spiders, and does their attractive force puzzle the male spider even as it draws him in? He wonders whether Jokić has an opinion on the subject. But he is certainly not going to ask. He has had enough of Jokić for one day, and Jokić, he suspects, has had enough of him.

"Will you have another beer?" he asks, pro forma.

"No, I must go."

Jokić must go. He must go. Where must they go, the two of them? The one, to an empty bed in Munno Para; the other, to an empty bed on Coniston Terrace, where he can lie awake all night, if he likes, listening to the ticking of the clock from the living-room. They might as well set up house together. Mutt and Jeff.

CHAPTER 20

It takes him the best part of an hour, stumping hither and thither across parkland, to track down Elizabeth Costello. In the end he finds her by the riverside, sitting on a bench, clustered around by ducks that she seems to be feeding. As he approaches, the ducks scatter in alarm and slide clamorously back into the water.

He props himself on the grass before her. Past six, but he can still feel the weight of the summer sun. "I am looking for Drago," he says. "Do you know where he can be found?"

"Drago? No idea. I thought he was staying with you. Aren't you going to ask about me? Are you not curious to hear how I spent the night after you so rudely turned me out?"

He ignores the question. "I have just had a meeting with Marijana's husband."

"Miroslav. Yes, poor fellow, he feels so humiliated. First by his own jealousy, and now to discover what sort of man his rival is. What did you say to him?"

"I asked him to think again. I asked him to put Drago's interests first. I repeated that there were no strings attached to my offer."

178

"No visible strings, you mean."

"No strings at all."

"What about heartstrings, Paul, strings of affection?"

"Strings of affection are beside the point. The money is for Drago's education. It is absurd to suggest that I am trying to buy his mother."

"Absurd? We should ask Marijana about that. She might have a different view. Tit for tat, she might say. For every tat there is a tit. You have offered the tat. Now the onus is on her to come up with the right tit, the appropriate tit."

"Don't be obscene."

"Well, I confess I have yet to appreciate what you see in your Balkan lady. To my eye she is somewhat tubby and rather the worse for wear. I would not have thought you liked your women that way. Tall man and stout woman: a bit of a comedy team. A fellow like you could do better. But *chacun ses goûts,* I suppose.

"My own opinion, for what it is worth, is that if it is requital you are after, requited love, you should give up on Mrs. Jokić. She is not for you. Your best option remains Marianna, Marianna of the two *ns*. An arrangement with Marianna, or someone like her, would work very well. For a single gentleman of your age, not keen because of his disability to appear in public, it would be quite appropriate to entertain in his home, one afternoon a week, a discreet woman friend like Marianna, someone who in return for favours

179

granted would now and again consent to accept a nice little present.

"Yes, Paul, presents, gifts. You must become accustomed to paying. No more free love."

"I may not love whom I choose?"

"Of course you may love whom you choose. But maybe from now on you should keep your love to yourself, as one keeps a head cold to oneself, or an attack of herpes, out of consideration for one's neighbours.

"However, if your verdict is that Marianna does not fit the bill, who am I to demur? In that case, why not telephone Mrs. Putts? Tell her you are in the market for a new nurse. Say you want someone not too young though not too old, with nice breasts and a well-turned calf, unattached, children no obstacle, preferably a non-smoker. What else? Of an eager temperament, eager and easily pleased.

"Or why bother with Mrs. Putts? Why submit to the rigmarole of hiring nurses and falling in love with them? Put an ad in the *Advertiser*. "Gent, sixtyish, childless, vigorous though of limited mobility, seeks lady, 35–45, with view to love, mystical parenthood. Nice breasts, et cetera. No chancers."

"Don't glare, Paul. I'm just joking, just keeping the conversation going. Be assured, I have learned my lesson. No more match-making, I promise. If you have made up your mind that no one can replace Marijana in your affections, that it has to be Marijana or nothing, I yield, I accept.

I should inform you, however, that Marianna, poor Marianna, the other one, is deeply hurt at the way she has been treated. Sobs into her handkerchief. *Be of good heart,* I tell her, *there are plenty of fish in the ocean.* But she will not be consoled. After what she put herself through for your sake, her pride has taken quite a knock. *He finds me too fat!* she wails. *Nonsense,* I say—*his heart is elsewhere, that is all.*

"But perhaps I misinterpret you entirely. Perhaps it is not requital of love that you are after. Or perhaps your quest for love disguises a quest for something quite different. How much love does someone like you need, after all, Paul, objectively speaking? Or someone like me? None. None at all. We do not need love, old people like us. What we need is care: someone to hold our hand now and then when we get trembly, to make a cup of tea for us, help us down the stairs. Someone to close our eyes for us when the time comes. Care is not love. Care is a service that any nurse worth her salt can provide, as long as we don't ask her for more."

She pauses for a breath; at last he has a chance to speak. "I came here looking for Drago," he says, "not to listen to you sharpening your wit upon me. I understand perfectly well the difference between love and care. I have never expected Marijana to love me. My hope, as a sixtyish gent, is simply to do what good I can for her and her children. As for my feelings, my feelings are my own business. I will certainly not thrust them on Marijana again.

181

"One word more, since you are determined to be sceptical. Don't underestimate the desire in each of us, the human desire, to extend a protective wing."

"In each of us?"

"Yes, in each of us. Even in you. If you are human."

Enough talk. His arms are aching, he is feeling the heat, he would like to sit. But if he were to settle down beside Mrs. Costello, they would look too much like what they are not: an old married couple taking a breather. And there is, after all, one more thing to be said.

"Why pour all this effort into me, Mrs. Costello? I am such a small fish, really. Have you never asked yourself whether taking me up might not have been a mistake—whether I might not be a mistake from beginning to end?"

A young couple in a pedal-boat in the shape of a giant swan pass by, smiling cheerily.

"Of course I have asked myself that, Paul. Many times. And of course, by some standards, you are a small fish. The question is, by what standards? The question is, how small? Patience, I tell myself: perhaps there is something yet to be squeezed out of him, like a last drop of juice out of a lemon, or like blood out of a stone. But yes, you may be right, you may indeed be a mistake, I will concede that. If you were not a mistake I would probably not still be here in Adelaide. I stay on because I don't know what to do about you.

"Should I therefore concede? Should I abandon

you and start anew somewhere else? I am sure that would make you happy. But I can't. Too much of a blow to my pride. No, I have to press on to the end."

"To the end?"

"Yes, to the bitter end."

He hopes to hear more. He hopes to hear what the end will be. But her mouth has snapped shut, she stares away from him.

"Anyway," he pursues, "in the course of trying to understand what you are doing in my life, I have come up with one hypothesis after another. I won't rehearse them all, though I will say that none is very flattering to you. The first, and still the most plausible, is that you want me as a model for a character in a book. In that case, let me repeat what I was saying a moment ago, and what you seem to have trouble accepting. Ever since the day of my accident, ever since I could have died but seem to have been spared, I have been haunted by the idea of doing good. Before it is too late I would like to perform some act that will be—excuse the word—a blessing, however modest, on the lives of others. Why, you ask? Ultimately, because I have no child of my own to bless as a father does. Having no child was the great mistake of my life, I will tell you that. For that my heart bleeds all the time. For that there is a *blessure* in my heart.

"Smile if you wish, Mrs. Costello. But let me remind you, once upon a time I was a pukkah little Catholic boy. Before the Dutchman uprooted us

183

and brought us to the ends of the earth I had my schooling from the good sisters of Lourdes. And as soon as we arrived in Ballarat I was committed to the care of the Christian Brothers. *Why would you want to do that, boy? Why would you want to commit a sin? Can you not see how Our Lord's heart bleeds for your sin?* Jesus and his bleeding heart have never faded from memory, even though I have long since put the Church behind me. Why do I mention this? Because I don't want to hurt Jesus any more by my actions. I don't want to make his heart bleed. If you want to be my chronicler, you will need to understand that."

"A pukkah little Catholic boy. I can see that, Paul. I can see it all too clearly. Don't forget, I am a proper Irish Catholic girl myself, a Costello from Northcote in Melbourne. But go on, go on, I find this rich, I find this fascinating."

"In my earlier life I did not speak as freely about myself as I do today, Mrs. Costello. Decency held me back, decency or shame. But you are a professional, I remind myself, in the business of confidences, like a doctor or a lawyer or an accountant."

"Or a priest. Don't forget the priests, Paul."

"Or a priest. Anyhow, since my accident I have begun to let some of that reticence slip. *If you don't speak now*, I say to myself, *when will you speak?* So: *Would Jesus approve?* That is the question I put to myself nowadays, continually. That is the standard I try to meet. Not as scrupulously as I should, I must admit. Forgiveness, for instance: I have no intention of forgiving the boy who drove his car into me, no matter what Jesus may say. But Marijana and her children—I want to extend a protective hand over them, I want to bless them and make them thrive. That is something you ought to take account of in me, and I don't think you do."

What he has said about discarding reticence, about speaking his heart, is not, strictly speaking, true. Even to Marijana he has not really opened his heart. Why then does he lay himself bare before the Costello woman, who is surely no friend to him? There can be only one answer: because she has worn him down. A thoroughly professional performance on her part. One takes up position beside one's prey, and waits, and eventually one's prey yields. The sort of thing every priest knows. Or every vulture. Vulture lore.

"Sit, Paul," she says. "I can't keep on squinting up at you."

He flops down heavily beside her.

"Your bleeding heart," she murmurs. The declining sun glances so piercingly off the surface of the water that she has to shade her eyes. The duck family, more than a family, the duck clan, is gathering for another assault on the land. Evidently he, the intruder, has been assessed and found harmless.

"Yes, my bleeding heart."

"The heart can be a mysterious organ, the heart

and its movements. Dark, the Spanish call it. The dark heart, *el oscuro corazón*. Are you sure you are not just a little dark-hearted, Paul, despite your many good intentions?"

He had thought he would make a peace overture; he had thought of offering the woman, if not a roof for the night, then at least an air ticket back to Melbourne. But now the old irritation comes flooding back. "And are you sure," he replies icily, "that you are not seeing complications where they do not exist, for the sake of those dreary stories you write?"

Mrs. Costello reaches into the plastic bag on her lap, crumbles a bread roll, and tosses it towards the ducks. There is huge commotion as they converge on their blessing.

"We would all like to be simpler, Paul," she says, "every one of us. Particularly as we near the end. But we are complicated creatures, we human beings. That is our nature. You want me to be simpler. You want to be simpler yourself, more naked. Well, I gaze in wonderment, believe me, upon your efforts to strip yourself down. But it comes at a cost, the simple heart you so desire, the simple way of seeing the world. Look at me. What do you see?"

He is silent.

"Let me tell you what you see, or what you tell yourself you are seeing. An old woman by the side of the River Torrens feeding the ducks. An old woman who happens to be running out of clean underwear. An old woman who irritates you with what you think of as her sly innuendoes.

"But the reality is more complicated than that, Paul. In reality you see a great deal more—see it and then block it out. Light of a certain stridency, for instance. A figure trapped by that light beside the softly fluent water. Lances of light that stab at her, threaten to pierce her through.

"Unnecessary complication? I don't think so. An expansion. Like breathing. Breathe in, breathe out. Expand, contract. The rhythm of life. You have it in you to be a fuller person, Paul, larger and more expansive, but you won't allow it. I urge you: don't cut short these thought-trains of yours. Follow them through to their end. Your thoughts and your feelings. Follow them through and you will grow with them. What was it that the American poet fellow said? There weaves always a fictive covering from something to something. My memory is going. I become vaguer with each passing day. A pity. Hence this little lesson I am trying to teach you. *He finds her by the riverside, sitting on a bench, clustered around by ducks that she seems to be feeding—* it may be simple, as an account, its simplicity may even beguile one, but it is not good enough. It does not bring me to life. Bringing me to life may not be important to you, but it has the drawback of not bringing you to life either. Or the ducks, for that matter, if you prefer not to have me at the centre of the picture. Bring these humble ducks to life and they will bring you to life, I promise.

187

Bring Marijana to life, if it must be Marijana, and she will bring you to life. It is as elementary as that. But please, as a favour to me, please stop dithering. I do not know how much longer I can support my present mode of existence."

"What mode of existence are you referring to?"

"Life in public. Life on the public squares, relying on public amenities. Life in the company of drunks and homeless people, what we used to call hoboes. Do you not recall? I warned you I had nowhere to go."

"You are talking nonsense. You can take a room in a hotel. You can catch a plane back to Melbourne or wherever else you want to go. I will lend you the money."

"Yes, you could do that. Just as you could get rid of the troublesome, volatile Jokićs and sell your flat and move into a well-regulated retreat for old people. But you don't. We are who we are, Paul. This, for the time being, is the life we are given to live, and we must live it. When I am with you I am at home; when I am not with you I am homeless. That is how the dice have fallen. Are you surprised to hear me say so? You should not be. But do not castigate yourself. I have become surprisingly good at this new life. Looking at me, you would not say that I live out of a suitcase, would you? Or that I have not eaten in days. Aside from a grape or two."

He is silent.

"Anyway, that is enough about me. As I keep telling myself, Have patience, Paul Rayment did not ask you to descend upon his shoulders. Nevertheless, it would be a great help if Paul Rayment would hurry up. As I mentioned, I may be nearing my limit. I can't begin to tell you how tired I am. And not with the kind of tiredness that can be fixed by a good night's sleep in a proper bed. The tiredness I refer to has become part of my being. It is like a dye that has begun to seep into everything I do, everything I say. I feel, to use Homer's word, *unstrung*. A word with which you are familiar, I seem to remember. No more tensile strength. The bowstring that used to be taut has gone as slack and dry as a strand of cotton. And not just the bodily self. The mind too: slack, ready for easeful sleep."

He has not looked at Elizabeth Costello in a long while, not properly. In part that is because she comes to him through a haze of irritation, in part because he finds her so colourless, so featureless, just as he finds her clothes so utterly without distinction. But now he gives her his full, deliberate attention, and indeed it is as she says: she has lost weight, the flesh on her arms hangs, her face is pallid, her nose peaked.

"If you had only asked," he says, "I would have helped, in practical respects. I am ready to help you now. But for the rest"—he shrugs—"I am not dithering, at least not in my own eyes. I am acting at a pace that comes naturally to me. I am not an exceptional person, Mrs. Costello, and I cannot make myself exceptional just for your sake. I am sorry."

He will help her. He means it. He will buy her a meal. He will buy her the ticket, go with her to the airport, wave her goodbye.

"You cold man," she says. She speaks the condemnatory word with lightness, with a smile. "You poor, cold man. I have tried my best to explain, but you understand nothing. You were sent to me, I was sent to you. Why that should be, God alone knows. Now you must cure yourself as best you can. I will try not to hurry you on any more."

She gets to her feet, not without difficulty, folds the empty bag. "Goodbye," she says.

For a long time after she has left he stays on, squinting out over the river, shaken. The ducks, used to being fed, encouraged by his stillness, come almost to his feet, but he pays them no attention.

Cold: is that really how he seems to outsiders? He wants to protest. He wishes well. His friends will attest to it—people who know him far better than the Costello woman does. Even the woman who used to be his wife will concede it: he wishes well, he wishes the best. How can someone be called cold who from his heart wishes well, who when he acts acts from the heart?

Cold was not a word his wife used. What she said was quite different: *I thought you were French,* she said, *I thought you would have some idea.* Some idea of what? For years after she left him he puzzled over her words. What were the French, even if only the French of legend, supposed to have an idea of? Of what will make a woman

190

happy? What will make a woman happy is a riddle as old as the Sphinx. Why should a Frenchman have the power to unknot it, much less such a notional Frenchman as he?

Cold, blind. Breathe in, breathe out. He does not accept the charge; he does not believe in its truth. Truth is not spoken in anger. Truth is spoken, if it ever comes to be spoken, in love. The gaze of love is not deluded. Love sees what is best in the beloved, even when what is best in the beloved finds it hard to emerge into the light. Who is Marijana? A nurse from Dubrovnik with a short waist and yellow teeth and not bad legs. Who except he, with the gaze of love, sees the shy, sloe-eyed gazelle hiding within?

That is what Elizabeth Costello does not understand. Elizabeth Costello thinks of him as a punishment brought down to blight the last days of her life, an incomprehensible penance she is sentenced to speak, to recite, to repeat. She looks on him with distaste, with dismay, with exasperation, with a sinking heart, with everything but love. Well, when he next catches up with her he will give her a lesson. *Not cold*, he will say, *and not French either. A man who sees the world in his own way and who loves in his own way. And a man who not too long ago lost part of his own body: do not forget that. Have a little charity*, he will say. *Then perhaps you may find it in you to write.*

CHAPTER 21

Drago. It continues to intrigue him, how little aware Drago seems to be of his own good looks. Not a narcissist; not reflective. On the other hand, if he were more self-aware he might lose some of that air of fearless candour, that warrior gaze.

Is there a feminine equivalent to Dragonian candour? Amazonian purity? Blanka, the sister, the unknown quantity: what is she like? Will he ever get to meet her?

Narcissus discovered a twin in the pool from whom he could not tear himself. Every time he smiled, the twin smiled back. Yet every time he bent to kiss those inviting lips, the twin would dissolve in ghostly ripples.

No narcissism in Drago: not yet, perhaps never. No narcissism in Marijana either. An admirable trait, in its way. Curious that he has fallen for Marijana, seeing that in the past he fell always for women who loved themselves.

He himself has never been at ease with mirrors. Long ago he draped a cloth over the mirror in the bathroom and taught himself to shave blind. One of the more irritating things the Costello woman did during her stay was to take down the drape. When she left he at once put it back.

He covers the bathroom mirror not just to save himself from the image of an ageing, ugly self. No: the twin imprisoned behind the glass he finds above all boring. *Thank God the day will come*, he thinks to himself, *when I will not have to see that one again!*

Four months have passed since he was released from hospital and allowed to return to his former life. Most of that time he has spent cloistered in this flat, barely seeing the sun. Since Marijana stopped coming he has not eaten properly. He has no appetite, does not bother to take care of himself. The face that threatens to confront him in the mirror is that of a gaunt, unshaven old tramp. In fact, worse than that. At a bookstall on the Seine he once picked up a medical text with photographs of patients from the Salpêtrière: cases of mania, dementia, melancholia, Huntingdon's chorea. Despite the untidy beards, despite the hospital nightshirts, he at once recognised in them soul mates, cousins who had gone ahead down a road he would one day follow.

He is thinking of Drago because, after the one night spent in his flat, Drago has not returned nor sent any word. And he is thinking of mirrors because of Mrs. Costello's story of the old man who turned Sinbad into his slave. Mrs. Costello wants to subject him to some fiction or other she has in her head. He would like to believe that, since the Marianna episode, he has resisted her schemes, held her at bay. But is he right? He shivers to think what the merest passing glimpse in a mirror might reveal: grinning over his shoulder, gripping his throat, the shape of a wild-haired, bare-breasted hag brandishing a whip.

He ought to write Marijana a letter, at her sister-in-law's or at home or wherever she is. *Please do not cut yourself off from me. Whatever I said, I promise never to repeat it. It was a mistake. I will not try to draw you into further intimacy. Even though you have done more for me, a great deal more, than duty requires, I have never been foolish enough to confuse your kindness with love, with the real thing. What I offer to Drago, and to you through Drago, is a token of gratitude, nothing more. Please accept it as such. You have taken care of me; now I want to give something back, if you will let me. I offer to take care of you, or at least to relieve you of some of your burden. I offer to do so because in my heart, in my core, I care for you. You and yours.*

Care: he can set the word down on paper but he would be too diffident to mouth it, make it his own speech. Too much an English word, an insider's word. Perhaps Marijana of the Balkans, giver of care, compelled even more than he to conduct her life in a foreign tongue, will share his diffidence. Or perhaps not. Perhaps she has accepted without afterthought what she was told by the accreditation board: that the profession into which she was being initiated was in the English-speaking world known as a caring profession; that her business would henceforth be taking care of people or caring for people; and that such caring should not be assumed to have anything to do with the heart, except of course in heart cases.

Yet is that not precisely what over the past four months he has mutated into—a heart case, *un cardiaque*? Once upon a time his heart was his strongest organ. Any one of its brother organs might let him down—bowels, spleen, brain—but his heart, tried and tested first on Magill Road and then in the operating theatre, would serve him faithfully to the end.

Then he met Marijana, and his heart suffered a change. No longer is his heart what it used to be. Now it aches to serve Marijana, Marijana and all who belong to her. As she gave to him, so his heart wants to give back. *To give back is not the same as to pay back*, he should add in a footnote. *Excuse the language lesson, I too am feeling my way, I too am on foreign soil.*

Dear Marijana, he writes, this time with a real pen on real paper, *Do you, or does your husband, truly think that in return for Drago's school fees I would try to inflict myself upon you? I would not dream of it; and anyway, Mrs. Costello is always hovering around, making sure I stay in line. "No woman with two eyes in her head would have a fellow like you," says Mrs. Costello. I could not agree more.*

You have had to see a great deal of me in the line

of duty, too much perhaps. Let me simply say these words: for the impartial care you have given me I will be thankful to my dying day. If I offer to take care of Drago's education, it is solely as a way of repaying that debt.

Miroslav and I have discussed the matter of a trust fund. If a trust fund is what it takes to make Miroslav feel easy, I will see about setting one up—for Drago, indeed for all three of your children.

I get your address from Mrs. Costello, who seems to know everything. Will you and Miroslav please reconsider, and do me the honour of accepting a gift that comes, as they say in English, with no strings attached.

Yours ever,
Paul Rayment

CHAPTER 22

The letter to Marijana is addressed care of Mrs. Lidija Karadžić, Elizabeth North. He hopes there is only one Karadžić in Elizabeth North; he hopes he has the diacritics right.

Marijana's reply comes two days later, in the form not of a letter—he never expected one, he can guess what a trial it would be for her to write in English—but of a telephone call.

"Sorry I don't come see you, Mr. Rayment," she says, "but we got all kind of problems. Blanka—you know Blanka?—she get in trouble." And a long story emerges about a silver chain, a chain that is not even real silver, that you can buy for one dollar fifty in the Chinese market, that some shopkeeper, some Jew, accuses Blanka of taking, though Blanka did not take it, a friend of hers took it and slipped it to her and she wanted to put it back but didn't have time; and the Jew says that the chain that is not real silver costs forty-nine ninety-five and he wants to take her to court for it, to youth court. So now Blanka is refusing to eat, is refusing to go to school, though exams are just a week away, is staying in her room all

197

day except yesterday evening she dressed up and went out she won't say where. And Mel doesn't know what to do and she doesn't know what to do. So does he, Paul Rayment, know someone he can talk to about Blanka, someone who can in turn talk to the Jew and make the charge go away?

"How do you know he is a Jew, Marijana?" he asks.

"OK, he is Jew, he is not Jew, is not important."

"Perhaps I am a Jew. Are you sure I am not a Jew?"

"OK, forget it. It slip from my tongue. Is nothing. You don't want to talk to me, say so, is finished."

"Of course I want to talk. Of course I want to help. Why am I on this earth but to help? Give me the particulars. Tell me when and where it happened, this business of the silver chain. And tell me more about Blanka's friend, the one who was with her in the shop."

"I got it here. Shop is Happenstance"—she spells the word—"on Rundle Mall, and Mr. Matthews is manager."

"And when did it happen, the business with Happenstance?"

"Friday. Friday afternoon."

"And her friend?"

"Blanka won't say her friend's name. Maybe Tracy. I don't know."

"Let me see what I can do, Marijana. I am not the best person for this kind of thing, but I will see what I can do. Where can I reach you?"

"You can phone, you got my number."

"Phone you at home? I thought you were staying with your sister-in-law. I wrote to you care of your sister-in-law. Didn't you get my letter?"

There is a long silence. "Is all finished," says Marijana at last. "You can phone me."

What Marijana wants is a man of influence, and he is not a man of influence, he is not even sure he approves of the phenomenon of the man of influence. But this must be how things are done in Croatia, so for Marijana's sake and the sake of her unhappy daughter, who must surely have learned her lesson by now—namely, to be more careful when she steals things—he is prepared to try. Is Marijana wrong, after all, to believe that a man with a smooth name like Rayment and a comfortable home in an eminently comfortable part of the city and money to give away can make things happen in a way that an auto mechanic with a funny name like Jokić cannot?

"Mr. Matthews?" he says.

"Yes."

"May I have a word with you in private?"

Happenstance—which sells what it calls *gear*—is not, however, the kind of establishment where one can have a word in private. It is, at most, five metres square. There are tightly packed racks of clothing, there is a counter and a till, there is music rattling from somewhere above them, and that is all. So what he has to say to Mr. Matthews has to be said in the open.

"A girl was detained here for shoplifting," he says. "Last Friday. Blanka Jokić. Do you recall the case?"

Mr. Matthews, who either is or is not a Jew, and who has been all affability thus far, stiffens visibly. Mr. Matthews is in his twenties; he is tall and slim; he has wide, dark eyebrows and bleached hair that stands up in spikes.

"My name is Paul Rayment," he presses on. "I am a friend of the Jokić family. May I tell you something about Blanka?"

The boy—what else is he but a boy?—nods guardedly.

"Blanka has never done anything like this before. Since last Friday she has been through a great deal of torment, self-torment. She is ashamed of what she did. She is reluctant to show her face in public. She has, I would venture to say, learned her lesson. She is just a child; I don't believe any good will be achieved by prosecuting her. So I have come to make a proposal. I want to pay for the item she took, which I understand was a silver chain retailing for fifty dollars."

"Forty-nine ninety-five."

"I am in addition, if you will agree to drop charges, prepared to buy goods from you to the value of, say, five hundred dollars. As a sign of good will. And all entirely above board."

Young Mr. Matthews shakes his head. "It's

company policy," he says. "Every year we lose five per cent of turnover, all branches, to shoplifting. We've got to send a signal to shoplifters out there: steal from us and you get prosecuted. The full weight of the law. Zero tolerance. That's our policy. I'm sorry."

"You lose five per cent but you build that five per cent back into your prices. I'm not criticising you, I'm just pointing out a fact. You have a policy aimed at shoplifters. Fair enough. But Blanka isn't a shoplifter. She is just a child thinking as a child thinks, stupidly. Bad luck is what happens to other people, she thinks, it won't happen to me. Well, now she knows bad things can happen to her too. If you wanted to teach her a lesson, you have taught her a lesson. She won't forget it. She won't steal again, it is not worth it, it has made her too miserable. So back to my offer. You make a phone call, retract the charge; I pay for the chain and in addition buy five hundred dollars worth of stuff, right here, right now."

Mr. Matthews is wavering visibly.

"Six hundred dollars. Here is my card. The police don't enjoy prosecuting these cases. They have better uses for their time."

"It's not a decision I can make, like, unilaterally. I'll speak to the manager."

"You are the manager."

"I'm just the manager of this outlet. There is our area manager. I'll speak to him. But I can't promise anything. As I say, it's company policy to

201

prosecute. That's the only way we can send a signal we are serious."

"Speak to your area manager now. Give him a call. I'll wait."

"Mr. DeVito is out of town. He'll be back Monday."

"Mr. DeVito may be out of town but he is not unreachable. Give him a call. Settle this business."

Young Mr. Matthews retreats behind the till, turns his back on him, and brings out his cell phone. Young Mr. Matthews is in the process of having his day spoiled, and by a cripple too. He is not a bully by nature, but probing for weakness in the boy, and then putting pressure on him, squeezing him, has been a not unpleasurable experience. Blanka Jokić: Matthews will not forget the name soon.

The assistant, a girl with ghastly white make-up and violet lips, has been watching them covertly. He signals her to come over. "Help me pick out some gear," he says. "Up-to-the-minute. For a fourteen-year-old."

A friend of the family. That is how he presents himself to Happenstance, that is how Happenstance sees him: as an elderly gent with a disability who for God knows what reason chooses to watch over the welfare of a girl with a funny name. And it is true. He is indeed that elderly gent, that good-hearted benefactor. True, but not the whole truth. If he battles the crowds on Rundle Mall, if he bargains and cajoles and pays for stuff he does not need, it is not, or not just, for the sake of a child he has never laid eyes on.

What does it look like to Marijana, this *will to give* with which he so doggedly pursues her? Has she had other clients like him, other doting old men? *Surely you must know. Surely a woman always knows. I love you.* How it must have jarred and irritated her: words of love from an object of mere nursing, mere care. Irritating but not, in the end, serious. The fantasy, working its way to the surface, of a man cooped up too long alone; an infatuation; not the real thing.

What would it take to make Marijana see him as the real thing? What is the real thing? Physical desire? Sexual intimacy? They have been intimate, he and Marijana, for some while now—for longer than some love affairs last, start to finish. But all the intimacy, all the nakedness, all the helplessness has been on one side. One-way traffic; no exchange; not even a kiss—not the merest peck on the cheek. Two ex-Europeans!

"You OK?" says a voice.

He is staring into the eyes, the entirely kindly eyes, of a young woman in blue uniform. A police officer.

"Yes. Why should I not be OK?"

She casts a glance at the man by her side, another officer. "Where do you live?"

"In North Adelaide. On Coniston Terrace."

"And how are you going to get home?"

"I am going to walk to Pulteney Street and take a taxi. Is there anything wrong with that?"

"Nothing. Nothing wrong."

He hooks the Happenstance bags over an arm, grips his crutches, and heaves himself up from the trash container against which he has been resting. Without a word, holding his head high, he picks his way through the crowd.

CHAPTER 23

"She cannot have it," says Marijana. "No. Is impossible."

He could not agree more. It is impossible. One is caught stealing a silver chain that is not even silver, no more silver than what one can get in the Chinese market for one dollar fifty, and what happens? One is rewarded with six hundred dollars worth of *gear*. Where is the justice in that? What will Drago say when he learns of it?

Blanka the black sheep of the family. Drago the shining light, the angel with the sword, defender of the family's honour. Commander Drago Jokić, R.A.N.

"Lock the stuff away in a cupboard," he says to Marijana. He is in high spirits. He and she are on the phone again, like old friends, old gossips. "That is what I would do. Bring it out as an incentive, piece by piece, if she will agree to go to school and so forth. But you will have to hurry. It will all be out of fashion in a month's time."

Marijana does not respond. He cannot remember her ever responding to his humour. Is he too frivolous for her taste? Does she find him too light, too

205

lightweight, too much of a joker? Or is she simply not sure enough of her English to bandy words? *It is just a game*, he should tell her. *Badinage it is called in some quarters. You should join in. It's not hard to play, it doesn't require a change of soul.*

Marijana's soul: solid, matter-of-fact. Miroslav less earthbound. Miroslav, who spent a year of his life putting together a duck out of cogs and springs, and appeared with his pet on Croatian television, must surely have a sense of humour. Drago too, with his wild, constrained laughter. Drago tossed between father and mother. A good tennis player, Marijana says. Back and forth. Three Balkan types. Three Balkan souls. But since when has he been an expert on lightness, or on the Balkans? "Many Croatians," says *Peoples of the Balkans*, "will deny that Croatia belongs to the Balkans. Croatia is part of the Catholic West, they will say."

"Always fighting," Marijana is saying on the telephone.

"Fighting? Who is fighting?"

"Drago and his father. Drago say he want to come stay in your store room."

"In my store room?"

"I say no. I say Mr. Rayment is good man, he have enough trouble from Jokićs."

"Mr. Rayment is not a good man, he is just trying to help. Drago can't take up residence in my store room or anyone else's, that is nonsense. But if relations are strained between him and his father, and if he has your blessing, tell him he is welcome to come back and stay here for a few days. What does he like to eat for supper? Pizza? Tell him I'll have them deliver a giant pizza every evening, just for him. Two giant pizzas, if he likes. He's a growing boy."

That is how it happens. In a flash, in a flesh. If there were any clouds, they have fled.

"They are what we call albumen prints," he tells Drago. "The paper is coated with diluted egg white in which silver chloride crystals are suspended. Then it is exposed to light under the glass negative. Then it is chemically fixed. It was a way of printing that had only just been invented in Fauchery's day. Look, here is a pre-albumen print to compare it with, on paper that has been soaked rather than coated—soaked in a solution of silver salts. Can you see how much more full and luminous the Fauchery is? That is because of the depth of the albumen coating. Less than a millimetre of depth, but that millimetre makes all the difference. Take a look through the microscope."

He wants to make himself interesting to Drago, that is to say, to an intelligent representative of the coming era, but it is not easy. What has he to offer? A broken bicycle. A truncated limb, probably more repellent than attractive. And a cabinet full of old pictures. In sum, not much. Not much with which to attach a boy to him as a mystical godson.

But Drago, excellent son of an excellent mother and—who is to say?—perhaps of an excellent father too, is nothing if not polite. Obediently he peers through the microscope, taking note of the millimetre of dried hen's egg that is claimed to make all the difference.

"You were a photographer yourself, weren't you, Mr. Rayment?"

"Yes, I ran a studio in Unley. For a while I also gave evening classes in photography. But I was never—how shall I put it?—an artist of the camera. I was always more of a technician."

Is that something to apologise for, not being an artist? Why should he apologise? Why should young Drago expect him to be an artist—young Drago, whose goal in life is to be a technician of warfare?

"Fauchery wasn't an artist himself," he says, "at least not until he came to Australia. He came out from Paris during the gold rush of the 1850s. Did some amateur gold-digging himself, in Victoria, to get a taste of it, but mainly took photographs." He gestures towards the group of women at the door of the wattle hut. "That was when he discovered his talent. Perfected his technique too. Took full command of his medium. As any great photographer needs to do."

"My mum wanted to be an artist, back in Croatia."

"Really!"

"Yeah. She went to art school. Then after art

school she went into restoration, you know, restoring old frescoes and things like that."

"How interesting! I did not know that about her. Restoration is a skilled profession. You might even call it an art in its own right, except that it is frowned on to be original. First rule of restoration: follow the intention of the artist. Never try to improve on him. Your mother must have found it hard to give up her art work and move to nursing. Does she still paint?"

"She has still got, you know, the brushes and equipment and stuff. But she hasn't got time any more."

"No, I'm sure she hasn't. Still, she is a first-rate nurse. She brings honour to the profession. I hope you know that."

Drago nods. "Where did you get these photographs, Mr. Rayment?"

"Collected them over many years. Went to antique shops, went to auction sales, bought old albums, bought up boxes full of old pictures, junk for the most part, but every now and again there would be something worth saving. When a picture was in poor condition, I did the restoring myself. Not nearly as difficult as restoring frescoes, but specialised work nonetheless. That was my hobby for years. That was how I spent my spare time. If your time is not worth much in itself, at least you can put it to a good use. So I told myself. On my death I will donate the collection. It will become public property. Part of our historical record." And he throws up his hands in an odd, unintended gesture. Astonishingly, he is close to tears. Why? Because he dares to mention his own death to this boy, this forerunner of the generation that will take over his world and trample on it? Perhaps. But more likely it is because of *our. Our record, yours and mine.* Because just possibly this image before them, this distribution of particles of silver that records the way the sunlight fell, one day in 1855, on the faces of two long-dead Irishwomen, an image in whose making he, the little boy from Lourdes, had no part and in which Drago, son of Dubrovnik, has had no part either, may, like a mystical charm—*I was here, I lived, I suffered*—have the power to draw them together.

"Anyway," he says, "if you get bored, if you have nothing else to do, feel free to look through the rest of the pictures. Just don't remove them from their sleeves. And make sure you put them back in order."

An hour later, as he is preparing for bed, Drago puts his head around the door. "Got a computer, Mr. Rayment?"

"Yes. You will find it on the floor under the desk. I don't use it much."

Soon Drago is back. "Can't find the connection, Mr. Rayment. For the modem."

"Sorry, I don't understand."

"The link. Do you have a cord somewhere that links you into the net?"

"No, it's not that kind of computer. I use it to

write letters now and again. What are you trying to do? What do you need it for?"

Drago gives him an unbelieving smile. "For everything. When did you buy your computer?"

"I don't remember. Years ago. Nineteen eighty something. It's not up to date. If you need something more advanced, I can't help you."

Drago does not let the subject rest there. They are in the kitchen the next evening, having supper. He has not ordered pizza, as he said he would. Instead he has cooked quite a nice risotto, with mushrooms and Sauternes.

"Do you hate things if they are new, Mr. Rayment?" says Drago out of the blue.

"No. Why do you say that?"

"I'm not, you know, blaming you. It's just the style, the style of everything." He sits back in his chair, waves a hand casually over, as he says, everything. "It's cool. I'm just asking. Isn't there anything new you like?"

The flat on Coniston Terrace is part of a refurbished pre-war block. It is high-ceilinged and spacious, yet not too large. He bought it after the divorce; it was exactly what he, as a rediscovered bachelor, wanted. He has lived here ever since.

Part of the deal when he bought the flat was that he should take over the previous owner's furniture. The furniture was heavy and dark and not to his taste; he has always meant to replace it, but has never found the energy. Instead, over the years, he has adjusted to his surroundings, growing a little more plodding, a little more sombre himself.

"I'll give you a straight answer, Drago, but not at the cost of being laughed at. I have been overtaken by time, by history. This flat, and everything in it, has been overtaken. There is nothing strange in that—in being overtaken by time. It will happen to you too, if you live long enough. Now tell me: what is this conversation really about? Is it about a computer that doesn't match up to your standards?"

Drago stares at him in shocked puzzlement. And indeed he surprises himself. Why such sharp words? What has the poor boy done to deserve them? *Do you hate things if they are new?* A fair enough question to an old man. What is there to be cross about?

"This was all, once upon a time, new," he says, waving a hand in exactly the same gesture Drago used. "Everything in the world was, once upon a time, new. Even I was new. The hour I was born I was the latest, newest thing on the face of the earth. Then time got to work on me. As time will get to work on you. Time will eat you up, Drago. One day you will be sitting in your nice new house with your nice new wife, and your son will turn around to the pair of you and say, *Why are you so old-fashioned?* When that day arrives, I hope you will remember this conversation."

Drago takes a last forkful of risotto, a last forkful of salad. "We went to Croatia last Christmas," he says. "Me and my mum and my sisters. To Zadar.

That's where Mum's parents live. They're pretty old now. They also got, like you said, overtaken by time. My mum bought them a computer and we showed them how to use it. So now they can shop on the internet, they can send e-mails, we can send them pictures. They like it. And they're pretty old."

"So?"

"So you can choose," says Drago. "That's all I'm saying."

CHAPTER 24

When he invited Drago to stay, there was, behind the invitation, nothing that he would deem—he picks up the primly disapproving word of the day, weighs it, tests it—*inappropriate*. His heart, as far as he can see into his heart, was and is pure, his motives innocent. He is fond of Drago with a measured, an appropriate fondness, as any man might be of an adopted son, or son-to-be.

The cohabitation he envisioned for the pair of them was to be on the mildest scale: a few companionable evenings together, Drago hunched over his homework at the dining table, he in an armchair with a book, while they waited for tempers in the casa Jokić to cool down.

But that is not how it turns out to be. Drago brings in friends; soon the flat has become as noisy and confused as a railway station. The kitchen is a mess of take-away cartons and dirty plates; the bathroom is forever occupied. None of the quiet growth in intimacy that he had looked forward to has come about. In fact, he feels that Drago is pushing him away. After the evening of the mushroom risotto they do not even eat together.

"I'm making myself an omelette for supper," he announces as casually as he can. "Shall I make one for you too? Ham and tomato?"

"Not for me," says Drago. "I'll be going out. One of my mates is picking me up. We'll get something to eat."

"You have money?"

"Yeah, thanks, my mum gave me money."

The mate in question is a pimply red-head named Shaun, to whom he has taken a dislike at first sight. Shaun, who according to Drago doesn't go to school much because he plays in a band, haunts the flat. He and Drago go out after dark, stay away till late, then return and shut themselves up in his ex-study, which has become Drago's room. Music and the murmur of their voices keep him awake into the early hours of the morning. Grumpy and miserable, he lies in the dark listening to the BBC.

"It is not just the noise," he complains to Elizabeth Costello. "Drago is used to a large family, I don't expect a monkish silence from him. No, what upsets me is the way he reacts when I dare to ask for a little consideration."

"How does he react?"

"A shutter falls. He does not see me any more. I might as well be a stick of furniture. Marijana says he and his father are always at loggerheads. Well, I begin to see why. I begin to sympathise with his father."

After her cold words at the riverside, he had thought he might not see Elizabeth Costello again. But no, she is back, perhaps because she cannot give up on him, but also perhaps because she is not well. She has lost weight; she looks more than a little frail; she has a persistent cough.

"Poor Paul!" she says. "So late in life, so monkish, as you say, so set in your ways, and now so grumpy too! What a reckless venture into childminding! In the abstract I am sure you would like to love young Drago, but the facts of life keep getting in the way. We cannot love by an act of the will, Paul. We have to learn. That is why souls descend from their realm on high and submit to being born again: so that, as they grow up in our company, they can lead us along the hard road of loving. From the beginning you have glimpsed something angelic in Drago, and I am sure you are not wrong. Drago has remained in touch with his other-worldly origins longer than most children. Overcome your disappointment, your irritation. Learn from Drago while you can. One of these days the last wisps of glory that trail behind him will vanish into the air and he will simply be one of us.

"You think I am crazy, don't you, or deluded? But remember: I have raised two children, real-life, unmystical children; you have raised none. I know what children are for; you are still ignorant. So pay heed when I speak, even when I speak in figures. We have children in order that we may learn to love and serve. Through our children we become the servants of time. Look into your heart. Ask yourself whether you have the reserves of fortitude you will need for the journey, and the stamina. If not, perhaps you should withdraw. It is not too late."

Speaking in figures. Angels from on high. It is the most mystifying speech she has made since the hocus-pocus about the woman with the dark glasses. Is she light-headed from fasting? Is she trying to make a fool of him again? Ought he to offer her more than a cup of tea? He gives her a hard look, as hard a look as he can. But she does not waver. She believes what she is saying, it would seem.

As for the contract solemnly concluded between Marijana and himself, that seems to have gone up in smoke. Day after day she stays away without a word of explanation. Her son, on the other hand, is blessed with frequent telephone calls. Of Drago's end of their conversations, which are in Croatian, he hears only a monosyllable here and there.

Then one afternoon, when he least expects it, Marijana drops in. Drago is not back from school; he is taking a nap.

"Mr. Rayment, I wake you? Sorry—I knock and no one come. You want I make you tea?"

"No, thank you." He is piqued at being caught asleep.

"How is your leg?"

"My leg? My leg is fine."

A stupid question and a stupid answer. How can his leg be fine? There is no leg. The leg in question was long ago hacked off and incinerated. *How is the absence of your leg?*: that is what she ought to be asking. *The absence of my leg is not fine, if you want the truth. The absence of my leg has left a hole in my life, as anyone with eyes in her head ought to be able to see.*

Marijana has brought Ljuba with her. For the sake of the child he tries to hide his irritation.

Marijana picks her way through the mess on the floor and perches at the foot of his bed. "You have nice life, nice and peaceful," she says. "Then *pfu!* car hit you. Then *pfu!* Jokić family hit you. Not so nice any more, eh? Sorry. No tea? You sure? How you and Drago get on?"

"Nothing to complain of. We get on well enough. It does me good, I am sure, to be with young people. Livens me up."

"You and him make friend, eh? Good. Blanka say thank you."

"It was nothing."

"Blanka come one day to say thank you in person. But not today. She is still, you know, father's girl." Which he takes to mean: There are still two camps among the Jokićs, the father's camp and the mother's camp. And all on account of you, Paul Rayment. Because of the tempest you have unleashed. Because of the inchoate passion for your cleaning lady that you were so foolish as to declare.

"So! You have new visitor!"

For a moment he cannot work out what she means. Then he recognises what she is holding up

218

for inspection: the nylon stocking that Mrs. Costello used to blindfold him, the stocking that for some reason he knotted around the base of the bedside lamp and forgot.

Marijana brings the stocking delicately within range of her nose. "Lemon flower!" she says. "Very nice! Your lady friend like lemon, eh? In Croatia, you know, we throw lemon flowers on woman and man when they get married in church. Old custom. Not rice, lemon flowers. So they have lots of children."

Marijana's humour. Nothing subtle about it. He ought to adjust, if he aspires to one day be her mystical bridegroom and be showered with lemon petals.

"It is not what it seems," he says. "I am not going to explain. Just accept what I tell you. It is not what you think."

Marijana holds the stocking at arm's length and ostentatiously lets it drop to the floor. "You want to know what I think? I think nothing. Nothing."

A silence falls. It is all right, he tells himself, we know each other well enough by now, Marijana and I, to have our little *contretemps*.

"OK," says Marijana. "Now I check your leg and give you wash and then we do exercise like usual. We fall behind our exercise, eh? Maybe you don't do exercise so good when you alone like. You sure you don't want *prosthese*?"

"I don't want a prosthesis, now or ever. The subject is closed. Please don't talk about it."

219

Marijana leaves the room. Ljuba continues to stare at him with the great black-eyed stare that he finds more and more eerie. "Hi, Ljuba," he says. "Ljubica." The endearment sounds foreign in his mouth, presumptuous. The child makes no reply.

Marijana returns with the big washing-bowl. "Private time for Mr. Rayment," she says. "Go make picture for Mama." She shepherds the child out, closes the door. She has taken off her sandals; her feet, he notices for the first time, are broad and flat; her toenails are painted a surprising dark red, almost purple, the colour of an angry bruise.

"You need help?" she says.

He shakes his head, slips his trousers off. "Lie down," she says. She spreads a discreet towel over his middle, lifts the stump onto her lap, deftly unwinds the bandage, gives the naked thing an approving pat. "No *prosthese*, eh? You think your leg grow again, Mr. Rayment? Only baby think like that—you cut it off, it grow again."

"Marijana, please stop. We have had this conversation before. I don't want to talk—"

"OK, OK, no more talk on *prosthese*. You stay at home, your lady friends come visit, better that way." She runs her thumb along the scar. "Cheaper. No pain? No itch?"

He shakes his head.

"Good," she says; and begins to soap the stump.

His bad humour is evaporating like the morning mist. *Anything*, he thinks to himself: *I would give anything for* . . . He thinks the thought with such fervour that it is impossible it does not communicate itself to Marijana. But Marijana's face is impassive. *Adored*, he thinks to himself. *I adore this woman! Despite all!* And also: *She has me in the palm of her hand!*

She finishes washing the stump, pats it dry, begins the first massage. After the first massage, the stretch exercises. After the stretch exercises, the second and concluding massage.

Let this go on for ever!

She must be used to it, all nurses must be used to it: men under their care growing physically excited. That must be why she is always so quick, so businesslike, why she declines to meet his eye. Presumably that is how they are taught to deal with male excitement. *It will sometimes happen that . . . It is important to understand that . . . Such motions are involuntary and are an embarrassment as much to the patient as to the nurse . . . It is best to . . .* Lively moments in an otherwise boring lecture.

Before the Fall, said Augustine, all motions of the body were under the direction of the soul, which partakes of God's essence. Therefore if today we find ourselves at the mercy of whimsical motions of bodily parts, that is a consequence of a fallen nature, fallen away from God. But was the blessed Augustine right? Are the motions of his own bodily parts merely whimsical? It all feels one to him, one movement: the swelling of the soul, the swelling of the heart, the swelling of desire. He cannot imagine loving God more than he loves Marijana at this moment.

Marijana is not dressed in her blue uniform, which means that she does not regard today as a working day, or at least did not regard it as such when she left home. Instead she is wearing an olive-green dress with a black sash and a brief slit up the left side that reveals a knee and a flash of thigh. Her bare brown arms, her smooth brown legs: *Anything!* he thinks again. *I would give anything!* And somehow this *anything!* and his approval of the olive-green outfit, which he finds irresistibly fetching, are no different from his love of God, who, if he does not exist, at least fills what would otherwise be a vast, all-devouring hole.

"Now on left side." She rearranges the towel to keep him decent. "So: press against me."

She presses the stump backward; he is supposed to press forward countervailingly. Briefly they hold the position, the two of them: she gripping the curtailed thigh with both hands, leaning her weight against him, he gripping the edge of the bed and resisting. *How far!* he thinks. *How near and yet how far!* Breast to breast they might as well be, pushing their fallen selves into each other. *If Wayne were to hear about this, what would he say!* But for Wayne Blight he would never have met Marijana Jokić; but for Wayne Blight he would not have known this pressure, this love, this urgency. *Felix, felix. Felix lapsus.* Everything is for the best, after all.

"OK, now relax," says Marijana. "Good. Now on front side."

She hitches up her dress and straddles him. On the radio, which sent him to sleep in the first place and which has not been switched off, a man is talking about the Korean car industry. Figures are up, figures are down. Marijana's hands slip under his shirt, her thumbs find a knot of pain high in the buttock and begin to caress it away. *Thank you, God*, he thinks. And thank God the Costello woman is not here to observe and comment.

"Što to radiš, mama?"

He opens his eyes with a start. From an arm's length away Ljuba is staring straight at him. There is no mistaking the severity of that gaze. Here he is, old and ugly and hairy and half naked and no doubt to her angelic nostrils smelly, wrestling with her mother, the two of them trapped in a posture that does not even have the repulsive majesty of intercourse.

For a moment, when the child spoke, he could feel Marijana freeze. Now she picks up the rhythm of the massage again. "Mr. Rayment has pain," she says. "Mama is nurse, remember?"

"That will be enough for today, Marijana," he says, hastening to cover himself. "Thank you."

Marijana clambers off the bed, slips on her sandals, takes Ljuba by the hand. "Don't suck thumb," she says. "Is ugly. OK, Mr. Rayment. Maybe pain go away now."

CHAPTER 25

It is Saturday. Marijana has closeted herself in the study with Drago; the two are having what sounds very much like a row. Her voice, rapid and insistent, rises every now and again above her son's, beating it down.

Ljuba is on the stairway, hopping up and down the stairs, making a clatter.

"Ljuba!" he calls. "Come and have some yoghurt!" The child ignores him.

Marijana emerges from the study. "Is OK I leave Ljuba here? She stay with Drago. No trouble. I come back later and fetch her."

He had been hoping to receive from Marijana a little more of what he pays her to provide, perhaps even another session of body-care; but evidently that will not be forthcoming. Twice a month, like clockwork, a little mechanism at the bank switches money from the Rayment account to the Jokić account. In return for his money, in return for the home from home that he provides for Drago, he receives—what? A shopping service, more and more irregular; infrequent ministrations of a health-professional kind. A not unadvantageous bargain, from Marijana's point of view. But then, as the Costello woman keeps telling him, if he wants to be a father he had better find out about fatherhood as it really is, fatherhood of the non-mystical kind.

Marijana has barely gone off when there are voices from the stairwell and Ljuba reappears with the Costello woman and Drago's friend Shaun in tow, Shaun clad today in a slack T-shirt and shorts down to his calves.

"Hello, Paul," says the Costello woman. "I hope you don't mind us breezing in. Ljuba darling, tell Drago that Shaun is here."

He and she are alone for a moment, the two seniors.

"Not quite in Drago's class, is he, our friend Shaun," says Costello. "But that is how gods and angels seem to be: they choose the most distressingly ordinary mortals to consort with."

He is silent.

"There is a story I keep meaning to tell, that I think will amuse you," she continues. "It comes from the distant past, from the time of my youth. One of the boys on our street was very much like Drago. Same dark eyes, same long eyelashes, same not quite human good looks. I was smitten with him. I must have been fourteen at the time, he a little older. I still used to pray in those days. 'God,' I would say, 'let him bestow on me just one of his smiles and I will be yours forever.'"

"And?"

"God paid no attention. Nor did the boy. My maiden longings were never requited. So, alas, I never became a child of God. The last I heard of Mr. Eyelashes, he was married and had moved to the Gold Coast, where he was making a killing in real estate."

"So is it all a lie then: Whom the gods love die young?"

"I fear so. I fear the gods no longer have time for us, whether to love us on the one hand or to punish us on the other. They have troubles enough in their own gated community."

"No time even for Drago Jokić? Is that the moral of your story?"

"No time even for Drago Jokić. Drago is on his own."

"Like the rest of us."

"Like the rest of us. He can relax. No spectacular doom hangs over his head. He can be sailor or soldier or tinker or tailor, as he chooses. He can even go into real estate."

It is the first exchange that he and the Costello woman have had that he would call cordial, even amiable. For once they are on the same side: two old folk ganging up on youth.

Might that be the real explanation for why the woman has descended on him out of nowhere: not to write him into a book but to induct him into the company of the aged? Might the whole Jokić affair, with his ill-considered and to this point fruitless passion for Mrs. Jokić at its centre, be nothing in the end but a complicated rite of passage through which Elizabeth Costello has been sent to guide him? He had thought Wayne Blight was the angel assigned to his case; but perhaps they all work together, she and Wayne and Drago.

Drago pokes his head around the door. "Can Shaun and me look at your cameras, Mr. Rayment?"

"Yes. But take care, and put them back in their cases when you have finished."

"Drago is interested in photography?" murmurs Elizabeth Costello.

"In cameras. He has never seen anything like mine. He knows only the new, electronic kind. A Hasselblad is like a sailing-ship to him, or a trireme. An antiquity. He also spends hours going through my photographs, the nineteenth-century ones. I thought it odd at first, but perhaps it is not so odd after all. He must be feeling his way into what it is like to have an Australian past, an Australian descent, Australian forebears of the mystical variety. Instead of being just a refugee kid with a joke name."

"That is what he tells you?"

"No, he would not dream of telling me. But I can guess. I can sympathise. I am not unfamiliar with the immigrant experience."

"Yes, of course. I keep forgetting. Such a proper Anglo-Adelaidean gentleman that I forget you are not English at all. Mr. Rayment, rhyming with *payment*."

"Rhyming with *vraiment*. I had three doses of the immigrant experience, not just one, so it imprinted itself quite deeply. First when I was uprooted as a child and brought to Australia; then when I declared my independence and returned to France; then when I gave up on France and came back to Australia. *Is this where I belong?* I asked with each move. *Is this my true home?*"

"You went back to France—I forgot about that. One day you must tell me more about that period of your life. But what is the answer to your question? *Is* this your true home?" She waves a hand in a gesture that encompasses not just the room in which they are sitting but also the city and, beyond that, the hills and mountains and deserts of the continent.

He shrugs. "I have always found it a very English concept, home. *Hearth and home*, say the English. To them, home is the place where the fire burns in the hearth, where you come to warm yourself. The one place where you will not be left out in the cold. No, I am not warm here." He waves a hand in a gesture that imitates hers, parodies it. "I seem to be cold wherever I go. Is that not what you said of me: *You cold man?*"

The woman is silent.

"Among the French, as you know, there is no *home*. Among the French to be at home is to be among ourselves, among our kind. I am not at home in France. Transparently not. I am not the *we* of anyone."

It is the closest he has come, with the Costello woman, to lamenting his lot, and it sickens him faintly. *I am not the we of anyone*: how does she manage to extort such words from him? A hint dropped here, a suggestion dropped there, and he follows like a lamb.

"And Marijana? Are you not desirous of joining the *we* of Marijana and Drago? And Ljuba? And Blanka, on whom you have yet to lay an eye?"

"That is another question," he snaps. And will not be drawn further.

Noon passes, and Marijana does not show up. Drago has strapped a doll to his little sister's back with rubber bands; she trots from room to room, her arms stretched out, making a droning noise like an aeroplane. Shaun has brought along some kind of electronic game. The two boys sit in front of the television screen, which emits low whoops and buzzes.

"You know, we don't have to put up with this," says Elizabeth Costello. "They don't need to be babysat, these young folk. We could make a quiet exit, go back to the park. We could sit in the shade and listen to the birds. We could look on it as our weekend excursion, our little adventure."

He is prepared to accept a helping hand from Marijana, who is after all a paid nurse, but not from a woman older than himself. He sends Costello to wait in the entranceway while he negotiates the stairs on his crutches.

On the way down he is passed by one of the neighbours, a slim, bespectacled girl from Singapore who with her two sisters, quiet as mice, occupies the flat above his. He nods to her; the greeting is not returned. In all their time on Coniston Terrace the girls have never acknowledged his existence. Each unto herself: that must be what they are taught in their island state. Self-reliance.

He and Costello find an empty bench. A dog trots up: it gives him a quick, jaunty once-over, then moves on to her. Always embarrassing when a dog pushes its snout into a woman's crotch. Is it reminding itself of sex, dog sex, or is it just savouring the novel, complex smells? He has always thought of Elizabeth as an asexual being, but perhaps a dog, putting its trust in its nose, will know better.

Elizabeth bears the investigation well, letting the dog have its way with her, then pushing it away good-humouredly.

"So," she says. "You were telling me."

"I was telling you what?"

"You were telling me the story of your life. Telling me about France. I was married to a Frenchman once. Didn't I tell you? My first marriage. Unforgettable times. He walked out on me, in the end, for another woman. Left me with a child on my hands. I was, according to him, too mutable. *Vipère*, was another of the terms he applied to me, which in England is an adder rather than a viper. *Sale vipère*, those were his words. He never knew where he was with me. Great ones for order, the French. Great ones for knowing where they are with you. But enough of that. We were talking about you."

"I thought you thought the French were great ones for passion. Passion, not order."

She turns a reflective eye on him. "Passion and order, Paul. Both, not one or the other. But proceed with the story of your love affair with France."

"It is not a long story. At school I was good at science. Not outstandingly good, I was not outstanding at anything, just good. So when I went to university I signed up for science. Science seemed a good bet in those days. It seemed to promise safety, and that was what my mother wanted above all for my sister and me: that we find some safe niche for ourselves in this foreign land where the man whom she had followed, God knows why, was retreating more and more into himself, where we had no family to fall back on, where she floundered in the language and could not get a grip on local ways of doing things. My sister went into teaching, which was one way of being safe, and I went into science.

"But then my mother passed on, and there no longer seemed much point to putting on a white coat and peering into a test tube. So I dropped out of university and bought a ticket to Europe. I stayed with my grandmother in Toulouse and found a job in a photo lab. That was how my career in photography began. But don't you

231

know all this? I thought you knew everything about me."

"It is news to me, Paul, I promise you. You came to me with no history attached. A man with one leg and an unfortunate passion for his nurse, that was all. Your prior life was virgin territory."

"I stayed with my grandmother and made overtures, as far as I could, to my mother's family, because in the France we came from, peasant France, family is everything. My cousins might be car mechanics and shop assistants and station foremen, but at heart they were still peasants, only one generation away from black bread and cow manure. I am talking about the 1960s, of course, a bygone age. It is different nowadays. All changed."

"And?"

"I was not successful. I was not, shall we say, embraced. I had missed too much of what should have been my *formation*: not just a proper French schooling but a French youth, including youthful friendships, which can be as intense as love, and longer-lasting. My cousins and the people I met through them, people of my age, were already settled into their lives. Even before they left school they knew what *métier* they were going to follow, what boy or girl they were going to marry, where they were going to live. They could not work out what I was doing there, this gangly fellow with the funny accent and the puzzled look; and I could not tell them because I did not know either. I was always the odd one out, the stranger in the corner at family gatherings. Among themselves they called me *l'Anglais*. It came as a shock, the first time I heard it, since I had no ties to England, had never even been there. But Australia was beyond their ken. In their eyes Australians were simply Englishmen, mackintoshes and boiled cabbage and all, transplanted to the end of the earth, scratching a living among the *kangourous*.

"I had a friend, Roger, who did deliveries for the studio where I worked. On Saturday afternoons he and I would pack our saddlebags and head off on our bicycles to Saint-Girons or Tarascon; or deeper into the Pyrenees as far as Oust or Aulus-les-Bains. We ate in cafés, spent nights in the open, rode all day, came back late on Sundays exhausted and full of life. We never had much to say to each other, he and I, yet now he seems to me the best friend I ever had, the best *copain*.

"Those were the days before the French romance with the automobile had taken off properly. The roads were emptier; roaming the countryside on a bicycle was not such an odd thing to be doing.

"Then I got involved with a girl, and suddenly I had other uses for my weekends. She was from Morocco: that really set me apart. The first of my unsuitable passions. She and I might have married if her family had not made it impossible."

"Struck by the lightning bolt of passion! And for an exotic maiden too! Material for a book in itself! How magnificent! How extravagant! You astonish me, Paul."

"Don't mock. It was all very decorous, very respectable. She was studying to be a librarian, until she was summoned home."

"And?"

"That is all. Her father summoned her, she obeyed, that was the end of the affair. I stayed on in Toulouse for another six months, then I gave up."

"You came home."

"Home . . . What does that mean? I told you what I think about home. A pigeon has a home, a bee has a home. An Englishman has a home, perhaps. I have a domicile, a residence. This is my residence. This flat. This city. This country. Home is too mystical for me."

"But you are Australian. You are not French. Even I can see that."

"I can pass among Australians. I cannot pass among the French. That, as far as I am concerned, is all there is to it, to the national-identity business: where one passes and where one does not, where on the contrary one stands out. Like a sore thumb, as the English say; or like a stain, as the French say, a stain on the spotless domestic linen. As for language, English has never been mine in the way it is yours. Nothing to do with fluency. I am perfectly fluent, as you can hear. But English came to me too late. It did not come with my mother's milk. In fact it did not come at all.

Privately I have always felt myself to be a kind of ventriloquist's dummy. It is not I who speak the language, it is the language that is spoken through me. It does not come from my core, *mon coeur*." He hesitates, checks himself. *I am hollow at the core*, he was about to say—*as I am sure you can hear*. "Don't try to load more onto this conversation than it will bear, Elizabeth," he says instead. "It is not significant, it is just biography of a rambling kind."

"But it is significant, Paul, truly it is! You know, there are those whom I call the chthonic, the ones who stand with their feet planted in their native earth; and then there are the butterflies, creatures of light and air, temporary residents, alighting here, alighting there. You claim to be a butterfly, you want to be a butterfly; but then one day you have a fall, a calamitous fall, you come crashing down to earth; and when you pick yourself up you find you can no longer fly like an ethereal being, you cannot even walk, you are nothing but a lump of all too solid flesh. Surely a lesson presents itself, one to which you cannot be blind and deaf."

"Really. A lesson. With a little ingenuity, it seems to me, Mrs. Costello, one can torture a lesson out of the most haphazard sequence of events. Are you trying to tell me that God had some plan in mind when he struck me down on Magill Road and turned me into a hobbler? What about yourself? You told me you have a heart condition. Interpret your heart condition to me. What lesson

235

did God have in mind when he struck you in the heart?"

"It is true, Paul, I do indeed have a heart condition, I was not telling a fib. But I am not the only one so afflicted. You have a heart condition of your own—do you really not know that? When I came knocking at your door, it was not to find out how a man rides a bicycle with one leg. I came to find out what happens when a man of sixty engages his heart unsuitably. And, if you don't mind my saying so, you have been a sorry let-down thus far."

He shrugs. "I was not put on this earth to entertain you. If you want entertainment"—he waves a hand at the runners, the cyclists, the good folk taking their dogs for a walk—"you have a wide range to explore. Why waste your time on someone who exasperates you with his obtuseness and keeps letting you down? Give me up as a bad job. Visit yourself on some other candidate."

She turns and bestows on him a smile that lacks, as far as he can see, any malice. "I may be capricious, Paul," she says, "but not as capricious as that. Capricious: goat-like, leaping from one rock to another. I am too old for leaping. You are my rock. I will stay with you, for the time being. As I told you—remember?—love is a fixation."

He shrugs again. *Love is a fixation.* One might equally well call love a bolt of lightning that strikes where it wills. If he is an ignorant baby when it comes to the maladies of love, he does not see that the Costello woman is any better.

But he is not going to argue with her. He is tired of arguing.

He is also thirsty. A cup of tea would go down very well. They could cross the bridge to the tea-room on the other bank. They could go back to the flat with its noise and disorder. Or they could forget about tea and go on dawdling here by the riverside, letting the afternoon pass, watching the waterfowl disport themselves. Which?

"Tell me about your marriage," says Elizabeth Costello. "You hardly ever mention your wife."

"I think not," he says. "It would not be proper. My wife would not thank me for offering her up as a minor character in one of your literary efforts. But if it is stories you want, I will tell you a story from the period of my marriage that does not involve my wife. You can use it to illustrate my character, or not, as you wish."

"All right. Shoot."

"It comes from the time I was still running the studio in Unley. I had two assistants, and one of them happened to fall in love with me. To be accurate, it was not love but adoration. She had no designs on me. That was why she could be so open about it. A perfectly intelligent girl. Pretty too. A fresh-faced, pretty, twenty-year-old girl in a solid, sturdy body, the body of a rugby player. Nothing she could do about it. No diet was going to save her, transfigure her into a sylph.

"I was teaching an evening course at the time, at what used to be the polytechnic. Principles of photography. Three evenings a week this girl came to my class. Sat in the back row and gazed at me. Took no notes.

"'Don't you think this is becoming excessive, Ellen?' I said to her. 'It's my only chance,' she replied. No blushes. She never blushed. 'Your only chance for what?' 'To be alone with you.' That was how she defined being alone with me: being free to sit in class and watch and listen.

"I had a rule: never get involved with employees. But in this one case I had a lapse. I broke the rule. I left a note for her: a time, a place, nothing else. She came, and I took her to bed.

"You probably expect me to say it was a humiliating experience, for her and therefore for me. But it wasn't humiliating at all. I would go so far as to call it joyous. And I learned a lesson from it: that love need not be reciprocated as long as there is enough of it in the room. This girl had enough love for two. You are the writer, the heart expert, but did you know that? If you love deeply enough, it is not necessary to be loved back."

The Costello woman is silent.

"She thanked me. She lay in my arms crying and gasping 'Thank you, thank you, thank you!' 'It's all right,' I said. 'No need for anyone to thank anyone.'

"The next day there was a note on my desk: 'Whenever you have need of me . . .' But I did not call on her again, did not try to repeat the experience. Once was enough, to absorb that lesson.

"She worked for me for another two years, keeping a correct distance because that was what I seemed to want. No tears, no reproaches. Then she disappeared. Not a word, just stopped coming to work. I spoke to her colleague, my other assistant, but she was in the dark. I telephoned her mother. Didn't I know, the mother said? Ellen had taken a new job and moved to Brisbane as a rep for a pharmaceuticals company. Hadn't she given notice? No, I said, this was the first I heard of it. Oh, said the mother, she told us she had spoken to you and you were quite cut up."

"And?"

"That's all. End of story. *I was quite cut up:* aside from the lesson in love, that was the part that interested me most. Because I wasn't cut up, not at all. Did the girl really think I would be cut up because she had left my employ? Or was the story about her boss being cut up just something she told her mother so that she would not seem too abject?"

"Are you asking my opinion? I don't know the answer, Paul. The claim that you, her boss, were cut up may be the part of the story that you find interesting, but it is not what interests me. What interests me is the *Thank you, thank you! Is Thank you, thank you!* what you plan to say to Marijana if and when she yields herself to you? Why didn't you say *Thank you, thank you!* to the girl I procured for you, the one you singled out for your attentions because she would not be able to witness you in your sadly reduced state?"

239

"I did not single her out. You were the one who brought her up."

"Nonsense. I merely took my cue from you. You singled her out in the hospital lift. You had dreams about her. Why did you not thank her, I repeat? Was it because you paid her, and if you pay you don't need to say thank you? Your rugby player had enough love for two, you say. Do you really think love can be measured? Do you think love comes by volume, like beer? That as long as you bring a case of it, the other party is permitted to come empty-handed—empty-handed, empty-hearted? Thank you, Marijana (Marijana with the *j* this time), for letting me love you. Thank you for letting me love your children. Thank you for letting me give you my money. Are you really such a dummy?"

He stiffens. "You asked me for a story, I gave you a story. I am sorry you don't like it. You say you want to hear stories, I offer you stories, and I get back nothing except ridicule and scorn. What kind of exchange is that?"

"What kind of love?, you might have added. I didn't say I didn't like your story. I found it interesting, and well told too, the story of you and your rugby player. Even the interpretation you give is interesting in its own right. But the question that nags me is: Why does he pick on *this* story to tell me, this above all others?"

"Because it is true."

"Of course it is true. But what does it matter if it is true? Surely it is not up to me to play God,

240

separating the sheep from the goats, dismissing the false stories, preserving the true. If I have a model, it is not God, it is the Abbé of Cîteaux, the notorious one, the Frenchman, the one who said to the soldiers in his pastoral care, *Slay them all—God will know who are His.*

"No, Paul, I couldn't care less if you tell me made-up stories. Our lies reveal as much about us as our truths."

She pauses, cocks an eyebrow at him. Is it his turn? He has nothing more to say. If truth and lies are the same, then speech and silence may as well be the same too.

"Do you notice, Paul," she resumes, "how conversations between you and me keep falling into the same pattern? For a while all goes swimmingly. Then I say something you don't want to hear, and at once you clam up or storm off or ask me to leave. Can't we get beyond such histrionics? We don't have much time left, either of us."

"Don't we."

"No. Under the gaze of heaven, in the cold eye of God, we don't."

"Is that the truth. Go on."

"Do you think I find this existence any less hard than you? Do you think I want to sleep outdoors, under a bush in the park, among the winos, and do my ablutions in the River Torrens? You are not blind. You can see how I am declining."

He gives her a hard stare. "You are making up stories. You are a prosperous professional woman, you are as comfortably off as I am, there is no need for you to sleep under bushes."

"That may be so, Paul. I may be exaggerating a little, but it is an apt story, apt to my condition. As I try to impress on you, our days are numbered, mine and yours, yet here I am, killing time, being killed by time, waiting—waiting for you."

He shakes his head helplessly. "I don't know what you want," he says.

"Push!" she says.

CHAPTER 26

On the hall table, a scrawled note: "BYE MR. RAYMENT. I'VE LEFT SOME STUFF, I'LL PICK IT UP TOMORROW. THANKS FOR EVERYTHING, DRAGO. PS PHOTOGRAPHS ALL IN ORDER."

The "stuff" Drago refers to turns out to be a garbage bag full of clothing, to which he adds a pair of underpants he finds among the bedclothes. Otherwise no trace of the Jokićs, mother or son. They come, they go, they do not explain themselves: he had better get used to it.

Yet what a relief to be by himself again! One thing to live with a woman; quite another to share one's home with an untidy and imperfectly considerate young man. Always tension, always unease when two males occupy the same territory.

He spends the afternoon tidying his study, putting things where they used to be; then he takes a shower. In the shower he by accident drops the flask of shampoo. As he bends to pick it up, the Zimmer frame, which he always brings into the cubicle with him, slips sideways. He loses his footing and falls, slamming his head against the wall.

Let nothing be broken: that is his first prayer.

Tangled in the frame, he tries to move his limbs. A flicker of exquisite pain runs from his back down his good leg. He takes a slow, deep breath. *Be calm*, he tells himself. *A slip in the bathroom, nothing to be alarmed about, it happens to many people, all may yet be well. Plenty of time to think, plenty of time to set things right.*

Setting things right (he tries to be calm and clear) will mean, one, disengaging himself from the frame; two, manoeuvring himself out of the cubicle; then, three, assessing what he has done to his back; and, four, proceeding to whatever comes next.

The problem lies between one and two. He cannot disengage himself from the Zimmer frame without sitting up; and he cannot sit up without a gasp of pain.

No one bothered to inform him, and he did not think to ask, who the Zimmer is or was who has come to play such a role in his life. For his own convenience he has imagined Zimmer as a thin-faced, tight-lipped figure of a man, dressed in the high collar and stock of the 1830s. Johann August Zimmer, son of Austrian peasants, determined to escape the drudgery of the family farm, toils by candlelight over his anatomy books while in the byre behind the house the milch-cow moans in her sleep. After scraping through his examinations (he is not a gifted student), he finds a posting as an army surgeon. The next twenty years he spends dressing wounds and cutting off limbs in the name of His Serene Imperial Majesty Carl Joseph August, nicknamed The Good. Then he retires from the service and after several wrong turns lands up at Bad Schwanensee, one of the lesser spas in Bohemia, prescribing for gentlewomen with arthritis. There he has the brainwave of adapting for the more frail among his patients the apparatus that back in Carinthia has for centuries been used to teach children to walk, thereby earning for himself a modest immortality.

Now here he is on the tiled floor, naked, immobile, with Zimmer's invention on top of him blocking the cubicle door, while water continues to pour down and leaking shampoo rises in a froth all around and the stump, which has taken a knock on its tender end, begins to throb with its own, unique variety of pain. *What a mess!* he thinks. *Thank God Drago does not have to witness it! And thank God the Costello woman is not here to make jokes!*

There are drawbacks, however, to having neither Drago nor the Costello woman nor anyone else within calling distance. One is that, as the supply of warm water runs out, he finds himself being douched with cold. The controls are beyond his reach. He is certainly free to lie here all night without risk of being laughed at; but by dawn he will have frozen to death.

It takes him a full thirty minutes to escape the prison he has made for himself. Unable to lift himself, unable to push Zimmer's frame out of the way, he finally grits his teeth and forces the door of the cubicle back until the hinges snap.

All shame is gone by now. He crawls across the floor to the telephone, calls Marijana's number, gets a child's voice. "Mrs. Jokić, please," he says through chattering teeth; and then, "Marijana, I have had an accident. I am OK but can you come at once?"

"What is accident?"

"I had a fall. I have done something to my back. I can't move."

"I come."

He drags the bedclothes down and huddles under them, but he cannot get warm. Not only his hands and foot, not only his scalp and his nose, but his very belly and heart are gripped with cold; spasms overtake him during which he grows too rigid even to shiver. He yawns until he is light-headed with yawning. *Old blood, cold blood*: the words drum in his brain. *Not enough heat in the veins*.

He has a vision of himself hung by the ankles in a cold chamber amid a forest of frozen carcases. *Not by fire but by ice*.

He falls into some kind of slumber. Then suddenly Marijana is bending over him. He tries to form his frozen lips into a smile, into words. "My back," he croaks. "Careful." No need, thank God, to explain how it happened. How it happened must be all too clear from the chaos in the bathroom, the hiss of the cold shower.

There is no tea left, but Marijana makes coffee, puts a pill between his lips, helps him to drink, then with surprising strength raises him bodily from the floor onto the bed. "You get scare, eh?" she says. "Now maybe you stop this shower business all alone."

He nods obediently, closes his eyes. Under the ministrations of this excellent woman and superlative nurse, he can feel the ice within him begin to thaw. No bones broken, no being reprimanded by Mrs. Putts, no being laughed at by Mrs. Costello. Instead, the soothing presence of an angel who has put aside all else to come to his aid.

No doubt for an ageing cripple the future holds further mishaps, further falls, further humiliating calls for help. What he needs at this moment, however, is not that dismaying and depressing prospect but this soft, consoling, and eminently feminine presence. *There, there, be calm, it is all over*: that is what he wants to hear. Also: *I will stay by your side while you sleep.*

So when Marijana rises and briskly dons her coat and picks up her keys, he has a quite childish sense of aggrievement. "Can't you stay a while longer?" he says. "Can't you spend the night?"

She sits down again on the bedside. "OK if I smoke?" she says. "Just one time?" She lights a cigarette, puffs, blows the smoke away from him. "We have talk, Mr. Rayment, fix up things. What you want from me? You want I must do my job, come back, be nurse for you? Then you don't say these things, like"—she waves the cigarette—"you know what I mean."

"I must not speak of my feelings for you."

"You go through bad time, you lose your leg and all that, I understand. You have feelings, man's feelings, I understand, is OK."

Though the pain seems to be dwindling, he cannot yet sit up. "Yes, I have feelings," he says, flat on his back.

"You have feelings, you say things, is natural, is OK. But."

"Labile. That is the word you are hunting for. I am too labile for your taste. Too much at the mercy of the feelings you refer to. I speak my heart too openly. I say too much."

"Mercy. What is mercy of feelings?"

"Never mind. I believe I understand you. I have an accident and am shaken to the core. My spirits rise, my spirits fall, they are no longer under my control. As a result I become attached to the first woman to cross my path, the first sympathetic woman. I fall, excuse the word, in love with her; I fall in love with her children too, in a different way. I, who have been childless, suddenly want children of my own. Hence the present friction between us, between you and me. And it can all be traced back to my brush with death on Magill Road. Magill Road shook me up so much that even today I let my feelings pour out without reckoning the consequences. Is that not what you are telling me?"

She shrugs but does not contradict him. Instead, drawing in the smoke luxuriously, blowing it out, she lets him run on. For the first time he sees what sensual pleasure there can be in smoking.

"Well, you are wrong, Marijana. It is not like that at all. I am not in a confused state. I may be labile, but being labile is not an aberration. We should all be more labile, all of us. That is my new, revised opinion. We should shake ourselves up more often. We should also brace ourselves and take a look in the mirror, even if we dislike what we will see there. I am not referring to the ravages of time. I am referring to the creature trapped behind the glass whose stare we are normally so careful to avoid. *Behold this being who eats with me, spends nights with me, says 'I' on my behalf!* If you find me labile, Marijana, it is not just because I suffered a knock. It is because every now and then the stranger who says 'I' breaks through the glass and speaks in me. Through me. Speaks tonight. Speaks now. Speaks love."

He halts. What a torrent of words! How unlike him! Marijana must be surprised. Is there indeed at this moment some stranger speaking through a mirror, taking over his voice (but which mirror?), or is the present outpouring just another bout of lability, the aftershock of the latest accident—the bump on the head, the strained back, the aching stump, the icy shower, and so forth—rising in his throat like bile, like vomit? In fact, might it simply be an effect of the pill Marijana gave him (what could the pill have been?), or even of the coffee? He should not have taken the coffee. He is not used to coffee in the evenings.

Speaks love. He cannot be sure, he is not wearing his glasses, but a flush seems to be creeping up from Marijana's throat. Marijana says she wants him to curb himself, but that is nonsense, she cannot really mean it. What woman would not want a torrent of love-words poured out on her every now and again, however questionable their origin? Marijana is blushing, and for the simple reason that she too is labile. And therefore? What comes next? *And therefore it does indeed all cohere!* Therefore behind the chaos of appearance a divine logic is indeed at work! Wayne Blight comes out of nowhere to smash his leg to a pulp, *therefore* months later he collapses in the shower, *therefore* this scene becomes possible: a man of sixty caught more or less rigid in bed, shivering intermittently, spouting philosophy to his nurse, spouting love. And the blood moves in her, responding!

Exulting, he stretches out (*Ignore the pain, who cares for pain!*) and places his large and (he notices) rather unattractively livid hand over Marijana's smaller, warmer hand with the tapering fingers that, according to his grandmother in Toulouse, signify a sensual temperament.

For a moment Marijana lets her hand rest under his. Then she frees herself, stubs out the cigarette, rises, and begins to button her coat again.

"Marijana," he says, "I make no demands, neither now nor in the future."

"Yes?" She cocks her head, gives him a quizzical look. "No demand? You think I know nothing about men? Men is always demand. I want, I want, I want. Me, I want to do my job, that is my demand. My job in Australia is nurse."

She pauses. Never before has she addressed him with such force, such (it seems to him) fury.

"You telephone, and is good you telephone, I don't say you must not telephone. Emergency, you telephone, OK. But this"—she waves a hand—"this shower business is not emergency, not medical emergency. You fall in bathroom, you call some friend. 'I get scared, please come,' that is what you say." She takes out a fresh cigarette, changes her mind, puts it back in the pack. "Elizabeth," she says. "You call Elizabeth, or you call other lady friend, I don't know your friends. 'I get scared, please come hold my hand. No medical emergency, just please come hold my hand.'"

"I was not just scared. I have injured myself. I cannot move. You can see that."

"Spasm. Is just spasm. I leave you pills for it. Back spasm is not emergency." She pauses. "Or else you want more, not just hold hand, you want, like you call it, the real thing, then maybe you join club for lonely hearts. If you got lonely heart."

She draws a breath, eyes him reflectively. "You

think you know how it is to be nurse, Mr. Rayment? Every day I nurse old ladies, old men, clean them, clean their dirt, I don't need to say it, change sheets, change clothes. Always I am hearing *Do this, do that, bring this, bring that, not feeling good, bring pills, bring glass of water, bring cup of tea, bring blanket, take off blanket, open window, close window, don't like this, don't like that.* I come home tired in my bone, telephone rings, any time, mornings, nights: *Is emergency, can you come . . ."*

Minutes ago she was blushing. Now he is the one who ought to blush. *An emergency . . . can you come?* Of course, in the language of the caring professions, this would not count as an emergency. One does not perish of cold in an air-conditioned flat on Coniston Terrace, North Adelaide. Even in the act of dialling the Jokić number he knew that. Yet he called anyhow. *Come, save me!* he called across the South Australian space.

"You were the first I thought of," he says. "Your name came to me first. Your name, your face. Do you think that is of no account—being first?"

She shrugs. There is silence between them. Of course it is a big word, an overbearing word to have hurled at one: *first.* But that is not the word that gives him pause. *Your name. Your name came to me. You came to me.* Words that rose in him without thought, came to him. Is this how it is when one is labile: words just come?

"I always thought," he presses on, "that nursing

was a vocation. I thought that was what set it apart, what justified the long hours and the poor pay and the ingratitude and the indignities too, such as those you mentioned: that you were following a calling. Well, when a nurse is called, a proper nurse, she doesn't ask questions, she comes. Even if it is not a real emergency. Even if it is just distress, human distress, what you call a scare." He has not lectured Marijana before, but perhaps the lecture is the mode in which, on this particular night, the truth will choose to reveal itself. "Even if it is just love."

Love: biggest of the big words. Nevertheless, let him sock her with it.

She takes the blow well this time, hardly blinking. The buttons of her coat are all done now, from bottom to top.

"Just love," he repeats with some bitterness.

"Time to go," she says. "Long drive to Munno Para. See you."

With considerable effort he quells a new bout of shivers. "Not yet, Marijana," he says. "Five minutes. Three minutes. Please. Let's have a drink together and simmer down and be ordinary. I don't want to feel I can never call you again, for shame. Yes?"

"OK. Three minutes. But no drink for me, I must drive, and no drink for you, alcohol and pills is not good."

Somewhat stiffly she resumes her seat. One of the three minutes passes.

"What exactly does your husband know?" he asks out of the blue.

She gets up. "Now I go," she says.

Distressed, remorseful, aching, uncomfortable, he lies awake all night. The pills that Marijana said she would leave are nowhere to be seen.

Dawn comes. Needing to go to the toilet, he gingerly tries to crawl out of the bed. Halfway to the floor the pain strikes again, immobilising him.

A sore back is not an emergency, says Marijana, whom he hired to save him from degradations of precisely this kind. Does being unable to control one's bladder count as an emergency? No, clearly not. It is just part of life, part of growing old. Miserably he surrenders and urinates on the floor.

That is the posture in which Drago—who ought to be at school but for reasons of his own seems not to be—finds him when he arrives to pick up his bag of stuff: half in bed, half out, his leg caught in the twisted bedclothes, stalled, frozen.

If he no longer hides anything from Marijana, it is because he cannot be more abject before her than he has already been. With Drago it is a different story. Thus far he has done his best not to make a spectacle of himself before Drago. Now here he is, a helpless old man in urinous pyjamas trailing an obscene pink stump behind him from which the sodden bandages are slipping. If he were not so cold he would blush.

And Drago does not waver! Does it run in the

family, this matter-of-factness about the body? As Drago's mother had helped him into bed, so now Drago helps him out; and when he tries to explain himself, to excuse his weakness, it is Drago who shushes him—"No worries, Mr. Rayment, just relax and we'll have you fixed up in a minute"— and then strips the bed and turns the mattress and (somewhat clumsily, he is after all just a boy) spreads fresh sheets; it is Drago who finds a fresh pair of pyjamas and patiently, averting his eyes as decency requires, helps him on with them.

"Thank you, son, good of you," he says at the end of it all. There is more he would like to say, for his heart is full, such as: *Your mother has abandoned me; Mrs. Costello, who jabbers on and on about care but takes care not to be around when care is needed, has abandoned me; everyone has abandoned me, even the son I never had; then you came, you!* But he holds his peace.

He has a passage of crying, old-man's crying which does not count because it comes too easily, and which he hides behind his hands because it embarrasses both of them.

Drago makes a phone call, comes back. "My mum says I should get you some pills for the pain. I've got the name here. She says she meant to leave you some but she forgot. I can go down to the pharmacy; but . . ."

"There is money in my wallet, in my desk drawer."

"Thanks. You got a mop somewhere?"

"Behind the kitchen door. But don't . . ."

"It's nothing, Mr. Rayment. It will take a minute."

The magic pills turn out to be nothing but Ibuprofen. "Mum says take one every four hours. And you should eat first. Shall I get you something from the kitchen?"

"Get me an apple or a banana if there is one. Drago?"

"Yes?"

"I'll be all right now. You don't have to stay. Thanks for everything."

"That's OK."

To complete the passage, Drago ought to say: *That's OK, you would do the same for me.* And it is true! If some cataclysm were to befall Drago, if some reckless stranger were to crash into him on his motorcycle, he, Paul Rayment, would move heaven and earth, spend every penny he had, to save him. He would give the world a lesson in how to take care of a beloved child. He would be everything to him, father and mother. All day, all night he would watch at his bedside. If only!

At the door Drago turns, waves, and flashes him one of the angelic smiles that must have the girls swooning. "See you!"

CHAPTER 27

The injury to his back is indeed, as Marijana told him, no great thing. By mid-afternoon he is able to move about, if cautiously, able to dress himself, able to make himself a sandwich. Last night he thought he was at death's door; today he is fine again, more or less. A dash of this, a dab of that, a smidgen of the other, mixed together and rolled into a pill in a factory in Bangkok, and the monster of pain is reduced to a mouse. Miraculous.

So when Elizabeth Costello arrives he is able to provide the briefest, calmest, most matter-of-fact recital of events. "I slipped in the shower and twisted my back. I called Marijana, and she came and fixed me up, and now I'm fine again." No mention of treacherous Johann August, no mention of the shivering and the tears, no mention of the pyjamas in the wash basket. "Drago dropped by this morning to check up. A nice boy. Mature beyond his years."

"And you are fine, you say."

"Yes."

"And your pictures? Your photograph collection?"

"What do you mean?"

"Is your photograph collection fine too?"

"I presume it is. Why should it not be?"

"Perhaps you should take a look."

It is not that any of the prints are actually missing. Nothing is actually missing. But one of the Faucherys has the wrong feel to it and, as soon as he brings it out of its plastic sleeve into the light, the wrong look too. What he is holding in his hands is a copy, in tones of brown that mimic the original sepia, made by an electronic printer on half-glazed photographic paper. The cardboard mount is new and slightly thicker than the original. It is the added thickness that first gives the forgery away. Otherwise it is not a bad job. But for Costello's prompting he might never have noticed it.

"How did you know?" he demands of her.

"How did I know Drago and his friend were up to something? I didn't know. I was merely suspicious." She holds up the copy. "I wouldn't be surprised if one of these diggers was great-grandfather Costello from Kerry. And look—look at this fellow." With a fingernail she taps a face in the second row. "Isn't he the spitting image of Miroslav Jokić!"

He snatches the photograph from her. Miroslav Jokić: it is indeed he, wearing a hat and open-necked shirt, sporting a moustache too, standing flank to flank with those stern-faced Cornish and Irish miners of a bygone age.

It is the desecration that he feels most of all: the

dead made fun of by a couple of cocky, irreverent youths. Presumably they did it using some kind of digital technique. He could never have achieved so convincing a montage in an old-fashioned dark-room.

He turns on the Costello woman. "What has become of the original?" he demands. "Do you know what has become of it?" He hears his voice go out of control, but he does not care. He smites the copy to the ground. *"The stupid, stupid boy! What has he done with the original?"*

Elizabeth Costello gives him a look of wide-eyed astonishment. "Don't ask me, Paul," she says. "It was not I who welcomed Drago into my home and gave him the run of my precious photograph collection. It was not I who plotted my way to the mother through the son."

"Then how did you know about this . . . this vandalism?"

"I did not *know*. As I said before, I was merely suspicious."

"But what made you suspicious? What are you not telling me?"

"Get a hold of yourself, Paul. Consider. Here we have Drago and his friend Shaun, two healthy Australian lads, and how do they spend their free time? Not racing their motorcycles. Not playing football. Not surfing. Not kissing the girls. No: instead they lock themselves up for hours on end in your study. Are they poring over smut? No: unless I am mistaken, you own singularly few dirty books. What then can it be that absorbs their attention but your photograph collection, a collection which according to you is so priceless that it must be donated to the nation?"

"But I don't see what motive they can have. Why should they go to all that trouble to fabricate"— he puts the tip of his crutch on the copy and grinds it into the carpet—"a dummy?"

"There I can't help you. That is for you to work out. But bear in mind: these are lively young chaps in a dozy city that does not provide outlets for all the restlessness in their bones, all the buzz of schemes and desires in their heads. Time is accelerating all around us, Paul. Girls have babies at the age of ten. Boys—boys take half an hour to pick up a skill that took us half a lifetime. They pick it up and get bored with it and move on to something else. Perhaps Drago and his friend thought it would be amusing: the State Library, a mob of worthy old gents and ladies fanning themselves against the heat, some boring bigwig or other unveiling the Rayment Bequest, and— hello, hello!—who is this at the centre of the *pièce de résistance* of the collection but one of the Jokić clan from Croatia! A capital jape—that's what Billy Bunter would have called it. Perhaps that is all it amounts to: an elaborate and rather tasteless jape that must have cost more than a little of their time and perhaps some expert guidance too.

"As for the original, your precious Fauchery print, who knows where it is? Perhaps it is still lying under Drago's bed. Or perhaps he and Shaun flogged it to a dealer. Be comforted, however. You may feel you have become the butt of a joke, and indeed you may be right. But there was no malevolence behind it. No affection, perhaps, but no malevolence either. Just a joke, an unthinking, juvenile joke."

No affection. Is it as plain as that, plain for all to see? It is as though the heart in his breast has suddenly grown too tired to beat. Tears come to his eyes again, but with no force behind them, just a watery exudation.

"Is that who they are then?" he whispers. "Gypsies? What else of mine have they stolen, these Croatian gypsies?"

"Don't be melodramatic, Paul. There are Croatians and Croatians. Surely you know that. A handful of good Croatians and a handful of bad Croatians and millions of Croatians in between. The Jokićs are not particularly bad Croatians, just a little callous, a little rough on the heart. Drago included. Drago is not a bad boy, you know that. Let me remind you: you did tell him, rather loftily I thought, that the pictures were not yours, you were merely guarding them for the sake of the nation's history. Well, Drago is part of that history too, remember. What harm is there, thinks Drago, in inserting a Jokić into the national memory, even if somewhat prematurely—grandpa Jokić, for instance? Just a lark, whose consequences he may not have thought through; but then, among the

unruly young, how many think through the consequences of their acts?"

"Grandpa Jokić?"

"Yes. Miroslav's father. You didn't think it was
Miroslav himself in the picture, did you? But
bear up, all is not lost. In fact, if you are lucky,
nothing is lost. Ten to one your beloved Fauchery
is still in Drago's hands. Tell him you will call
the police if it is not returned at once."

He shakes his head. "No. He will just take fright
and burn it."

"Then speak to his mother. Speak to Marijana.
She will be embarrassed. She will do anything to
protect her first-born."

"Anything?"

"She will take the blame on herself. She is, after
all, the picture-restorer in the family."

"And then?"

"I don't know. What happens after that is up to
you. If you want to go on and make a scene, you
can make a scene. If not, not."

"I don't want a scene. I just want to hear the
truth. Whose idea was this, Drago's or what's-
his-name's, Shaun's, or Marijana's?"

"I would call that a fairly modest circumscription
of the truth. Would you not like to hear more?"

"No, I don't want to hear more."

"Would you not like to hear why you were
chosen as the victim, the dummy?"

"No."

"Poor Paul. You flinch away even before the blow

can fall. But perhaps there will be no blow. Perhaps Marijana will prostrate herself before you. *Mea culpa. Do with me as you wish.* And so forth. You will never be sure unless you have a scene with her. Can't I persuade you? Otherwise what will you be left with? An inconsequential story about being taken for a ride by the gypsies, the high-coloured gypsy woman and the handsome gypsy youth. Not the main thing at all, the distinguished thing."

"No. Absolutely not. I refuse. No scenes. No threats. If you knew, Elizabeth, how sick and tired I am of being nudged by you this way and that to further these crazy stories in your head! I can see what you want. You would like me to—what is the word?—*exploit* Marijana. Then you hope the husband will find out and shoot me or beat me up. That is the kind of *main thing* you are hoping I will produce, isn't it?—sex, jealousy, violence, action of the most vulgar kind."

"Don't be ridiculous, Paul. You don't resolve a crisis like the present one, whose essence is moral, by beating someone up or shooting him dead. Even you must recognise that. But if my suggestion offends you, I withdraw it. Don't speak to Drago. Don't speak to his mother. If I can't persuade you, I certainly can't force you. If you are happy to lose your precious picture, so be it."

Speak to Marijana, the Costello woman tells him. But what can he say? *Marijana? Hello, how are you?*

I want to apologise for what I said the other night, the night I tripped in the shower, I don't know what came over me. I must have lost my head. By the way, I notice that one of the photographs in my collection is missing. Do you think you could ask Drago to look in his rucksack and see if he hasn't packed it by mistake?

Above all he must not accuse. If he accuses, the Jokićs will deny, and that will be the end of whatever tenuous status he still holds among them—patienthood, clientship.

Rather than telephone Marijana, perhaps he should write another of his letters, suppressing the lability this time, taking the utmost care with the wording, giving a cool, sensible exposition of his situation vis-à-vis her, vis-à-vis Drago, vis-à-vis the missing photograph. But who writes letters nowadays? Who reads them? Did Marijana read his first letter? Did she even receive it? She gave no sign.

A memory comes back: a childhood visit to Paris, to the Galeries Lafayette; watching scraps of paper being screwed into *cartouches* and shot from one department to another along pneumatic tubes. When the hatch in the tube was opened, he remembers, there came from the bowels of the apparatus a subdued roar of air. A vanished system of communication. A vanished world, rationalised out of existence. What happened to them, all those silvery *cartouches?* Melted down, probably, for shell casings or guided missiles.

But perhaps with Croatians it is different. Perhaps back in the old country there are still aunts and grandmothers who write letters to their far-flung family in Canada, in Brazil, in Australia, and put stamps on them, and drop them in the mailbox: Ivanka has won the class prize for recitation, the brindled cow has calved, how are you, when will we see you again? So perhaps the Jokićs will not find it so odd to be addressed through the mails.

Dear Miroslav, he writes.

I tried to break up your home, so no doubt you feel I ought to shut up and accept whatever punishment the gods visit on me. Well, I will not shut up. A rare photograph belonging to me has disappeared and I would like it back. (Let me add that Drago will not be able to sell it, it is too well known in the trade.)

If you don't know what I am talking about, ask your son, ask your wife.

But that is not why I am writing. I am writing to make a proposal.

You suspect me of having designs upon your wife. You are right. But do not jump to conclusions about what kind of designs they are.

It is not just money that I offer. I offer certain intangibles too, human intangibles, by which I mean principally love. I employed the word godfather, if not to you then to Marijana. Or perhaps I did not utter the word, merely thought it. My proposal is as follows. In return for a substantial loan of indefinite term, to cover the education of Drago and perhaps other of your children, can you find a place in your hearth and in your home, in your heart and home, for a godfather?

I do not know whether in Catholic Croatia you have the institution of the godfather. Perhaps yes, perhaps no. The books I have consulted do not say. But you must be familiar with the concept. The godfather is the man who stands by the side of the father at the baptismal font, or hovers over his head, giving his blessing to the child and swearing his lifelong support. As the priest in the ritual of baptism is the personification of the Son and intercessor, and the father is of course the Father, so the godfather is the personification of the Holy Ghost. At least that is how I conceive of it. A figure without substance, ghostly, beyond anger and desire.

You live in Munno Para, some distance from the city. It is no easy matter for me, in my present reduced state, to come visiting. Nevertheless, will you in principle open your home to me? I want nothing in return, nothing tangible, beyond perhaps a key to the back door. I certainly harbour no plan to take your wife and children away from you. I ask merely to hover, to open my breast, at times when you are elsewhere occupied, and pour out my heart's blessings upon your family.

Drago should have no trouble, by now, in comprehending what place I aspire to in the household. The younger children may find it more difficult. If you choose to say nothing to them for the present, I will understand.

I know a proposal of this kind was not what you expected when you began to read this letter. I mentioned

266

to an acquaintance of mine what has been going on in my flat—the disappearance of the item from my photograph collection and so forth—and she suggested that I call in the police. But nothing could be further from my mind. No, I am just using the opening created by this unpleasant incident to let my pen run and my heart speak (besides, how many letters does one have a chance to write nowadays?).

I don't know how you yourself feel about letters. Given that you come from an older and in some respects better world, perhaps you will not find it strange to take up the pen in turn. If on the other hand letters are alien to you, there is always the telephone (8332 1445). Or Marijana can bear a message, or Drago. (I have not turned my back on Drago, far from it: tell him that.) Or Blanka. And finally there is always silence. Silence can be full of meaning.

I am going to seal and stamp this missive now, and before I have second thoughts make the trek to the nearest mailbox. I used to have lots of second thoughts, I had second thoughts all the time, but now I abhor them.

Yours most sincerely,
Paul Rayment.

CHAPTER 28

"**D**on't you think you should see a doctor?" he says to the Costello woman.

She shakes her head. "It's nothing, just a chill. It will pass."

It does not sound like a chill at all. It is a cough, and it has a soggy quality, as if the lungs are trying to expel, a fistful at a time, a layer of deeply settled mucus.

"You must have picked it up under the bushes," he says. She looks back uncomprehendingly.

"Didn't you say you were sleeping under the bushes in the park?"

"Ah yes."

"I can recommend eucalyptus oil," he says. "A teaspoon of eucalyptus oil in a pan of boiling water. You inhale the steam. It does wonders for the bronchial passages."

"Eucalyptus oil!" she says. "I haven't heard of eucalyptus oil in ages. People use inhalers nowadays. I have one in my bag. Quite useless. My standby used to be Friar's Balsam, but I can't find it in the shops any more."

"You can get it in country stores. You can get it in Adelaide."

"Can you. As our American friends say, that figures."

He will get the eucalyptus oil out for her. He will boil a pan of water. He will even hunt in the medicine cabinet to see whether he has Friar's Balsam. She has only to ask. But she does not ask.

They are sitting on the balcony with a bottle of wine between them. It is dark, there is a strong breeze blowing. If she really is ill she would be better off indoors. But she does nothing to hide her distaste for the flat—"your Bavarian funeral parlour," she called it yesterday—and he is not her keeper.

"No word from Drago? No news from the Jokićs?" she inquires.

"No word. I have written a letter, which I have yet to mail."

"A letter! Another letter! What is this, a game of postal chess? Two days for your word to reach Marijana, two days for her word to come back: we will all expire of boredom before we have a resolution. This is not the age of the epistolary novel, Paul. Go and see her! Confront her! Have a proper scene! Stamp your foot (I speak metaphorically)! Shout! Say, 'I will not be treated like this!' That is how normal people behave, people like Marijana and Miroslav. Life is not an exchange of diplomatic notes. *Au contraire*, life is drama, life is action, action and passion! Surely

269

you, with your French background, know that. Be polite if you wish, no harm in politeness, but not at the expense of the passions. Think of French theatre. Think of Racine. You can't be more French than Racine. Racine is not about people sitting hunched up in corners plotting and calculating. Racine is about confrontation, one huge tirade pitted against another."

Is she feverish? What has brought on this outburst?

"If there is a place in the world for Friar's Balsam," he says, "there is a place for old-fashioned letters. At least, if a letter does not sound right, you can tear it up and start again. Unlike speeches. Unlike outbursts of passion, which are irrevocable. You of all people ought to appreciate that."

"I?"

"Yes, you. Surely you don't scribble down the first thing that comes into your head and mail it off to your publisher. Surely you wait for second thoughts. Surely you revise. Isn't the whole of writing a matter of second thoughts—second thoughts and third thoughts and further thoughts?"

"Indeed it is. That is what writing is: second thoughts to the power of n. But who are you to preach second thoughts to me? If you had only been true to your tortoise character, if you had waited for the coming of second thoughts, if you had not so foolishly and irrevocably declared your passion to your cleaning lady, we would not be in our present pickle, you and I. You could be happily set up in your nice flat, waiting for visits from the lady with the dark glasses, and I could be back in Melbourne. But it is too late for that now. Nothing left for us but to hold on tight and see where the black horse takes us."

"Why do you call me a tortoise?"

"Because you sniff the air for ages before you stick your head out. Because every blessed step costs such an effort. I am not asking you to become a hare, Paul. I merely plead that you look into your heart and see whether you cannot find means *within* your tortoise character, *within* your tortoise variety of passion, of accelerating your wooing of Marijana—if it is indeed your intention to go on wooing her.

"Remember, Paul, it is passion that makes the world go round. You are not analphabete, you must know that. In the absence of passion the world would still be void and without form. Think of Don Quixote. *Don Quixote* is not about a man sitting in a rocking chair bemoaning the dullness of La Mancha. It is about a man who claps a basin on his head and clambers onto the back of his faithful old plough-horse and sallies forth to do great deeds. Emma Rouault, Emma Bovary, goes out and buys fancy clothes even though she has no idea of how she is going to pay for them. *We only live once,* says Alonso, says Emma, *so let's give it a whirl!* Give it a whirl, Paul. See what you can come up with."

"See what I can come up with so that you can put me in a book."

"So that someone, somewhere *might* put you in a book. So that someone might *want* to put you in a book. Someone, anyone—not just me. So that you may be *worth* putting in a book. Alongside Alonso and Emma. Become major, Paul. Live like a hero. That is what the classics teach us. Be a main character. Otherwise what is life for?

"Come on. Do something. Do anything. Surprise me. Has it occurred to you that if your life seems repetitive and circumscribed and duller by the day, it may be because you hardly ever leave this accursed flat? Consider: somewhere in a jungle in Maharashtra State a tiger is at this very moment opening its amber eyes, *and it is not thinking of you at all*! It could not care less about you or any other of the denizens of Coniston Terrace. When did you last go for a walk under the starry sky? You have lost a leg, I know, and ambulating is no fun; but after a certain age we have all lost a leg, more or less. Your missing leg is just a sign or symbol or symptom, I can never remember which is which, of growing old, old and uninteresting. So what is the point of complaining? Hark!

I am, yet what I am none cares or knows.
My friends forsake me like a memory lost.
I am the self-consumer of my woes.

"Do you know the lines? John Clare. Be warned, Paul: that is how you will end up, like John Clare,

272

sole consumer of your own woes. Because no one else, you can be sure, will give a damn."

He never knows, with the Costello woman, when he is being treated seriously and when he is being taken for a ride. He can cope with the English, that is to say the Anglo-Australians. It is the Irish who have always given him trouble, and the Irish strain in Australia. He can see that someone might want to turn him and Marijana, the man with the stump and the mobile Balkan lady, into comedy. But despite all her gibing comedy is not quite what Costello seems to have in mind for him, and that is what baffles him, that is what he calls the Irish element.

"We should move indoors," he says.

"Not yet. O starry sky . . . How does it go on?"

"I don't know."

"O starry sky, o something something. How has it come about, do you think, that I am stuck with so incurious, so unadventurous a man as you? Can you explain? Does it all come down to the English language, to your not being confident enough to act in a language that is not your own?

"Ever since you reminded me of your French past, you know, I have been listening with pricked ears. And yes, you are right: you speak English, you probably think in English, you may even dream in English, yet English is not your true language. I would even say that English is a disguise for you, or a mask, part of your tortoiseshell armour. As you speak I swear I can hear words being selected, one after the other, from the word-box you carry around with you, and slotted into place. That is not how a true native speaks, one who is born into the language."

"How does a native speak?"

"From the heart. Words well up within and he sings them, sings along with them. So to speak."

"I see. Are you suggesting I return to French? Are you suggesting I sing *Frère Jacques*?"

"Don't mock me, Paul. I said nothing about returning to French. You lost touch with French long ago. All I say is, you speak English like a foreigner."

"I speak English like a foreigner because I am a foreigner. I am a foreigner by nature and have been a foreigner all my life. And I don't see why I should apologise. If there were no foreigners there would be no natives."

"A foreigner by nature? No, that is not it, don't put the blame on your nature. You have a perfectly good nature, if a little underdeveloped. No, the more I listen the more convinced I am that the key to your character lies in your speech. You speak like a book. Once upon a time you were a pale, well-behaved little boy—I can just see you—who took books too seriously. And you still are."

"I still am what? Pale? Well-behaved? Under-developed?"

"A little boy afraid of sounding funny when you open your mouth. Let me make a proposal, Paul. Lock up this flat and bid farewell to Adelaide.

Adelaide is too much like a graveyard. There is no more life for you here. Come and live with me in Carlton instead. I will give you language lessons. I will teach you how to speak from the heart. One two-hour lesson a day, six days a week; on the seventh day we can rest. I will even cook for you. Not as expertly as Marijana, but serviceably enough. Then after dinner, should the spirit move you, you can tell me more stories from your treasure-hoard, which I will afterwards tell back to you in a form so accelerated and improved that you will hardly recognise them. What else? No rough pleasures—you will be relieved to hear that. As clean as the blessed angels we will be. In all other respects I will take care of you; and perhaps in return you will learn to take care of me. When the appointed day arrives, you can be the one to close my eyelids and stuff cotton wool up my nostrils and recite a brief prayer over me. Or vice versa, if I am the one left behind. How does that sound to you?"

"It sounds like marriage."

"Yes it is, marriage of a kind. Companionate marriage. Paul and Elizabeth. Elizabeth and Paul. Companions on the way. Or if Carlton doesn't appeal to you, we could buy a camper van and tour the continent taking in the sights. We could even catch a plane to France. How about that? You could show me your old haunts, the Galeries Lafayette, Tarascon, the Pyrenees. No end of options. Come on, what do you say?"

She may be Irish, but she sounds sincere, or half sincere. Now his turn.

He rises and stands propped against the table before her. Can he, for once, make his voice sing? He closes his eyes, empties his mind, waits for words to come.

"Why me, Elizabeth?" come the words. "Why, of all the many people in the world, me?"

The same old words, the same disappointing old song. He cannot get beyond it. Yet until he has an answer to his question, whatever in the heart does the singing will be clogged.

Elizabeth Costello is silent.

"I am dross, Elizabeth, base metal. I am not redeemable. I am of no use to you, to anyone, of no value. Too pale, too cold, too frightened. What made you choose me? What gave you the idea you could make anything of me? Why do you stay with me? *Speak!*"

She speaks.

"You were made for me, Paul, as I was made for you. Will that do for the present, or do you want me to give it to you *plenu voce*, in full voice?"

"Speak it in so full a voice that even a poor dullard like me can understand."

She clears her throat. "For me alone Paul Rayment was born and I for him. His is the power of leading, mine of following; his of acting, mine of writing. More?"

"No, that is enough. Now let me ask you straight out, Mrs. Costello: Are you real?"

"Am I real? I eat, I sleep, I suffer, I go to the bathroom. I catch cold. Of course I am real. As real as you."

"Please be serious for once. Please answer me: Am I alive or am I dead? Did something happen to me on Magill Road that I have failed to grasp?"

"And am I the shade assigned to welcome you to the afterlife—is that what you are asking? No, rest assured, a poor forked creature, that is all I am, no different from yourself. An old woman who scribbles away, page after page, day after day, damned if she knows why. If there is a presiding spirit—and I don't think there is—then it is me he stands over, with his lash, not you. *No slacking, young Elizabeth Costello!* he says, and gives me a lick of the whip. *Get on with the job now!* No, this is a very ordinary story, very ordinary indeed, with just three dimensions, length, breadth and height, the same as ordinary life, and it is a very ordinary proposal I am making to you. Come back with me to Melbourne, to my nice old house in Carlton. You will like it, it has many mansions. Forget about Mrs. Jokić, you don't stand a dog's chance with her. Take a chance on me. I'll be your best *copine*, the *copine* of your last days. We will share our crusts while we still have teeth. What do you say?"

"What do I say from the word-box I carry around with me or from the heart?"

"Ah, you've got me there, what a quick fellow you are! From the heart, Paul, just for once."

He has been watching her mouth as she speaks,

it is a habit of his: other people watch the eyes, he watches the mouth. *No rough pleasures*, she said. But right now he cannot help imagining what it would be like to kiss that mouth, with its dry, perhaps even withered lips and the trace of down above. Does companionate marriage include kissing? He drops his eyes; if he were less polite he would shudder.

And she sees it. She is not a higher being, but she sees it. "I bet that as a little boy you didn't like it when your mother kissed you," she says softly. "Am I right? Ducked your head, let her peck you on the forehead, nothing more? And your Dutch stepfather not at all? Wanted to be a little man from the beginning, your own little man, owing nothing to anyone; self-made. Did they disgust you, your mother and her new husband—their breath, their smell, their pawing and fondling? How on earth could you expect someone like Marijana Jokić to love a man with such an aversion to the physical?"

"I have no aversion to the physical," he protests coldly. What he wants to add, but does not, is: *My aversion is to the ugly*. "What do you think life has consisted in ever since Magill Road but being rammed into the physical day after day? It is a testament to my faith in the physical that I have not done away with myself, that I am still here."

Yet even as he speaks it is clear to him what the woman meant about the box of words. *Done away with myself!* he thinks. *How artificial! How insincere! Like all the confessions she leads me into!* And at the very same moment he is thinking: *If we had*

*had but five minutes more, that afternoon, if Ljuba
had not come prowling like a little watchdog, Marijana
would have kissed me. It was coming, I am sure, I
felt it in my bones. Would have bent down and ever
so lightly touched her lips to my shoulder. Then all
would have been well. I would have taken her to me;
she and I would have known what it was to lie side
by side, breast to breast, in each other's arms, breathing
each other's breath. Home country.*

"Would you not concede, Paul" (the woman is
still talking), "that I have kept my humour exceed-
ingly well, from the day I turned up on your
doorstep to the present? Not a curse, not a cross
word, lots of jokes instead, and a leavening of Irish
blarney. Let me ask you: Do you think that is how
I am by nature?"

He holds his tongue. His mind is elsewhere. He
does not care how Elizabeth Costello is by nature.

"I am a tetchy old creature by nature, Paul, and
given to the blackest rages. A bit of a viper, in
fact. It is only because I vowed to myself to be
good that I have been such a light burden for you
to bear. But it has been a battle, believe me. Many
is the time I have had to restrain myself from
flaring up. Do you think what I have said is the
worst that can be said of you—that you are slow
as a tortoise and fastidious to a fault? There is
much beyond that, believe me. What do we call
it when someone knows the worst about us, the
worst and most wounding, and does not come out
with it but on the contrary suppresses it and

continues to smile on us and make little jokes? We call it affection. Where else in the world, at this late stage, are you going to find affection, you ugly old man? Yes, I am familiar with that word too, *ugly*. We are both of us ugly, Paul, old and ugly, As much as ever would we like to hold in our arms the beauty of all the world. It never wanes in us, that yearning. But the beauty of all the world does not want any of us. So we have to make do with less, a great deal less. In fact, we have to accept what is on offer or else go hungry. So when a kindly godmother offers to whisk us away from our dreary surroundings, from our hopeless, our pathetic, unrealisable dreams, we ought to think twice about spurning her.

"I will give you a day, Paul, twenty-four hours, to rethink. If you refuse, if you insist on holding to your present dilatory course, then I will show you what I am capable of, I will show you how I can spit."

His watch shows 3.15. Three hours yet to dawn. How on earth will he kill three hours?

There is a light on in the living-room. Elizabeth Costello lies asleep at the table she has annexed, her head cradled in her arms atop a mess of papers.

His inclination is to leave her strictly alone. The last thing he wants to do is wake her and open himself to more of her barbs. He is weary of her barbs. Half the time he feels like a poor old bear in the Colosseum, not knowing which way to turn. The death of a thousand cuts.

Nevertheless.

Nevertheless, ever so gently, he lifts her and slips a cushion in under her head.

In a fairy story, this would be the moment when the foul hag turns into a fair princess. But this is not a fairy story, evidently. Since the exploratory handclasp when they met, he and Elizabeth Costello have had no physical contact. Her hair has a life-less feel to it, a lack of spring. And beneath that hair is the skull, within which activities go on that he would prefer not to know about.

If the object of his care were a child—Ljuba, for instance, or even handsome, heart-breaking, treacherous Drago—he might call the act tender. But in the case of this woman it is not tender. It is merely what one old person might do for another old person who is not well. Humane.

Presumably, like everyone else, Elizabeth Costello wants to be loved. And like everyone else faces the end gnawed by a feeling that there is something she has missed. Is that what she is looking for in him: whatever it is she has missed? Is that the answer to his recurring question? If so, how ludicrous. How can he be the missing piece when all his life he has been missing himself? *Man overboard!* Lost in a choppy sea off a strange coast.

Somewhere in the distance are the two Costello children he read about in the library, children she does not talk about, probably because they do not love her, or do not love her enough. Presumably, like him, they have had enough of Elizabeth Costello's barbs. He does not blame them. If he had a mother like her he would keep his distance too.

All alone in Melbourne in an empty house, entering upon her last days, starved for love, and to whom does she turn for relief but a man in another state, a retired portraitist, an utter stranger, yet one who has suffered a blow of his own and has his own need of love. If there is a human, a humane explanation for her situation, that must be it. Almost at random she has lighted on him, as a bee might alight on a flower or a wasp on a worm; and somehow, in ways so obscure, so labyrinthine that the mind baulks at exploring them, the need to be loved and the storytelling, that is to say the mess of papers on the table, are connected.

He glances at what she is writing. In fat letters: *(EC thinks) Australian novelist—what a fate! What does the man have running in his veins?* Under the words, a line across the page scored savagely into the paper. Then: *After the meal they play a game of cards. Use the game to bring out their differences. Blanka wins. A narrow, intense intelligence. Drago no good at cards—too careless, too confident. Marijana smiling, relaxed, proud of her offspring. PR tries to use the game to make friends with Blanka, but she draws back. Her icy disapproval.*

A meal and then a game of cards. PR and

Blanka. Are they to be a family together after all, he with the ice-water in his veins and the Jokićs, so full of blood? What else is Costello plotting in that busy head of hers?

The scribbler sleeps, the character prowls around looking for things to occupy himself with. A joke, but for the fact that there is no one around to catch it.

The scribbler's busy head lies at rest on the pillow. From her chest, if he listens carefully, a faint rattle as the air pumps in, pumps out. He switches off the lamp. He seems to be turning into the kind of person who falls asleep early and wakes up in the dark hours; she would seem to be the kind who stays up late, spinning her fantasies into the night. How could they possibly set up house together?

CHAPTER 29

"Not an unannounced visit," he says. "I don't
like people visiting me unannounced and
I don't make unannounced visits myself."
"Nevertheless," says Elizabeth Costello, "break
your rule just once. It is so much more spontaneous
than writing letters, so much more neighbourly.
How else will you get to see your mystical bride on
home ground, *chez elle*?"

His mind goes back to his childhood, to Ballarat
in the days before the spread of telephones, when
the four of them would get into the Dutchman's
blue Renault van on a Sunday afternoon and set
off to pay unannounced visits. What tedium! The
only visits he remembers with any pleasure were to
the smallholding of their stepfather's horticultural
friend Andrea Mittiga. It was at the Mittigas',
among the spider webs in the cramped space behind
the huge water tank, that with Prinny Mittiga he
carried out his first breathless explorations into the
difference between male and female.

"Come back next Sunday, promise," Prinny
Mittiga would whisper when the visit was over,
when, with the raspberry juice drunk and the

284

almond cake eaten, they were getting back into the van, weighed down with tomatoes or plums or oranges from the Mittigas' garden, for the drive back to Wirramunda Avenue. And he would have to shrug. "Dunno," he would have to say, his face impassive, though he burned to go on with the lessons.

"Paulie and Prinny were playing doctor again," announced his sister from their makeshift seat in the back of the van.

"Weren't!" he protested, and dug her in the ribs.

"*Allez, les enfants, soyez sages!*" admonished his mother. As for the Dutchman, hunched over the wheel, dodging the bumps and holes in the Mittigas' road, he never listened.

The Dutchman drove at bottom speed, in fourth gear. That was his theory of driving, learned in Holland. When they came to hills, the engine of the van would hammer and choke; other cars would queue up behind and hoot. The hooting had no effect on him. "*Toujours pressés, pressés!*" he would say in his grating Dutch voice. "*Ils sont fous! Ils gaspillent de l'essence, c'est tout!*" He was not going to *gaspiller* his own *essence* for anybody. So they would crawl on, into the dark, with no lights, to save the battery.

"*Oh la la, ils gaspillent de l'essence!*" he and his sister would whisper to each other in the back of the van that smelled of rotten dahlia bulbs, rasping their consonants in the barbaric Dutch way, snorting with laughter, holding back their snorts, while the proper cars, the Holdens and Chevrolets and Studebakers, accelerated past. *"Merde, merde, merde!"*

The Dutchman had taken to wearing shorts. Nothing could be more embarrassing than the Dutchman in his baggy shorts with his pale legs and his ankle-length check socks among the real Australians. Why did their mother ever marry him? Did she let him do *it* to her in her bedroom in the dark? When they thought of the Dutchman with his *thing* doing *it* to their mother they could explode with shame and outrage.

The Dutchman's Renault van was the only one in Ballarat. He had bought it second-hand from some other Dutchman. *Renault, l'auto la plus économique*, he would enounce, though in fact there was always something wrong with the van, it was always in the repair shop waiting for some part or other to arrive from Melbourne.

No Renault vans here in Adelaide. No Prinny Mittiga. No playing doctor. Only the real thing. Should they pay a last unannounced visit, for old times' sake? How will the Jokićs take it? Will they slam the door in the faces of their surprise visitors; or, coming from the same world, broadly speaking, as the Mittigas, a world gone or going, will they make them welcome and offer them tea and cake and send them home laden with gifts?

"A real expedition," says Elizabeth Costello. "The dark continent of Munno Para. I'm sure it will take you out of yourself."

"If we visit Munno Para it will not be in order to take me out of myself," he says. "There is nothing in me that I need to escape from."

"And so good of you to invite me along," continues Elizabeth Costello. "Would you not prefer to go by yourself?"

Always gay, he thinks. How tiring it must be to live with someone so resolutely gay.

"I would not dream of going without you," he says.

Years ago he used to cycle through Munno Para on the way to Gawler. Then it was just a few houses dotted around a filling station, with bare scrub behind. Now tracts of new housing stretch as far as the eye can see.

Seven Narrapinga Close: that was the address on the forms he had to sign for Marijana. The taxi drops them in front of a colonial-style house with green lawn around an austere little rectangular Japanese garden: a slab of black marble with water trickling down its face, rushes, grey pebbles. ("So real!" enthuses Elizabeth Costello, getting out of the car. "So authentic! Would you like me to give you a hand?")

The driver passes him his crutches; he pays the fare.

The door is opened a hand's width; they are inspected suspiciously by a girl with a pale, stolid face and a silver ring in one nostril. Blanka, he presumes, the middle child, the shoplifter, his unwilling protégée. He had half hoped she might be a beauty like her sister. But no, she is not.

"Hello," he says. "I am Paul Rayment. This is Mrs. Costello. We were hoping to see your mother."

Without a word the girl disappears. They wait and wait on the doorstep. Nothing happens.

"I reckon we go in," says Elizabeth Costello at last.

They find themselves in a living-room furnished in white leather, dominated to one side by a large television screen and to the other by a huge abstract painting, a swirl of orange and lime green and yellow against a white field. A fan spins overhead. No dolls in folk costume, no sunsets over the Adriatic, nothing to put one in mind of the old country.

"So real!" says Elizabeth Costello again. "Who would have thought it!"

He presumes these remarks about the real are in some sense aimed at him; he presumes they are made with irony. What their point might be he cannot guess.

The putative Blanka puts her head around the door. "She's coming," she intones, and withdraws.

Marijana has made no effort to pretty herself up. She wears blue jeans and a white cotton top that does nothing for her thick waist. "So, you bring your secretary," she says without preliminaries. "What you want?"

"This is not meant to be a confrontation," he says. "We have a slight problem on our hands, and

I thought the best way of clearing it up would be to have a quiet talk. Elizabeth is not my secretary and has never been. She is just a friend. She came along because it is a nice day, we thought we would take a drive."

"A drive in the country," says Elizabeth. "How are you, Marijana?"

"Good. So, sit down. You like some tea?"

"I would love a cup of tea, and so would Paul. If there is one thing Paul misses about the old way of life, it is dropping in on friends for a cup of tea."

"Yes, Elizabeth knows me better than I know myself. I need barely open my mouth."

"That's good," says Marijana. "I make tea."

The blinds are angled against the fierce sun, but through the slats they can see two tall gum trees in the yard and a hammock slung between them, empty.

"A lifestyle," says Elizabeth Costello. "Isn't that what they call it nowadays? Our friends the Jokićs have a lifestyle to support."

"I don't see why you sneer," he says. "Surely one is as much entitled to a lifestyle in Munno Para as in Melbourne. Why else should they have left Croatia if not for the lifestyle of their choice?"

"I'm not sneering. On the contrary, I'm full of admiration."

Marijana returns with the tea. Tea, but no cake.

"So, why you come?" she says.

"Could I speak to Drago, just briefly?"

She shakes her head. "Not at home."

"All right," he says, "I have a proposal to make. Drago has a key to my flat. On Tuesday morning I will be going out, and will be away most of the day. I will have left by nine and I won't be back before three. Could you tell Drago it would be nice, when I get home, to find everything as it was before."

There is a long silence. Marijana is wearing blue plastic sandals. Blue sandals and purple toenails: he may be an ex-portrait photographer and Marijana may be an ex-picture restorer, but their aesthetics are worlds apart. Very likely other things about them are worlds apart too. Their attitude towards mine and thine, for instance. A woman he had dreamed of prising away from her husband. *I want to look after you. I want to extend a protective wing over you.* What would it be like in reality, looking after her and her two hostile daughters and her treacherous son? How long would he last, he and his protective wing? On the other hand . . . On the other hand, how proud her breasts, how comely!

"I don't know nothing about this key," says Marijana. "You give Drago keys?"

"Drago had a front door key during the time he was living with me. During the time he was using my flat. You have one key and Drago has another key. He can take things out of the flat and he can bring things back. Whether I am at home or not. Using his key. I don't see how I can express myself more clearly."

There is a chrome cigarette lighter on the table in the shape of a nautilus shell. Marijana lights a cigarette. "You also have complains?" she says to Elizabeth. "You also think my son is thief?"

Elizabeth shrugs theatrically. "I wouldn't know what to think, I am sure," she says. "The young are subject to so many temptations nowadays . . . That word *thief* . . . So large, so heavy, so final. In America they use the word *larceny*. Grand larceny, petty larceny, and all the grades between. My guess is that what Paul has in mind is a petty larceny, one of the pettiest, so petty that it merges into mere borrowing. Is that not what you would want to be saying, Paul? That Drago or more likely one of Drago's friends borrowed one or two items that you would like returned?"

He nods.

"That is what you come for?" says Marijana. "No telephone, just bang on door like police? What he take? What you say he take?"

"A photograph, from my collection. A Fauchery. A copy has been substituted for the original, a copy which has been doctored, for what purpose I can't say. And we are not the police. That is ridiculous. The police don't come by taxi."

Marijana waves towards the telephone. Are they being dismissed? He has not even finished his tea. "Original?" she says. "What is this thing, original photograph? You point camera, click, you make copy. That is how camera works. Camera is like photocopier. So what is original? Original is copy already. Is not like painting."

"That is nonsense, Marijana. Sophistry. A photograph is not the thing itself. Nor is a painting. But that does not make either of them a copy. Each becomes a new thing, a new real, new in the world, a new original. I have lost an original print which is of value to me and I want it back."

"I talk nonsense? You make photograph, or this man, how you say, Fauchery, make photograph, then you make prints, one two three four five, and these prints all original, five times original, ten times original, hundred times original, no copies? What is nonsense now? You come here, you say to Drago he must find originals. For what? So you can die and give originals to library? So you can be famous? Famous Mister Rayment?" She turns towards Elizabeth Costello. "Mr. Rayment offer us money. You know that? He offer to take me away from nursing. He offer us all new life. He offer Drago new school, fancy school in Canberra. Offer to pay. Now he say we steal from him."

"That is only half true. I offered to take care of you. I offered to take care of the children too. But I did not offer a new life. I am not as stupid as that. There is no such thing as a new life. We have only one life, one each."

"So why you say Drago steal?"

"I don't believe I ever used the word *steal*, and if I did I take it back unreservedly. Drago, or more likely Drago's friend Shaun, removed a photograph from my collection, borrowed it, and made a copy which he proceeded to doctor, I don't pretend I know how, you understand these things better than I do. Now I would like the original back. After which there will be no more questions and everything will be as it was before. Drago can come visiting, his friends can come visiting, he can stay overnight if he likes. It is not good, Marijana, to get into habits of borrowing and not returning, not good for a growing boy. They won't stand for it at this new school of his, Wellington College."

"Wellington finished. We have no money for Wellington."

"I offered to pay for Wellington, my offer stands. Nothing has changed. I will pay for other things too. Money is not the issue."

"So is not money, so why you so angry? Why you come bang on door? Sunday and you come bang on door like police. Bang bang."

He has never been good at arguments. Women in particular run rings around him in an argument. That was certainly true of his wife. In fact, now that he comes to think of it, perhaps that was why the marriage ended: not that there were too many arguments but that he was always losing them. Perhaps if he had won an argument once in a while he and Henriette might have stayed together. How boring to be tied to a man who can't even put up a fight!

And the same with Marijana. Perhaps Marijana wants him to try harder. Perhaps in her secret

293

heart she would like it if he won. If he could tip the balance back he might yet hold on to her.

"No one is angry, Marijana. I have a letter to deliver, and I thought it would be quicker to bring it in person. I will leave it here." He places the letter on the coffee table. "It is addressed to Mel. He can read it at his leisure. I also thought"—he casts a glance at Elizabeth Costello—"we also thought it would be nice to drop by for a cup of tea and a chat, as one used to do in the old days. It's a nice practice, sociable, friendly. It would be a pity if it died out."

But Elizabeth Costello is no help. Elizabeth Costello is leaning back, eyes shut, abstracted. Thank God Ljuba is not around to treat him to one of her glares.

"Only people which come bang on door is police," says Marijana. "If you telephone first, you say you come for tea, then you don't make frightening, like police."

"Give you a fright. Yes. I'm sorry. We should have telephoned."

"I agree," says Elizabeth, rousing herself. "We should have telephoned. That is what we should have done. That was our mistake."

Silence. Is that the conclusion of the bout? Plainly he has lost; but has he lost honourably, honourably enough to get a rematch, or has he lost abjectly?

"You want taxi?" says Marijana. "You want to call taxi?"

He and the Costello woman exchange looks. "Yes," says Elizabeth Costello. "Unless Paul here has something more to say."

"Paul here has nothing more to say," he says. "Paul came in the hope of getting his property back, but as of now Paul gives up."

Marijana rises, gives an imperious wave. "Come!" she says. "You want to see what kind of thief is Drago, I show you."

He tries to get up from the sofa. Though she can see what an effort it costs him, she makes no move to help. He casts a glance at Elizabeth Costello. "Go on," says Elizabeth Costello. "I'll stay here and catch my breath before the next act begins."

He struggles erect. Marijana is already halfway up the stairs. One step at a time, gripping the banisters, he follows.

PRIVATE, says the glaring sign on the door. *THIS MEANS YOU*. "Drago's room," says Marijana, and throws open the door.

The room is functionally furnished in blond pine: bed, desk, bookcase, computer workstation. It could not be more clean and orderly.

"Very nice," he says. "Very neat. I'm surprised. Drago was never so neat when he stayed with me."

Marijana shrugs. "I say to him, Mr. Rayment let you make mess so you will like him, but here you don't make mess, is not necessary, is your home here. I also say to him, you want to go to navy, you want to live in submarine, you learn to be neat."

"True. If you want to live in a submarine you had better be neat. Is that what Drago wants to do: live in a submarine?"

Marijana shrugs again. "Who knows. Is young. Is just a kid."

His own opinion regarding Drago, an opinion he does not voice, is that if he keeps his room shipshape, that is probably because his mother is always breathing over his shoulder. Quite intimidating, Marijana Jokić, when she wants to be. Quite a presence to bear with you into the future.

Pinned to the wall over Drago's bed are three photographs blown up to poster size. Two are Faucherys: the group of miners; and the women and children in the doorway of the wattle hut. The third, in colour, shows eight lithe male bodies caught in midair as they dive into a swimming pool.

"So," says Marijana. With hands on hips she waits for him to speak.

He steps closer and examines the second photograph. Mounted on the body of the little girl with the muddy hands is the face of Ljuba, her dark eyes boring into him. The fit is less than perfect: the orientation of the head does not quite match the hang of the shoulders.

"Just playing," says Marijana. "Is not serious thing. Is just—how you say it?—slips."

"Shapes. Images."

"Is just images. Play with images on computer, what is thief in that? Is modern thing. Images, who they belong to? You want to say, I point camera at you"—she stabs a finger at his chest— "I am thief, I steal your image? No: images is free—your image, my image. Is not secret what Drago is doing. These photographs—" she waves towards the three photographs on the wall—"all on his website. Anyone can see. You want to see website?"

She gestures towards the computer, which is humming softly.

"Please not," he says. "I don't understand computers. Drago can make all the copies he likes, I couldn't care less. I just want the originals back. The original prints. The ones touched by Fauchery's hand."

"Originals." All of a sudden she smiles, and not without kindliness, as if it has dawned on her that if he does not understand computers or the concept of the original or anything else, it is not out of wilfulness but because he is a fool. "OK. When Drago come home I ask him about originals." She pauses. "Elizabeth," she says—"she come live with you now?"

"No, we have no such plan."

She is still smiling. "But is good idea maybe. Then you not alone when it comes, you know, emergency."

Again she pauses, and in that pause he senses that her purpose in bringing him upstairs may not just have been to show him Drago's pictures.

"You a good man, Mr. Rayment."

"Paul."

"You a good man, Paul. But you get too lonely in your flat—you know what I mean? I get lonely too, in Coober Pedy, before we come to Adelaide, so I know, I know. Sit at home all day, kids at school, just baby and me—Ljuba was baby then—you get, you know, negative. So maybe you get negative too in your flat. No children, nobody. Very . . ."

"Very gloomy?"

She shakes her head. "No, I don't know how you say it. You grab. Anything come, you grab." With one hand she shows him how one grabs.

"Clutch at straws," he suggests. It is the first intimation she has given that the makeshift English she employs is not enough for her. If only he could speak Croatian! In Croatian, perhaps, he would be able to sing from the heart. Is it too late to learn? Can he find a teacher here in Adelaide? Lesson one: the verb to love, *ljub* or whatever.

"Anyway," she says, "Elizabeth come live with you, then you forget Marijana. Forget godfather too. Is no-good idea, godfather, is not realistic like. Because where he lives, this godfather? You want godfather come live in Narrapinga Close? Is not realistic—you see?"

"I never asked to come and live with you."

"You come live here, where you sleep? You sleep in Drago's bed, where is Drago sleeping? Or you want to sleep with me and Mel, two man, one

298

woman?" She is bubbling over with laughter now. "You want that?"

He cannot laugh. His throat is dry. "I could live in your back yard," he whispers. "I could have a shed put up. I could live in a shed in your back yard and watch over you. Over all of you."

"OK," she says briskly, "is enough talking. Elizabeth come live with you, she fix up everything, no more gloomy."

"Gloom."

"No more gloom. Is funny word. In Croatia we say *ovaj glumi*, doesn't mean he is gloomy, no, means he is pretending, he is not real. But you not pretending, eh?"

"No."

"Yeah, I know that." And, to his surprise, perhaps to her own surprise too, she rises on tiptoe and gives him a kiss, two kisses, one on each cheek. "Come, we go down now."

CHAPTER 30

Elizabeth Costello is not by herself. Standing over her is a strange figure: a man in baggy white overalls, his head hidden under what looks like a canvas bucket. The man seems to be speaking, but his words are irretrievably muffled by the mask.

Swiftly Marijana crosses the floor. "*Zaboga, zar opet!*" she exclaims, laughing. "His hair is catched! Every time he put it on"—she gestures towards the strange headgear—"his hair catch, then I must . . ." She makes twisting motions with her fingers.

She grasps the man by the shoulders—it is Miroslav—turns him around, and begins to disengage the mask from his long hair. Miroslav stretches backward with his hands, groping for her hips. She sways out of the way, frees the mask. He lifts it up: his face is ruddy from the heat; he seems to be in a good humour.

"It's the bees," he explains. "I've been moving hives."

"My husband is beekeeper," says Marijana. "You meet my husband? Is Mrs. Costello, she is friend to Mr. Rayment. Mel."

"How do you do, Mel," says Elizabeth Costello. "Elizabeth. I have heard about you but we have never met in the flesh, so to speak. You keep bees?"

"It's just a hobby like," says Mel or Miroslav.

"My husband, his family always keeping bees," says Marijana. "His father, and before him his greatfather. So he is keeping bees too, here in Australia."

"Just a few hives," says Mel. "But it's good honey, from the gum trees mainly. Got the eucalyptus tang, you know."

The ease between the two of them tells all—that and Marijana's laughter and the freedom of her fingers in his hair. Not an estranged couple at all. On the contrary, intimate. An intimate relationship with a row every now and again, Balkan style, to add a dash of spice: accusations, recriminations, plates smashed, doors slammed. Followed by remorse and tears, followed by heated lovemaking. Unless the whole story of the fight and the flight to Aunt Lidie was a lie, a fabrication. But why? Can he be the object of an extended plot, a plot he does not begin to understand?

"Pretty hot in overalls," says Mel. "I'll go change." He pauses. "You come to inspect the bike?"

"The bike?" he says. "No. What bike?"

"We would love to see the bike," says Elizabeth. "Where is it?"

"It's not finished," says Mel. "Drago hasn't worked on it for a while. There's a couple things still needs to be done. But you can take a look, seeing as you have come all the way. He won't mind."

"We would love that," says Elizabeth. "Paul has been looking forward to it so much."

"Go on then. I'll meet you outside."

They troop out of the house. Miroslav rejoins them, wearing shorts and sandals and a T-shirt that says Team Valvoline. He rolls up the garage door. There stands the familiar red Commodore, and beside it what Miroslav calls the bike.

"My, my!" exclaims Elizabeth. "What a strange contraption! How does it work?"

Miroslav wheels the machine out of the garage; then, with a smile, turns to him. "Maybe you can explain."

"It's what they call a recumbent bicycle," he says. "On this model you don't pedal, you turn the cranks with your hands instead."

"And Drago built it?" says Elizabeth. "All by himself?"

"Yeah," says Miroslav. "Only the brazing I did. Over in the workshop. Brazing is specialist like."

"Well, what a splendid gift," says Elizabeth. "Don't you think so, Paul? It will set you free again. Free to go wandering."

"Drago want to say thank you," says Marijana. "Thank you to Mr. Rayment for everything."

All eyes are on him, Mr. Rayment. Out of nowhere Ljuba has appeared. Even Blanka, who disapproved of him from the first, has joined the group. Slim body. A supple mover. Her father's daughter. No beauty, but then, some women develop late. Is Blanka going to have a turn to thank him too? Has she been busy as a bee, working on a gift? What will it be? An embroidered wallet? A hand-dyed tie?

He can feel a blush creeping over him, a blush of shame, starting at his ears and creeping forward over his face. He has no wish to stop it. It is what he deserves. "It's magnificent," he says. And, since it is expected of him, and since it is the right thing to do, he takes a step forward on his crutches and inspects his prize more closely. "Magnificent," he repeats. "A magnificent gift." *Munificent too*, he might add, but does not. He knows what he pays Marijana; he can guess what Miroslav earns. *Much more than I deserve.*

The wheel at the front is of standard bicycle size, with a set of cogs and a chain; the smaller wheels at the back merely roll. Spraypainted a vivid red, the bicycle—in fact a tricycle—stands less than a metre high. On the street the rider will be near to invisible, beneath a car driver's line of sight. So behind the seat Drago has mounted a fibreglass wand with an orange-coloured pennant at its tip. Fluttering above the rider's head, the brave little pennant is meant to warn off the Wayne Blights of the world.

A recumbent. He has never ridden one before, but he dislikes recumbents instinctively, as he dislikes prostheses, as he dislikes all fakes.

"Magnificent," he says again. "I am running out of words. May I take it for a spin?"

Miroslav shakes his head. "No cables," he says. "No gear cables, no brake cables. Drago hasn't put them in yet. But while we got you here we can adjust the seat. You see, we mounted the seat on a rail, so you can adjust it backward or forward."

He lays his crutches down, takes off his jacket, allows Miroslav to help him aboard. The seat feels odd.

"Marijana help with the seat," says Miroslav. "You know—for your leg. She design it, then we mould it in fibreglass."

Not just hours. Days, weeks. They must have spent weeks on it, father, son; mother too. The blush has not left his face, and he does not want it to.

"You can't get this kind of thing in bike shops, so we thought we make it like one-off, custom made. I'll give you a push, so you get the feel. OK? I'll give you a push but I'll keep a hold because, remember, there's no brakes."

The onlookers stand aside. Miroslav trundles him out onto the paved driveway.

"How do I steer?" he asks.

"With your left foot. There's a bar here—see?— with a spring. Don't worry, you'll get the hang of it."

No cars on Narrapinga Close. Miroslav gives a gentle push. He leans forward, grips the crank handles, gives them an experimental turn, hoping the contraption will steer itself.

Of course he will never put it to use. It will go into the store room at Coniston Terrace and there gather dust. All the time and trouble the Jokićs have put into it will be for nothing. Do they know that? Did they know all along, while they were building it? Is this driving lesson just part of a ritual they are all performing, he for their sake, they for his?

The breeze is in his face. For a moment he allows himself to imagine he is rolling down Magill Road, the pennant fluttering brightly overhead to remind the world to have mercy on him. A perambulator, that is what it is most like: a perambulator with a grizzled old baby in it, out for a ride. How the bystanders will smile! Smile and laugh and whistle: *Good on you, grandpa!*

But perhaps, in a larger perspective, that is exactly what the Jokićs mean to teach him: that he should give up his solemn airs and become what he rightly is, a figure of fun, an old gent with one leg who when he is not hopping around on his crutches roams the streets on his home-made tricycle. One of the local sights, one of the quaint types who lend colour to the social fabric. Till the day Wayne Blight guns his engine and comes after him again.

Miroslav has not left his side. Now Miroslav turns the machine in a wide arc that allows them to return to the driveway.

Elizabeth claps her hands; the others follow suit.

"Bravo, my knight," she says. "My knight of the doleful countenance."

He ignores her. "What do you think, Marijana?" he says. "Should I take up riding again?"

For Marijana has not so far uttered a word. Marijana knows him better than her husband does, better than Elizabeth Costello. She has seen from the beginning how he has striven to save his manly dignity, and has never jeered at him for it. What does Marijana think? Should he go on battling for dignity or is it time to capitulate?

"Yeah," says Marijana slowly. "It suits you. I think you should give it a whirl."

With her left hand Marijana holds her chin; with her right hand she props up her left elbow. It is the classic posture of thought, of mature reflection. She has given his question its full due, and she has answered. The woman the touch of whose lips he still feels on his cheek, the woman who, for reasons that have never been fully clear to him, though now and then he has a flicker of illumination, holds his heart, has spoken.

"Well then," he says (he was going to say *Well then, my love,* but forbears because he does not want to hurt Miroslav, though Miroslav must know, Ljuba must know, Blanka certainly knows, it is written all over his face), "well then, I'll give it a whirl. Thank you. In all sincerity, all heartfelt sincerity, thank you, each one of you. Thank you most of all to the absent Drago." *Whom I have misjudged and wronged,* he would like to say. "Whom I have misjudged and wronged," he says.

"No worries," replies Miroslav. "We'll put it on the trailer and bring it over next weekend maybe. Just a couple more things to fix, the cables and suchlike."

He turns to Elizabeth. "And now we must take our leave, must we not?" he says; and to Miroslav: "Can you give me a hand?"

Miroslav helps him up.

"PR Express," says Ljuba. "What does PR Express mean?"

And indeed, that is what is painted on the tubing of the tricycle, in lettering that artfully suggests the rush of wind. *PR Express.*

"It means I can go very fast," he says. "PR the rocket man."

"Rocket Man," says Ljuba. She gives him a smile, the first she has ever given. "You aren't Rocket Man, you're Slow Man!" Then she breaks into giggles, and embraces her mother's thighs, and hides her face.

"A debacle," he says to Elizabeth. They are in a taxi, heading south, heading home. "A rout, a moral rout, nothing less. I have never felt so ashamed of myself."

"Yes, you did not come out well. All that fury! All that self-righteousness!"

Fury? What is she talking about?

"Just think," she continues: "you were on the

point of losing a godson, and for what? I could not believe my ears. For an old photograph! A photograph of a bunch of strangers who could not care less about you. About a little French boy who hasn't even been born yet."

"Please," he says, "please let there not be another argument, I have not the stomach for it. What entitles Drago to take over my photographs I still don't see, but let it pass. Marijana tells me that the photographs are now on Drago's website. I am such an ignoramus. What does it mean, to be on a website?"

"It means that anyone in the world who feels curious about the life and times of Drago Jokić can inspect the photographs in question, in their original form or perhaps in their new, revised and augmented form, from the privacy of his or her home. As for why Drago chooses to publish them in this way, I am not the right one to ask. He will be coming next Sunday to deliver your conveyance. You can quiz him then."

"Marijana claims that the whole forgery business is just a joke."

"It is not even a forgery. A forger is out to make money. Drago could not care less about money. Of course it is just a joke. What else should it be?"

"Jokes have a relation to the unconscious."

"Jokes may indeed have a relation to the unconscious. But also: sometimes a joke is just a joke."

"Directed against—"

"Directed against you. Whom else? The man who doesn't laugh. The man who can't take a joke."

"But what if I had never found out? What if I went to the grave in total ignorance of this so-called joke? What if the joke were to go unnoticed at the State Library too? What if it were to go unnoticed to the end of time? *Take a look at these pictures, kids. The Ballarat diggers. Look at that bloke with the fierce moustaches!* What then?"

"Then it will become part of our folklore that brigand moustaches were in fashion in 1850s Victoria. That's all. This is really not a matter worth going on about, Paul. What counts is that you have left your flat and visited Munno Para, where you have had words in private with your beloved Marijana and got to see her husband's beekeeping outfit and the bicycle her son is building for you. That is the only outcome of the so-called forgery that matters. Otherwise the episode is of the utmost insignificance."

"You forget the missing print. Whatever opinion you may hold on photographs and their relation to the real, the fact is that one of my Faucherys, a genuine national treasure, worth more than mere money, has disappeared."

"Your precious photograph has not disappeared. Look in your cabinet again. Ten to one it is there, misfiled. Or else Drago will find it in his stuff and return it to you next Sunday, with apologies."

"And then?"

"Then the matter will be closed."

"And then?"

"After that? After Sunday? I am not sure there will be any more, after Sunday. Sunday may well mark the last of your dealings with the Jokićs, Mrs. Jokić included. Of Mrs. Jokić nothing alas but memories will remain to you. Of her supple calves. Of the splendid line of her bust. Of her charming malapropisms. Fond memories, shaded with regret, which will fade with the passage of time, as memories tend to do. Time, the great healer. However, there will still be the quarterly bills from Wellington College. Which I have no doubt you will pay, as a man of honour. And Christmas cards: *Wishing you a happy Christmas and a prosperous new year— Marijana, Mel, Drago, Blanka, Ljuba.*"

"I see. And what more do you care to reveal of my future, Mrs. Costello, while you are in prophetic vein?"

"You mean, will there be someone to replace Marijana or is Marijana the end of the line for you? That depends. If you stay on in Adelaide, I foresee only nurses, a gallery of nurses, some pretty, some not so pretty, none of whom will come near to touching your heart as Marijana Jokić has done. If you come to Melbourne, on the other hand, there will be me, faithful old Dobbin. Though my calves are not, I suspect, up to your exacting standard."

"And what of the state of your heart?"

"My heart? It has its ups and downs. It hammers

and gasps like an old car when I climb the stairs. I dare say it will not last much longer. Why do you ask? Are you anxious you might turn out to be the one doing the nursing? Never fear—I would never demand that of you."

"Then is it not time you called upon your children? Is it not time your children did something for you?"

"My children are far away, Paul, across the broad waves. Why do you mention my children? Do you want to adopt them too, become their stepfather? That will surprise them no end. They haven't even heard of you.

"But no, to answer your question, I would not dream of imposing myself on my children. If all else fails, I will check myself into a nursing home. Though the kind of care I seek is, alas, not provided in any nursing home I am aware of."

"And what kind of care might that be?"

"Loving care."

"Yes, that is indeed hard to come by nowadays, loving care. You might have to settle for mere good nursing. There is such a thing as good nursing, you know. One can be a good nurse without loving one's patients. Think of Marijana."

"So that would be your advice: settle for nursing. I disagree. If I had to elect between good nursing and a pair of loving hands, I would elect the loving hands any day."

"Well, I do not have loving hands, Elizabeth."

"No, you do not. Neither loving hands nor a

loving heart. A heart in hiding, that is what I call it. How are we going to bring your heart out of hiding?—that is the question." She clutches his arm. "Look!"

Three figures on motorcycles flash past in quick succession, going the other way, towards Munno Para.

"The one in the red helmet—wasn't it Drago?" She sighs. "Ah for youth! Ah for immortality!"

It was probably not Drago. Too much of a co-incidence, too neat. Probably a trio of unrelated young men, though with the blood running equally hot in their veins. But let them pretend neverthe-less that the one in the red helmet was Drago. "Ah Drago," he repeats dutifully, "ah for youth!"

The taximan drops them on Coniston Terrace in front of his flat.

"So," says Elizabeth Costello. "The end of a long day."

"Yes."

This is the moment when he ought to invite her indoors, offer her a meal and a place to sleep. But he speaks no word.

"Just the right gift, isn't it," she says—"your new bicycle. So thoughtful of Drago. A thoughtful boy. Now you are free to ride wherever you wish. If you are still nervous of Wayne Blight, you can confine yourself to the river path. It will give you exercise. It will improve your moods. You will develop strong arms in no time. Is there space for a passenger, do you think?"

"Space for a child behind the rider, yes. But not for another grown-up."

"Just joking, Paul. No, I wouldn't want to be a burden on you. If I were to go riding I would want a contraption of my own, preferably one with a motor. Do they still sell those little motors that you fasten to bicycles that go putt-putt and help you up the hills? They had them in France, I remember. *Deux chevaux*, two horses."

"I know what you mean. But they are not called *deux chevaux*. *Deux chevaux* is something else."

"Or a bath chair. Perhaps that is what I really ought to get for myself. Do you remember bath chairs, the kind with a tasselled sunshade and a steering-bar? We can scout around the antique shops, I'm sure we will find one, Adelaide is just the place for a bath chair. We can ask Miroslav to fix a couple of *chevaux* to it. Then we will be ready to set out on our adventures, you and I. You already have your nice orange flag and I will get another for myself, with a design."

"How about a mailed fist? A mailed fist in black on a white field, and beneath it the motto *Malleus maleficorum.*"

"*Malleus maleficorum.* Excellent! You really are turning into quite a wit, Paul. Who would have suspected you had it in you. *Malleus maleficorum* for me and *Onward and upward* for you. We could tour the whole land, the two of us, the whole of this wide brown land, north and south, east and west. You could teach me doggedness and I could teach you to live on nothing, or nearly nothing. They would write articles about us in the newspapers. We would become a well-loved Australian institution. What an idea! What a capital idea! Is this love, Paul? Have we found love at last?"

Half an hour ago he was with Marijana. But Marijana is behind them now, and he is left with Elizabeth Costello. He puts on his glasses again, turns, takes a good look at her. In the clear late-afternoon light he can see every detail, every hair, every vein. He examines her, then he examines his heart. "No," he says at last, "this is not love. This is something else. Something less."

"And is that your last word, do you think? No hope of budging you?"

"I am afraid not."

"But what am I going to do without you?"

She seems to be smiling, but her lips are trembling too.

"That is up to you, Elizabeth. There are plenty of fish in the ocean, so I hear. But as for me, as for now: goodbye." And he leans forward and kisses her thrice in the formal manner he was taught as a child, left right left.

AUTHOR'S NOTE

For their generous advice and assistance, my thanks to Arijana Božović, Catherine Lauga du Plessis, Peter Goldsworthy, Peter Rose, John Williams, and Sharon Zwi.